Search for Death

A Mortician Murder Mystery-Book 4

A. E. Howe

**Books in the
Mortician Murder Mystery Series
(in order):**

Return to Death
Gambling on Death
Memorial for Death
Search for Death

CHAPTER ONE

Lee Lamberton stepped lightly down the stairs of the funeral home on a Tuesday morning in August, wearing a contented smile. It had been six months since their biggest competitor had imploded, and he found himself busy and the business solvent for the first time since his father had died and left it to him and his sister.

"You've got a message. I put it under the edge of your plate. Come on and sit down for a little breakfast." Ruby Bowen, the funeral home's cook and housekeeper, was standing in the doorway to the kitchen, waving a spatula at him.

"I would never miss one of your breakfasts." Lee turned at the bottom of the stairs and followed Ruby into the kitchen where the table was set for him and his sister, Kay. "Where's Lester?" Lester Andrews, his apprentice, was almost always the first one to the table and the last one to leave. Lee couldn't understand how he stayed so skinny.

"You know he's helping Alison move stuff around at the store. He told you that last night at dinner." Ruby was piling scrambled eggs onto his plate as she talked.

"He works over there more than he does here," Lee grumbled, though he didn't really mind.

Lee and Alison Dobbs had been going out off and on for almost a year now and, with his business finally doing well, he was starting to think it was time to get serious about their relationship. In the meantime, letting Lester help out at the electronics store Alison had inherited from her father kept Lee in touch with what was going on in her life even when he couldn't be with her. Lester always gave him a full rundown of everything happening at the store. It wasn't that Lester was purposely reporting on Alison, but he just couldn't help himself. Lester's mouth had two settings: wide open or full of food.

"Better read that note," Ruby reminded Lee as she buttered a stack of toast.

Lee picked it up and saw that the message was from Dwayne McKenzie, a local farmer. Ruby had written detailed notes in her flowery cursive, including the fact that a dead man had been found on McKenzie's hunting property north of town.

"He asked for you to call him as soon as you can," Ruby said.

"You know, you could have led with that." Lee stood up and walked over to the phone on the wall.

"You should finish your breakfast first," Ruby insisted, frowning at him with her hands on her hips.

Lee waved her away as he spun the dial on the phone. He knew McKenzie's number because he'd grown up with his son, Matt. The McKenzies farmed over two thousand acres in the county, mostly hay and watermelons.

"Lee, thanks for getting back with me," McKenzie said gratefully. "I've got a situation at our hunting property. A man who was camping out there was found dead, and I need you to pick up the body."

"Is it still at the property?"

"Yeah, it's at our old cabin on the pond out past Snake

Creek. The guys driving the ambulance said that the coroner has to come out and take a look at it."

"When was the body found?" Lee asked.

"About two hours ago."

"Do you know how long it's been out there?"

"No more than a day or two at most," McKenzie said.

"I can get there in about thirty minutes."

"You know where it is?"

"Out on County Road 5 just past the gristmill bridge?"

"That's it. I just got the call from the coroner's office and I'm heading back out there to meet them. A deputy's there now."

Lee hung up and returned to his place at the table, but instead of sitting down he took two pieces of toast and made a scrambled egg sandwich.

"That's no way to eat your breakfast," Ruby scolded him while pouring coffee into a paper cup. "Go on. I'll walk out to the hearse with you."

She started to follow him as he grabbed a set of keys off the wall, then changed her mind. "Wait, you'll need to take Lester with you. I'll make him a bacon sandwich." Ruby treated all of them like her children, but none more so than Lester.

Ruby made sure Lee finished his egg sandwich before she let him pull the hearse out of the driveway. "When she comes down, tell Kay I'm picking up a body," he said as he drove away, shaking his head at Ruby's maternal behavior.

Dobbs Appliances and Electronics was still closed when Lee arrived, so he had to tap on the back door several times before Alison came to open it.

"Sorry, but I need to collect your helper," Lee joked.

"Fine. We've already moved the truck-sized console TVs." She gave Lee a quick kiss before backing away from the door.

The kiss made his heart feel as though it was growing inside his chest like the Grinch. Smiling a little stupidly, Lee looked around and admired the rearranged shop. "The place looks bigger."

"It should. I feel like I've been pushing the walls out." Lester was sweating as he came out of the back room. "What's up, boss?"

"A body to pick up."

"Anybody we know?"

"I didn't ask. Dwayne McKenzie called me. Sounds like it was someone working for him or something."

"McKenzie owns half the land in the county," Lester said.

"Close," Lee said. "Come on. We need to get going."

"Did Ruby send over any breakfast?"

"Out in the car." Lee waved toward the door.

As Lee drove out to McKenzie's property, Lester kept up a one-sided conversation between bites of bacon sandwich, going on and on about the new electronic gizmos that had come into Alison's store over the past week.

"This is the place," Lee finally said, pointing through the windshield as he turned off of the main road and through an open metal gate. The driveway, little more than a dirt track wide enough for one car, looked like it had seen a lot of traffic that morning.

"We're in the country now," Lester observed as they navigated a path surrounded by pine trees, scrub oaks and palmettos.

"Matt used to invite the guys out here during high school. Made for a safe place to drink beer and talk about girls."

"Did you ever have girls out here?" Lester asked.

"We never had much luck talking them into joining us. To be honest, we didn't have much luck talking to girls, period."

"But you were good at talking *about* girls."

"Exactly. Matt was a great guy," Lee said with a hint of nostalgia in his voice.

"Was?"

"It was horrible. He got a scholarship to play football at the University of Alabama, but during his second semester he was killed in a car accident. I helped Dad with the funeral. It was huge. The first time I'd buried a friend."

After almost half a mile, the driveway ended at a clearing surrounding a rustic cabin near a small pond. A sheriff's patrol car was parked near the cabin, and Lee saw a young deputy that he recognized leaning against the trunk. Next to the patrol car was a van from the coroner's office.

Deputy Henry Booker waved as Lee and Lester climbed out of the hearse.

"You still driving Bertha?" Henry asked, looking at the beat-up old Lincoln. "I remember you showing up at the prom with your date in that thing. I think I was a little jealous. Ain't no doubt it was cooler than the Impala station wagon my parents let me borrow."

Lee shook Henry's hand and grinned. "You know it."

"You remember the last time we were out here?" Henry asked.

"Yep, it was a month before my graduation. You and Tom came out to celebrate me, Matt and R. C. finally catching up with you."

"Matt and R. C. went off to college that summer. I haven't seen R. C. since… the funeral." Henry glanced off into the distance for a moment.

"How about Tom? Is he doing any better?" Lee asked.

"Sutton arrested him last month for stealing half a dozen lawnmowers and trying to sell them. You'd think he would have hit rock bottom by now."

"I tried to help him out a bit a couple of years ago. Didn't do any good," Lee said with a shrug.

"Times change and people change too," Henry said philosophically.

"Tom *was* always the crazy one," Lee pointed out.

Henry nodded.

"Is the body in the cabin?" Lee asked, getting back to the purpose of their trip.

"Nope, you can't have it that easy. The guys from the coroner's office are at the scene, which is about three hundred yards on the other side of the pond." Henry pointed past the cabin.

The rumble of a truck coming down the dirt road caused them both to turn and look. A blue-and-white two-tone Chevy C10 pickup pulled up next to the hearse and Dwayne McKenzie stepped out. He was in his late fifties with a thick, white beard and wearing overalls and a ballcap.

"Did he show you where the body is?" McKenzie asked as he walked over to them.

"I was just getting to that." Henry nodded.

Lee waved to Lester, who'd been leaning against the hearse while the two high school friends reminisced. The four of them followed a trail past the cabin, around the pond and back into the woods to another clearing.

"This is one of our food plots to attract deer," McKenzie said, only partly explaining the sight that met their eyes.

A large wooden deer stand sat on the edge of the clearing. Halfway down the ladder, the body of an older man hung upside down with his head only a couple of feet above the ground. The man's left foot was caught between two rungs of the ladder, keeping the body suspended in the air. Two men in white overalls were walking around the ladder.

"Wow!" Lester exclaimed.

"That's Professor Roger Harrington." McKenzie shook his head sadly. "I was letting him stay here and search around the place."

"Looks like an accident, but we're going to have to do an autopsy," the taller of the two men in overalls told them. Lee recognized the man as a long-time employee at the morgue named Mitch.

"We just have to figure out how to get him down without making a mess of it." Mitch looked irritated that the man hadn't had the decency to die on the ground.

"We'll help," Lee offered, looking at the corpse. The man's face was badly discolored as all his blood had settled to the lowest point of his body after death.

"Old guy probably slipped and got his foot caught," Mitch said. "Either he was knocked out or just couldn't get unstuck and died from asphyxiation, heart attack or a stroke. Hanging upside down like that puts pressure on your lungs and increases your blood pressure. It's okay for a couple of minutes, but if you do it for too long, especially an old guy like this, it isn't going to end well."

"How long do you think he's been dead?" Henry asked.

"We'll take his temperature when we get him down." Mitch reached out and tried to move Harrington's arm. "There's still some rigor. An educated guess would be since sometime yesterday morning."

"The sooner we get him down, the better," the younger morgue attendant said.

"Open the bag and we'll try to ease him down onto it," Mitch told him.

With the body bag in place and Lester, the most agile of the group, standing above the corpse on the ladder, Lee and the two attendants got ready to take the weight of Harrington's body. When Mitch told him to, Lester unhooked Harrington's foot and the others slid the body down onto the bag.

"How long will the autopsy take?" Lee asked once the

bag was zipped up.

"There were a couple of bad accidents in Gainesville this weekend, a shooting on Monday and a co-ed was stabbed. We're stacked up." Mitch sounded like a mechanic telling a customer why his car would take a while to fix. "Maybe a couple of days. Does he have any family?"

"An ex-wife is all that I know of. He never talked about anyone else," McKenzie said.

"The office will be in touch. If you can dig up the name of the ex-wife or any other kin, that would be great," Mitch told McKenzie and then turned to Lee. "We'll let you know when you can pick up the body."

"What was Harrington doing out here?" Lee asked McKenzie as the coroner's van pulled away.

"The Professor was a little touched in the head if you ask me," McKenzie said. "Maybe I shouldn't have humored him, but he was a nice guy with the gift of gab, as my mother would say. He told me some story about there being buried treasure out here or some such. I didn't see any harm in letting him look around and dig a few holes. All I asked was that he leave things the way he found them. Dig a hole, fill it in. Open a gate, close it."

"What was his full name?" Lee asked Henry.

"Roger Arthur Harrington, sixty-two years old. The address on his license is an apartment on the southeast side of Gainesville," the deputy said.

"Most people around here just called him the Professor. He taught Spanish history at the university for years," McKenzie said.

"You said he was looking for treasure?" Lee asked skeptically.

"It was a crazy story." McKenzie looked unsure.

"That sounds mysterious."

"More odd than mysterious. Maybe it was a mistake to let

him look around the place. I just thought it was harmless." McKenzie sighed. "Look, don't let this get around 'cause people might go wild. I don't want a bunch of nuts tearing up my place looking for a pot of gold."

"Gold?" Lester perked up. He'd gone back to leaning against the hearse and looking bored before he heard the word "gold."

"See, it's just like in *Jaws*," McKenzie said. "You say 'barracuda,' everyone goes: 'Huh?' But you say 'gold' and you've got a rush on your hands. According to the Professor, he found some old Spanish manuscript that described where a bunch of gold and jewels were buried near here. I mean, this document was from the sixteen hundreds. What are the odds you could follow the description and find the gold even if it *was* buried around here?"

"Where did the gold come from?" Lee felt drawn in despite himself.

"Long story short, there was a wreck on the Gulf Coast and the Spaniards on board decided to abandon the ship and attempt to cross the state in order to reach their settlement at St. Augustine. According to this document, they made it this far before they had to bury the gold and go on without it."

"Do you think there really is anything to the story?"

McKenzie shrugged. "No idea."

"Did he offer you a share of the gold?" Lester asked.

"We didn't even talk about that. He asked if he could look around and I said he could. I knew he'd had a few setbacks recently. Wife left him. He quit his job."

"Wow. Just think about all that gold." Lester looked around like he expected to see a treasure chest hidden under a palmetto bush.

"How's your wife doing?" Lee asked McKenzie to change the subject before Lester started digging holes.

"She's doing fine. Her mother has some health issues, though. Of course, when the time comes, we'll want you to take care of the arrangements."

"You know we'll be glad to take care of her final wishes," Lee said in his mortician's voice.

"Beth appreciated how you handled her father's funeral and of course… Matt's." A shadow passed over McKenzie's face at the mention of his son.

Everyone was quiet for a moment out of respect for the dead. Then McKenzie took a deep breath and gave Lee a small smile.

"Sorry I had you come all the way out here for nothing. I didn't think about the coroner taking the body for an autopsy."

"No problem. I'll pick it up as soon as they're done. If you find a next of kin, have them give me a call."

CHAPTER TWO

Kay Lamberton had slept in after a late night out with Alan Eckhart. After a quick, hot shower, she came downstairs just in time to hear Lee backing Bertha out of the driveway.

"Where's he headed?" Kay asked Ruby, who was already filling up a plate with more food than she could possibly eat.

"There's a body out in the woods. You want bacon with your eggs? Toast?" She'd already put both onto Kay's plate. "I can whip up some pancakes too, if you'd like."

"The eggs are fine," Kay said, pouring herself a glass of inky black coffee. "The stronger, the better" was a motto she'd adopted when she was an Army nurse in Vietnam.

"How was your date?" Ruby asked.

"Fine. We went to a movie and then had dinner." Kay sprinkled pepper on her eggs.

"What'd you see?"

Kay knew that Ruby didn't care about the movie. Instead, she had an intense interest in Kay's relationship with Eckhart that bordered on voyeurism.

"We saw that movie with Richard Gere. *An Officer and a Gentleman.* It was good."

"You could do worse than Alan Eckhart." Ruby sat down with her own plate of eggs and bacon.

"I don't know if I'm looking for anything steady."

"You like him 'cause he's a doctor," Ruby said, then shook her head quickly when she saw the look on Kay's face. "I don't mean that you're looking for a rich husband like some showgirl on the prowl. I just mean he reminds you of your career."

Kay stopped eating and looked hard at Ruby. The woman had an uncanny ability to know things that she shouldn't have been able to know. Kay had thought the very same thing when she was in the shower. Hearing Alan talk about his work at the emergency room brought back memories of her own career working as an ER nurse, though many of them had to be held off at arms' length. They were bloody and painful. Still, the exhilaration she had felt when she was able to step in and take a situation that was deteriorating fast and stabilize it, even turn it around, was the biggest high she'd ever known.

"I liked being a nurse," Kay told Ruby, her words conveying more than simple facts.

"The tides of life take us to different ports. Not always the ones we want, but always the ones that need us. Would you like me to read the tarot cards or tea leaves?"

"I'll pass." Kay could never decide how much of Ruby's gypsy persona was real and how much was put on like backstage greasepaint.

"Yin likes you. He's not as smart as Yang, but he has a bigger heart," Ruby said, referring to her two sibling tabby cats. Kay found them cute, but slightly spooky. They were perfect companions for Ruby.

"Yin *is* sweet," Kay agreed.

"That's settled then," Ruby said cryptically. "What do you think about Bigfoot?" Another of Ruby's quirks was abruptly changing the subject in the middle of a conversation. "I was watching that show with Spock where he talks about strange things."

"You mean Leonard Nimoy?" Kay said, trying to keep up with Ruby's thoughts.

"*In Search of.* That's the name of it. This episode was about Bigfoot. I'd love to meet him," Ruby said with a wave of her fork.

Kay didn't know if Ruby meant that she wanted to meet Leonard Nimoy or Bigfoot.

"The soldiers I patched up in Vietnam told me some wild stories about what they saw in the jungle." As soon as the words were out of her mouth, Kay regretted it. Ruby's eyes focused on her with rapt attention.

"What kind of things?"

"Oh…" Kay would have preferred not to bring up some of those memories, but she'd learned long ago that getting Ruby off the scent once she was dogging you wasn't possible.

"Well, there was a young soldier, Clark, who had been accidently shot by another member of his squad. Clark said a band of ape-men had been throwing rocks and stalking their squad for almost two days. The second night, everyone's nerves were on edge. They were miles deep in thick jungle under a second lieutenant who didn't want to admit that he was out of his depth. When the creatures started pummeling the soldiers at three in the morning, one of the men started shooting and then everyone else got spooked and fired wildly into the jungle. Clark was hit, but he didn't blame his buddies. He said they were all scared to death at that point. Of course, no one above the rank of captain would admit that the creatures existed."

"Did the locals believe in them?"

"The farmers called them Batututs."

"Batututs." Ruby rolled the word over her tongue, listening to the sound of it.

"It means something like wild men or men of the woods."

"There must of have been some women in the woods too," Ruby joked.

"Did Lester go with Lee?" Kay wanted to move the conversation on from the rock apes of Vietnam. She didn't even understand how they'd gotten on the subject to begin with.

"Lester was helping Alison at the shop this morning, so Lee went to pick him up."

"We have enough business now that Lester doesn't have to do part-time work for Alison," Kay said, even though she knew that Lee's relationship with Alison was a big part of the reason he let Lester continue to work there whenever Alison needed the help.

"Now you know Lester loves the gadgets and Lee… well, Lee's in love too," Ruby said with a sly smile.

"Do you think it's serious?" Kay had wondered if Lee was really in love or just infatuated with Alison.

"He's smitten. I'm not sure about Alison. She likes him… but…"

"Do you think it's the funeral home?" Not everyone was ready to be in a relationship with a mortician.

"She's a practical girl," Ruby said. "I don't think she'd let a few dead bodies in the parlor bother her. Right now, she's just more interested in running the shop."

"That's understandable. She seems to be good at business and loves the gadgets as much as Lester does."

"I saw Mr. Harman at the store yesterday, and he bought

one of those video recorders from her. Lots of other folks have too." Ruby sounded surprised.

"I don't know if she's going to sell enough of them to keep her movie rental business afloat."

"I love old movies," Ruby said wistfully. "Maybe I'll buy one with my bonus."

"What bonus?" Kay looked up at Ruby and saw the teasing grin on her face.

"You *did* say the business was doing well."

"Christmas is four months away."

"I think she has a layaway plan."

"I need to go check on some supplies Lee ordered." Kay ignored Ruby's last comment and got up from the table.

As she sat at her father's old roll-top desk, going through records and calling suppliers, Kay's mind wandered again to the idea of going back to work as a nurse. She was pulled out of her musings by the sound of Lee and Lester coming in the back door.

"How did it go?" she asked as Lee walked past the open door of the office.

Lee stopped abruptly and turned toward her.

"The body was hanging from a ladder," he said as he came into the office. He glanced up at a photograph of his father on the wall as he sat down in a chair by the desk. In the photograph, his dad was standing by the funeral home's sign on the day that it had been installed. The sign, now almost thirty years old, was still lit up every night to announce to the world that the old Victorian house was the Lamberton Funeral Home. Only recently had Lee been able to meet his father's eyes when he looked at the picture. Before now, the funeral home had been bleeding money to the point that he'd been convinced he would lose the business and have to take the sign down.

"Was he hanged?" Kay asked.

"No, he caught his foot in the ladder of a deer stand. He was hanging upside down with his head about two feet from the ground."

"That's kind of gruesome." Kay made a face. "Was it an accident?"

"That or a natural death. The guy was in his sixties. Could have been a heart attack. The guys from the coroner's office took the body so there'll be an autopsy."

"Strange way to die."

"Seemed odd to me too," Lee agreed. "I almost can't see how it can be an accident. Still, who's going to hang a guy up by his foot?"

"I've seen something like that," Kay said, having a flashback. Maybe it was brought on by the conversation about Batututs in Vietnam or just the idea of a man hanging upside down, but she suddenly remembered an incident where a soldier had been left hanging in a Viet Cong camp. "I'll be interested in what the autopsy says."

"Really?" Lee was surprised because Kay wasn't normally interested in the bodies. She preferred to stick to the business side of the funeral home.

"I just... I have an odd feeling about this."

"It's going to be a day or two."

"Let me know when you pick up the body," Kay said, feeling puzzled. She didn't understand why she felt something was wrong. Maybe it was just the fact that anything that stirred up her memories of Vietnam uncorked emotions she'd spent a lot of time bottling up.

On Friday, Lee pulled Bertha, bearing the body of Roger Harrington, into the driveway of the funeral home. Lester helped him roll the man into the cooler at the back of the embalming room.

"Are we going to embalm him this afternoon?" Lester asked as they closed the door on the cooler.

"I need to call Dwayne McKenzie and see if he has any more information on Harrington's relatives."

"Didn't he mention an ex-wife? Wouldn't she know who his closest relative is?"

"The ex is apparently hard to get ahold of."

"I could at least clean him up. I'll have time after we get done with Mrs. Evans," Lester offered. Even though the coroner's office had removed the soiled clothes and cleaned the body enough to examine it, the corpse still needed to be washed properly before it could be embalmed.

"That'd be fine," Lee told him before he went to find Kay. He was still curious about her interest in Harrington's death.

"We picked up Mr. Harrington today," he informed Kay when he entered the office.

"What did the autopsy reveal?"

"Preliminary report is positional asphyxiation due to accidental causes," Lee said, picking up the phone on the desk. "I need to find out if McKenzie ever contacted any of Harrington's relatives."

"Shouldn't the sheriff's department notify the next of kin?"

"McKenzie told Henry he'd do it. I just need the next of kin to authorize his embalming or tell me who to turn the body over to." Lee dialed the phone.

"Yeah?" Dwayne McKenzie answered after half a dozen rings.

"Mr. McKenzie?" Lee could hardly hear him over the sound of an engine running in the background.

"Who's this?"

"Lee Lamberton at the funeral home. Were you able to get up with Harrington's ex-wife or someone from his family?"

McKenzie cursed and then apologized. "I've been running full-throttle with a thousand acres of hay to cut and bail. I've left a couple of messages with his ex-wife, but she hasn't called me back. Or if she did, she didn't leave a message on my answering machine. Look, I'm spending sixteen hours a day in the fields right now. The only reason you caught me was because I needed more bailing twine. I'll pay you if you just take on the responsibility for all this. We have a window with the weather, and I need to take advantage of it."

"Don't worry about the money. We'll take care of it."

"'Preciate it. Let me know what you find out and I'll help out with the arrangements," McKenzie shouted over the rumble of a diesel engine.

"No problem," Lee assured him.

"That didn't sound encouraging," Kay said as Lee hung up the phone. "I'd like to see the body."

Lee raised his eyebrows and headed for the door. "Sure. Lester just rolled him into the cooler."

The embalming room, an addition to the back of the Victorian structure, was the largest room in the house. There was room for several embalming tables and lots of shelves for all of the fluids and supplies used in the business, as well as the walk-in cooler where several bodies could be stored at any one time.

Lester was preparing Mrs. Evans for embalming when Lee and Kay came in.

"What are you doing in here?" Lester asked, startled to see Kay.

"I own half the business, remember?" Kay shook her head. "It's true that I'm not a fan of the embalming process, but it's not like I avoid the room."

"You don't come in very often," Lester said, oddly

embarrassed at the nude body of the septuagenarian on the embalming table. "I was just getting ready to… you know." He held up the tube and needle used to drain the body of blood and replace it with embalming fluid.

"Don't let me stop you."

"She just wants to see the Professor," Lee assured Lester.

"He's in the cooler," Lester said, still looking confused.

Lee rolled the Professor's corpse, still in a body bag, out on the gurney and positioned it under a chrome lamp before unzipping the bag.

Kay reminded herself that this was her idea as she reluctantly stepped up next to the gurney. The odor was unpleasant, but not unexpected. The body was discolored and bore the classic "Y" incision across the chest from the autopsy. The stitching was clunky and distracting. Kay knew that during the embalming process, Lee would take out the crude stitches and sew the chest neatly back together. The worst of it was Harrington's face, purple and bloated from the blood that had settled in the head as he hung upside down.

"Some gloves." Kay held out her right hand.

"You're serious about this." Lee pulled out a pair of latex gloves and handed them to her.

With the gloves on, she gently lifted the man's head and felt along the neck for any damage.

"Can you lift him up?"

"Lester, give me a hand," Lee called out.

They bent the body at the waist, allowing Kay to examine the Professor's back.

"What are you looking for?" Lee was genuinely curious.

"If he had fallen backward on the ladder with his foot caught in the rungs, wouldn't you expect there to be some damage to his head or shoulders?"

"Yeah, but it's kind of hard to tell with all the lividity,"

Lee said.

"Still, you'd expect to see some type of abrasion. Maybe even a cracked skull. You can put him down."

As they eased the body back down on the gurney, Kay went to the other end.

"Which foot was he hanging by?"

Lee looked up, trying to remember. "The left. Wasn't it?" he asked Lester.

"I climbed up and… Yeah, it was the left," Lester affirmed.

Kay took Harrington's left leg out of the bag. She rotated it, feeling the bones in the foot and ankle.

"You'd also think that his ankle or foot might have been broken."

"If it had been broken badly enough, he probably would have slipped out and fallen to the ground," Lee pointed out.

"True. It's almost hard to imagine how he could have *not* fallen all the way to the ground."

"What's your point?" Lee didn't like the way this was going.

"I saw a man hanging by his foot in a village in Vietnam. A group of us were taken there to help some wounded locals. Colonel Mims was one of the few officers who was willing to go out of his way and commit resources to helping the villagers who'd been caught in the crossfire. This particular village had been held by the Viet Cong for almost a week before we retook it. Anyway, behind one of the huts, the VC had rigged up a bamboo tripod that stood about eight feet high. Tangled inside this tripod was a middle-aged Vietnamese man. I knew at a glance that he was dead, so I went to work helping the wounded instead."

"That's awful," Lester said.

"Later, when I was taking a break, I asked a sergeant why the man had been strung up that way. He told me that the man was one of our friends and the VC had been trying to get information out of him. The sergeant explained that, if you hang a man upside down, you can ask him questions and when he starts to pass out, you bend him at the waist and hold him up for a minute until he recovers. At that point, you let him hang down again and the process can be repeated over and over. It's a slow, passive form of torture. They would sometimes pour water on the subject as added torment."

"What's that got to do with the Professor?" Lee asked, almost afraid to hear her answer.

"Maybe it's nothing. Still, the only way I can think of for him to be hung up like that without more physical damage was if someone put him there." She sighed. "Ruby got me talking about my time overseas the other day. I could just be dredging all of that up in my head and making a mountain out of a molehill."

"Murder seems… a little hard to believe." Lee frowned and looked down at Harrington.

"You're right. Why would someone torture an older guy like this?" Lester frowned.

Lee and Lester looked at each other.

"What?" Kay asked them.

"I mean… It's probably nothing." Lee looked uncomfortable.

"Is there a reason someone might have tortured him?"

"Gold!" Lester blurted.

"What?"

"He was out in the woods hunting for gold," Lee explained reluctantly.

"There's no gold around here. The closest place to find gold is in North Georgia."

"No, not natural gold. He thought the Spanish hid a bunch of gold and jewels around here."

"You're kidding?"

"He taught history at the University of Florida and found some Spanish manuscript that apparently suggested that the crew of a wrecked galleon buried the gold around here."

"Why here?" Kay asked dubiously.

"They wrecked on the west coast and were trying to reach St. Augustine. At some point either the natives, disease, the weather or a combination of all of that wore them down and they decided to bury the treasure. The Professor here thought it was on McKenzie's land or close by."

"And that's what he was doing when he died?" Kay was having a hard time believing the story.

"Apparently. Now you're talking about him being tortured. I can't think of a better reason to torture someone than to find a fortune in gold." Lee looked up at the ceiling as though to ask the heavens why he always ended up in these crazy situations.

"Do you think he knew where the gold was?" Lester asked.

"If he knew where it was, then wouldn't he have come forward and told someone?" Kay asked.

"Think about the *Atocha*," Lee said. "After eight years in court, they just settled the claim last month."

Kay nodded. "I read about that. They searched for years for the wreck of that Spanish galleon before finally finding it near Key West."

"The salvage company has been fighting for the rights to the treasure since the mid-seventies. So you might not want to just pop up with a bunch of treasure without studying the legal issues first."

"And the *Atocha* was, like, twenty miles out to sea," Kay mused.

"Exactly," Lee said. "Finding treasure on dry land would

really get the government after you. Even if you planned on coming clean about finding it, you might want to talk to a lawyer first."

"Or maybe someone just *thought* he'd found the gold," Lester suggested.

"Out of the mouths of babes," Kay joked. "Bad guys often aren't very smart."

"So what should we do with Mr. Harrington?" Lee asked her.

"What are the odds we can convince the coroner to reconsider his verdict?"

"It's not final until they get all the lab reports back. I just got the CliffsNotes version of the preliminary autopsy report."

"What's your friend think?"

"I haven't talked to Glen about it." Lee's friend Glen Doyle was an assistant at the coroner's office. He had been a pathologist but lost his license years ago, so the morgue treated him like a red-headed stepchild and he was frequently assigned the night shift.

"But he'll have some insight into the decision-making process?"

"He has all night to sit there and read reports… if he wants to." Lee knew that Glen spent most evenings reading horror stories and furtively sipping Scotch from a flask.

"I'd like to ask him some questions about the autopsy," Kay said with a determined look.

"I'll talk to him. It only costs me a bottle of Scotch." Lee was already considering how he would approach Glen when another roadblock occurred to him. "We need to find out who the next of kin is. Mr. Harrington might not even be our responsibility."

"I see your point." Kay felt oddly deflated. Did she really want to get entangled in another murder investigation? "You said Harrington taught at the university. They should have a record of the next of kin."

"He has an ex-wife too. She might still live in Gainesville," Lester added.

"We've got to finish with Mrs. Evans, and the Wilkins viewing is tonight," Lee said, wondering when he'd have the time to track down Harrington's relatives. Tiger Wilkins had been a local football star back in the late forties and had run several businesses in town. At only sixty, he'd left a grieving family and community behind that wanted to show how much they were going to miss him. The viewing would be well attended, and the funeral would be even larger.

"I'll do all the legwork," Kay assured him. "But go ahead and ask your friend at the morgue if we can come over there and talk to him about the autopsy."

"Are we sure we want to start something we might have a hard time finishing?" Lee wasn't sure he wanted to get too deep into this. With the business going well, he found himself more reluctant to rock the boat.

"Wasn't it Dad who always said we had to do everything we could for our clients?" Kay asked.

"This is a role reversal. I'm usually the one telling *you* what Dad would want." Lee frowned and looked down at the sad remains of Roger Harrington. "I guess if Mr. Harrington was murdered then we should try and get someone to look into it."

"Maybe we'll find the gold," Lester said with a grin.

"I've seen *The Treasure of the Sierra Madre*. Let's hope there isn't any gold," Lee told him. "I'll call Glen and ask if he'll look over Harrington's autopsy report."

"And I'll see what I can find out at the university," Kay said.

"I guess I'll do all the work around here," Lester muttered with a wry grin.

CHAPTER THREE

Kay put on her most professional clothes for her trip to Gainesville. If she was going to be schmoozing with people at the university, she wanted to look the part. While she changed, she tried to think of who she knew at the school. Surely someone from her high school must work there. Then she remembered Vince Edwards. *How about someone I* haven't *already pulled into a murder investigation*, she told herself firmly. With a sigh, she realized she'd have to call Zach Terrill.

Zach would know, but she was uncomfortable with the idea of calling him. They'd reconnected when she first come back home to Lang, and she had been surprised to learn that Zach had had a crush on her when they were in school together. They'd gone on a few dates, but Kay hadn't felt any sparks, just a companiable friendship, and she'd decided that it was unfair to continue dating him. They had stayed in touch, but she still felt a little uncomfortable around him.

Zach worked for the Melon County building department, so she decided to head over to his office at the courthouse.

It would be better than a phone call, but much less awkward than visiting him at home.

"He just stepped out," an older woman sitting at a desk outside his office told her.

"When do you expect him back?" Kay asked.

"He just went around the corner to the copy machine. That little room just to the left of the door."

Pleased with this opportunity to appear as if she were running into Zach by accident, Kay headed in the direction the woman had pointed. Zach almost bumped into her as he came out of the copy room, his hands full of file folders.

"Kay!" he said with a wide grin. "What are you doing at the courthouse?"

"Just needed to renew my tag. I wondered if I'd see you."

"Sorry." He held up the folders. "I've got my hands full. Let me put these in my office, then we can go out back and talk. I need a break anyway."

Soon they were sitting on a bench under the shade of a spreading live oak tree that was picturesquely draped in Spanish moss. A storm was brewing a few miles away, bringing a wet, cool breeze that chased off the summer heat.

"I lied. I came here to talk to you," Kay said, feeling the need to come clean.

"You know I'm always glad to see you." Zach gave her his most disarming smile. "Even if it has to be platonic."

"I know our friendship got a little weird when we weren't on the same wavelength."

"My fault, and I won't make the same mistake twice. Let's start fresh. So why did you come to see me?"

"I'm looking for an insider at UF."

"Are you thinking about going back to school?"

"I'm looking for information about a professor. I think he retired or resigned or something about a year ago."

Zach narrowed his eyes. "What are you getting into

now?"

"We're just checking up on… a body that came into the funeral home." Kay tried to look innocent and failed miserably.

"The truth?"

"I wish I was a better liar," Kay sighed. "Okay, Lee got a call to pick up a body on a piece of land owned by the McKenzies. One they use for hunting. Anyway, the body was an older guy who was—and this is the odd part— hanging upside down with his foot caught in the ladder of a deer stand."

"Was it an accident?"

"That's what the coroner thinks."

"But you aren't sure. We've been down *this* road before."

"I'll admit that Lee and I have stuck our noses into some situations that turned out to be a little precarious. Trouble is, I can't ignore my instincts. And I really think this is not what it seems."

"Okay." Zach nodded. "Getting past the question of whether this is a good idea or not, you're looking into this ex-professor's background. What's his name?"

"Roger Harrington."

"I know that guy!" Zach's face lit up in recognition until he remembered they were talking about a dead man. "Wow. I liked him. He was in the courthouse a lot in the last… Oh, I guess six months or so."

"Why?"

"He was looking at old plat maps. I asked him about it, and he told me he was looking for a lost treasure. Something about the crew from a Spanish galleon."

"Did you believe him?"

"That it existed? No. That he was looking for it? That much was obvious. The old guy had a gleam in his eye. He had gold fever, for sure." Then Zach shook his head. "That's not exactly true. I think it was more about proving that he was right than it was about finding the gold. He talked a bit about how his colleagues thought he was crazy and how they would swallow their words when he found the treasure and wrote his book."

"Did you see anyone else with him or talking to him?"

"All the time. He talked to everyone. He had that professor thing going on where he wanted to tell you all about what he was doing and the history of the galleon that sank. Everything. Honestly, once he started talking, it was hard to get away from him. You think someone killed him?"

Kay described her experience in Vietnam and the similarities with the Professor's death.

"I admit it's an interesting coincidence. Still, it seems like a stretch," Zach said.

"I'm not saying he was killed. I just want to look into the possibility since the sheriff's office isn't going to do it."

"Harrington was a nice guy. If there's any doubt, he deserves to have someone look into his death." Zach seemed to gather his thoughts. "I remember he said he taught Spanish history. Claimed he was fluent in medieval Spanish. Oh yeah, he mentioned an ex-wife a few times too. When he talked about her there was a little, not bitterness, but maybe irritation. Like he wanted to prove something to her."

"Do you know someone I can talk to at the university? I was hoping that one of our old classmates might be working there."

"Do you remember Elma Rutledge?"

"Thin, blonde, smart, never said much?"

"That's her. Elma went to UF and never left. She received a doctorate in sociology and now she's on a tenure track. I can give you her number."

"You kept up with her?"

"Her parents still live in town. Her father is a general

contractor, so I run into him sometimes when he's pulling a permit for a project."

Kay caught the look in his eye. "Did you go out with her?" she teased.

He rolled his eyes and blushed a little. "We went out a couple of times. It's been a few years. Hey, there's also Ken Bailey. He's with the campus police."

"I don't remember Ken."

"He's a little younger than us. Your brother might know him. My dad was friends with his dad, so we all went camping and fishing together. I was irritated sometimes that I had to babysit him, but he was a good kid. Became more of an outdoorsman than I did. Heck, Ken still goes on trips with our dads."

They reminisced a little longer, then Zach finally said, "I need to go back to work."

They stood up and Kay reached out to take his hand. "Thanks."

"Don't get into any trouble." Zach gave her hand a gentle squeeze before he walked away.

Kay headed straight to Gainesville. *Strike while the iron is hot and all that stuff,* she told herself.

She decided to start with Elma and lucked into a visitor parking space only a quarter of a mile away from the sociology building. The summer session was winding down, and there were less people on campus than there would have been during the fall or spring semesters. Walking across the green, she wanted to stop the self-involved young people she passed and explain that the university was an imaginary world that had little to do with the real world they would soon be in.

When did I get so jaded? I'm only ten years older than most of them, Kay wondered, then reminded herself: *But a couple of tours in a war zone adds more than a decade to your age.* The idea that life could be ended in an instant and as capriciously as the flip of a coin would take most of these students many more years to learn.

She found Elma Rutledge in her office, grading final exams. She knocked gently on the doorframe and said, "Elma?"

The woman looked up and pulled a pair of reading glasses from her face. "You must be a ghost from my past. I don't use Elma anymore." She smiled at Kay. "I do know you, but I can't quite put my finger on it."

"Kay Lamberton. We were in high school together."

"That's right! Call me Ellie." She held out her hand. "Elma always made me think I should be a recurring character on *Little House on the Prairie*."

"I like Ellie better."

"Aw, thanks. I think I've come a long way from that shy girl who was afraid to speak in class," Ellie said. "And now I stand up in front of hundreds of students every day.

"So what's your story? I remember you were always running around with the high achievers." She grimaced. "I heard about the murders last year. Who'd have thought that… Wait, why don't we go sit down somewhere that we can talk?"

"That would be great," Kay said, surprised but pleased at the woman's chatty demeanor.

"We can walk over to the Rathskeller," Ellie suggested.

They chatted a bit about mutual high school memories as they walked. The combination beer hall and restaurant was located in the basement of a building on campus. It was dimly lit and smelled of grease and stale beer.

"Can I buy you lunch?" Ellie asked as they sat down at a booth along the wall.

"Just iced tea."

"I know I shouldn't eat here, but…" Ellie shrugged. "I think I'm addicted to the grease."

Ellie placed her order, then settled back in her seat expectantly.

"I guess you're wondering why I looked you up," Kay said.

"I figured you'd get around to it in your own time. But I *am* curious."

"I'm trying to get some information on a professor, Roger Harrington. He taught Spanish history here about a year ago."

"Dr. Harrington." Ellie shook her head. "I didn't really know him, but I'm friends with his ex-wife, Joyce."

"Does she teach here too?"

"She quit at the end of the spring semester. Now she's over at Flagler College in St. Augustine. Truth is, she went there to be with a man she's been having an affair with. I guess it's not an affair now that she's divorced from Roger. Why are you interested in Roger?"

"He's dead," Kay said, belatedly realizing that she'd been a little blunt. "My brother picked up his body this morning. We don't have a next of kin so…"

"Oh my! Roger's dead? Wow. Not that I knew him that well. I've just heard Joyce talk about him for years. I need to call her."

"I'm not sure she knows yet."

"Really?"

"Like I said, we were asked to attend to his body, but the person who called us just owns the property where he died. They weren't close friends."

"That's odd. Of course, Joyce said Roger went a little loopy when he found out she was having an affair."

"You know Joyce well?"

"We met three years ago. A mutual friend of ours is a tenured professor in the English department and she created this informal group to help any women who are on the tenure track. There are about twenty of us that get together a couple of times each semester for wine and gossip. The more wine, the more gossip. Seriously, though, it's been a big help to all of us. Just having a chance to bitch about some of the treatment we receive from the department heads, the men, the students and, frankly, other women. Like they say, knowing you aren't alone prevents you from being alone."

"Did you ever meet Roger Harrington?"

"Once or twice, before he and Joyce got divorced. He was one of those guys... What would you call them? Enthusiasts! You know the type. Sometimes it's model cars, or fishing or the stock market. With Roger, it was Spanish colonial history. Once he got wound up, there was no stopping him telling you everything you ever wanted to know about colonial Spain but were afraid to ask." She chuckled at her own joke. "Having said that, he seemed like a nice guy."

"You said she was having an affair. Who was the other man?" Kay asked.

"Another academic. I think his name is Hugo something-or-other. Apparently, he's a real scholar. Almost the same field as Roger. Spanish artifacts or documents or something. I haven't met him."

They traded a few stories about life after Melon County High School while Ellie ate her lunch. Before they went their separate ways, Ellie wrote down Joyce Harrington's number for Kay.

Kay's next stop was the university's security office. The man at the front desk didn't even blink when Kay told him that she wanted to speak with Ken Bailey. He just pulled out his radio and called for Ken to come to the office.

Ken was six inches shorter than Kay and had a jaunty walk that appeared almost belligerent. That, combined with his red hair, made him look like he'd been sent from central casting to fill the role of an Irish cop.

"You looking for me?" Ken asked, giving Kay a big smile.

"I'm Kay Lamberton." She held out her hand.

"Lamberton… Oh sure, the funeral home over in Lang." He stepped forward and pumped her hand for half a dozen shakes. "What can I do for you?"

"Is there somewhere we can talk?"

"Sure, we've got an interview room." He looked past Kay to the man behind the counter. "I'll be back in a few."

"It's quiet. Take your time." The man sounded bored.

Ken led Kay down the hall to a room with a table and three chairs. There was a window, but the blinds were down. Ken waved her to one of the metal chairs.

"Sorry, the room is bleak on purpose. Makes the suspects nervous and more likely to talk." He took a chair across the table from her. "How can I help you?"

"My brother picked up Roger Harrington's body from a piece of hunting land owned by Dwayne McKenzie. We're trying to get ahold of the Professor's next of kin."

Ken looked shocked. "Professor Harrington is dead? What happened?"

"The coroner is satisfied that it was an accident or natural causes."

"But you aren't?" he asked shrewdly.

"I didn't say that. We're just trying to let his next of kin know that we have his body." Kay was trying not to become defensive, but it was hard with Ken staring straight into her eyes and asking probing questions.

"I know all about your last couple of forays into detective work." Now there was a hint of admiration in his voice.

"We were sort of forced into it since the sheriff wasn't going to pursue the cases."

"I understand. My goal when I was a kid was to become a deputy with the Melon County Sheriff's Office, but when I got old enough to understand how bad our sheriff was I... Well, I took this job until I can get on with a bigger department."

"Okay, here's the deal." Kay decided to be honest with him and went on to explain how Harrington's body had been found and about his search for Spanish gold. After she was done, she leaned back in her chair and looked at Ken to gauge his response.

He seemed contemplative for a few moments. "I met Professor Harrington twice. Once professionally and once when I needed someone to act as a translator. He seemed like a nice guy who talked too much and could be taken advantage of. I see victims like him all the time. They are so mesmerized by their own ideas that they don't have time to wonder what the other guy is thinking."

"You said you met him professionally. What do you mean?"

"He and his wife were having an argument in one of the classrooms and it got out of hand."

"They were violent?"

Ken shook his head. "It might have come to that. But, no, they were just yelling so loudly that they were disturbing a class in the room next door. They settled down pretty quickly when another officer and I showed up. Both of them were still spitting mad but were able to listen to our advice and go their separate ways."

"What did you think of Joyce Harrington?"

"Typical professor. She looked right through me. The only time she took notice of me was when I threatened to call in the Gainesville police and have her arrested. That got her attention. Of course, I got a call from my supervisor the next day that a faculty member had made a complaint against me. My boss and I talked about it, and he went back to her and explained that I could make a fuss and have her dirty laundry aired in public. She dropped the complaint. Needless to say, I wasn't sorry when she left the university."

"I was told she's teaching in St. Augustine now."

"I wouldn't know."

"What was the argument about?"

"Ha! She was cheating on him."

"He caught her?"

"No, I think that's what got her so worked up. I'm not sure he cared. Like I said, Harrington was a very self-involved guy. He was upset that she was going to divorce him. Said she wasn't going to take him to the cleaners. Something like that."

"Hard to understand why he'd want to force her to stay in the marriage when she was cheating on him."

"I can think of some reasons. One, he didn't want to have to pay alimony. Two, pride. Three, he might have figured that was the best way to punish her."

"Did you ever hear anything about the other man?"

Ken rolled his eyes. "There's enough drama on campus without me looking into every professor having an affair. Only thing I know about him is that he wasn't teaching here. I asked her about that after I broke up the argument. I didn't want another person getting involved in the fight. Once I found out he was from out of town, I told them to go their separate ways and that if we heard anything else out of them, they'd both go to jail. Of course, that was a big bluff. Unless they started throwing punches or shooting at each other, the university would do its best to keep it in-house."

"Did either of the Harringtons have any conflicts with other people at the university?"

"I'm sure they did. This place is crazy with backstabbing and sordid affairs. I keep my nose clean and deal with the problems the university wants me to deal with. Parking, theft, parking, drunken students, parking, fights and more parking."

Kay thanked him and headed back to her car. She had at least gotten Joyce's phone number and some insight into the Harringtons' relationship. *Did it have anything to do with his death?* Kay wondered. *I guess it all depends on where Joyce and her boyfriend were at the time.*

CHAPTER FOUR

After Kay had left, Lee spent some time supervising Lester as he started the embalming process on Mrs. Evans. Lester had entered an official apprenticeship program with Lee as he worked his way toward his own mortician's license. Lee was trusting him with more responsibilities, but he liked to be on hand to make sure Lester didn't slip up.

"You're doing good work. Of course, this is the easy stuff."

"You need to let me prepare the next… challenging body that comes in," Lester said.

"We'll see. There's challenging and then there's challenging."

"I mean a case where there can be an open casket." Lester was carefully gluing Mrs. Evans's eyelids shut.

"Understood. As busy as we've been, I may not have a choice soon." Lee took a deep breath, still surprised that he was in the position to say what he was about to say. "I talked to Kay. Now that you're an apprentice and are taking on more of the responsibilities around here, we're going to raise your salary to two-hundred-and-fifty dollars a week."

Lester looked up. "Really? That's like half again what I was making."

"We're bringing in more money, so you deserve to share in our success. Though I encourage you to put some of that into a savings account. If our good fortune doesn't hold, we'll all have to take a cut. Understand?"

"Yeah, sure, that's great! I'll work hard to make sure we have lots of business," Lester said enthusiastically, then added, "Well, you know, short of actually killing anyone myself."

Lee grinned. "I see you're already developing a mortician's dark humor. You know, with the raise you won't need anymore free meals from Ruby."

Lester looked genuinely panicked. "You're kidding, right?"

"I guess," Lee said, leaving Lester to finish up with Mrs. Evans while he went to check on the final arrangements for her viewing.

After several calls to the family, the florist and the newspaper, he dialed Glen Doyle's home number.

"What?" Glen answered brusquely.

"It's Lee."

"You know I work the nightshift, right?" Glen mumbled.

"It's…" Lee looked at his watch "Two o'clock."

"Which means I have another three hours of sleep before I have to get up." Glen gave a heavy sigh. "Okay, to what do I owe the honor of this phone call?"

"It's about an autopsy."

"And I'm not at the office. Call me tonight and I'll look it up."

"You have a pen?" Lee was used to Glen's surly attitude. "The man's name is Harrington. I picked his body up today.

He died with one foot hooked in a ladder."

"I'm not awake enough to make sense of anything you're saying, let alone take notes. Give me twenty minutes," Glen said and hung up on him.

Half an hour later, Glen sounded more friendly. "Okay, that's better. I got ahold of Becket at the office. He was able to fill me in on your case. They didn't find anything that set off alarm bells. The basic bloodwork didn't indicate intoxication. The rest of the labs will take a couple of weeks. Full report to follow."

"We think there's more to it."

"Of course you do," Glen said, and Lee could almost see him shaking his head. "Becket isn't Grade A, but he's not the worst pathologist we've got. What makes you think he's wrong?"

"That's what I want to talk to you about. Not just me. My sister wants to ask you a few questions as well."

"So ask."

"I'd rather you come over here and look at the body. That way we can go over the details in person."

"I work tonight," Glen reminded him.

"Two bottles of premium Scotch."

There was a prolonged silence from Glen's end of the phone line, which surprised Lee.

"No, not this time. Look, Lester's been telling me about that cook you've got. I haven't had a homecooked meal in… maybe a year."

"I don't know what she's making tonight." Lee was taken aback by the request.

"Anything is better than what I've been eating."

"We'll set a place for you. Get here by five and we can go over Harrington's case before dinner."

"I'll swing by the office and get a look at the autopsy before I come out there."

"Thanks," Lee said, but Glen had already hung up.

Lee and Lester were putting the final touches on the viewing room where Tiger Wilkins was laid out when they heard the door open in the hallway.

"Death is so lovely at your end. You can tell he really enjoyed those Friday night lights."

Glen Doyle stood in the doorway, taking in the site of Tiger Wilkins lying in his mahogany coffin that was draped in the colors of the high school football team. The coffin was flanked by a number of floral arrangements in the same colors.

"We do our best." Lee nudged a torchiere lamp on the right side of the coffin slightly to the left and stood back to make sure it was symmetrical with the one on the other side.

"Where's the body you want me to look at?" Glen's clothes always looked like he'd picked them up at a thrift shop without worrying about the size. The Hawaiian shirt he wore was too large even for his ample frame and the pants were too short.

"In the cooler," Lee said, coming over and shaking his hand. "I really appreciate this."

"I'll get my butt kicked if word gets back to the morgue I'm giving out information on an autopsy that hasn't been finalized."

"We won't tell anyone," Lester piped up.

"All we're asking is for a private... assessment," Lee assured Glen as they walked back toward the embalming room. "Did you get a look at the report?"

"Not a problem. This is Becket's day to sneak out early for a round of golf. He's a walking stereotype." He stopped and turned toward the kitchen. "What's cooking?"

"A pot of ham and green beans that Ruby will serve with

the best meatloaf on this side of the galaxy." Lester smiled.

"Remember, the deal is for the meal." Glen tapped Lee on the arm.

"It made Ruby's day when I told her you were going to have dinner with us," Lee said.

As they passed the office, Kay stepped out into the hall.

"Glen, you remember my sister, Kay."

"Of course." Glen winked at Kay, who rolled her eyes.

"Let's go look at the body," she said, waving them toward the embalming room. She was already starting to wonder if she was making too big of a deal out of the circumstances of Harrington's death, but she had gone this far and was determined to see it through.

Lee rolled Roger Harrington's body out of the cooler and under a lamp, which he flipped on before stepping back.

"Take a look," he said, inviting Glen over with a gesture toward the body bag.

Glen frowned as he stepped forward and unzipped the bag.

"We just want your unbiased opinion," Kay promised.

After a meticulous examination of Harrington's body, Glen stepped back and looked at the naked corpse, which seemed strangely deflated. The assistant to the pathologist had made a half-hearted attempt to fill the cavity with Styrofoam inserts, one of many materials Lee had seen used for this purpose, including newspaper and wood shavings. Despite the effort, the body remained a testament to the corruptibility of the flesh in the absence of the spirit.

"Interesting." Glen pursed his lips. "I was hoping your suspicions were unfounded."

"What'd you find?" Lee asked eagerly.

Glen stepped back up to the body and pointed. "There are several bruises, hematomas that occurred within an hour of death. Here, around both upper arms, and on the leg that wasn't locked in the rung of the ladder. Besides that, there are no abrasions to the back of the head or elbows. Those are the places I would have expected to see them if the subject had fallen backward from the ladder."

"See?" Kay said, nodding at Lee.

"He's not a big man. How sturdy was the ladder?" Glen asked.

"It was a well-built ladder and firmly attached to a deer stand," Lee assured him.

"Did it seem reasonable that he could have fallen and not brought the ladder over on top of himself?"

"It was nailed to the platform which was secured to the tree. Even a larger man could have fallen and the ladder would have held."

"Then nothing contradicts the preliminary cause of death, which is listed as asphyxiation caused by inversion suspension."

"Did they call it an accident?" Kay asked.

"No. They didn't try to explain how he became inverted." Glen shook his head. "While it's suspicious, I would have done the same thing. Put the cause of death without trying to answer the question of how he got in the physical position that *led* to his death. If there was clear evidence that another party had been involved, or if it would have been physically impossible for him to have accidently ended up the way he was found… well, that would be a different story."

"You don't think the bruises and the lack of a head injury aren't proof that he was murdered?"

"The superficial injuries might have been caused by a number of things other than a killer gripping him during the course of the crime."

"What about the injuries that aren't present?" Kay insisted.

"Maybe he slipped and half caught himself before he lost the battle and wound up hanging upside down. Can you say it didn't happen that way?" Glen raised his eyebrows as he posed the question to Kay.

"A hundred percent? No," Kay admitted.

"Beyond a reasonable doubt?" Glen said with a thoughtful look at the body.

"Close," Kay said.

"It does seem unlikely that he could have gotten *gently* hung up in the ladder." Lee laid a couple of pounds of sarcasm on the words.

"He was killed for the gold," Lester blurted.

"What gold?" Glen looked at Lester, then back at Lee.

Lee filled Glen in on what Professor Harrington had been doing on McKenzie's property.

"So he'd found the gold?" Glen asked.

"Maybe, and maybe they were torturing him to find out where it was." Lester looked at Glen, then pointed at Kay. "That's her idea."

With everyone staring at her, Kay explained to Glen what she'd seen during her time in Vietnam.

"Interesting theory. I can see why it would be an effective way to torture someone. Almost killing them and then letting the blood rush back into the brain and air back into the lungs would be similar to holding someone underwater until they're close to drowning." Glen looked back at Harrington's body. "Poor man. Either way, he didn't have an easy death."

"Without the coroner declaring it a murder, we'll never get the sheriff's office to investigate," Lee said.

"Have you talked to Jerome?" Kay asked.

"I didn't see the point in getting him worked up until we knew something definitive." Lee looked at Glen. "But I guess that's not going to happen."

"Sorry. A dead body can only answer so many

questions."

"Jerome's coming in to help with the viewing, so he'll be here for dinner. We can throw it out to him and see what he thinks," Lee said, thinking that he already knew what Jerome would say. Jerome Carter was a full-time sheriff's deputy who worked part-time for the funeral home as security and an occasional extra driver.

"The sheriff isn't going to listen to him," Lester said bluntly.

They all knew Lester was right. Sheriff Tommy Pratt had been elected more for his glad-handing with the powerful people in the county rather than his dedication to enforcing the laws of the state.

"Dinner!" They all jumped at the sound of Ruby yelling from the kitchen.

Lester and Glen almost got jammed against each other in the kitchen doorway in their eagerness to get to the table. As they all found seats, the back door opened and Jerome joined the group.

"Makes my heart sing seeing the table full!" Ruby declared.

"Hey Glen," Jerome said, looking a little puzzled. "What are you doing here?"

"Glen came over for a meal and to talk about our latest client," Lee explained.

"Fill your plates first. No one is going away hungry tonight." Ruby was in her element as she handed Glen a plate.

"We aren't helping ourselves from the stove?" Kay asked, knowing it would rankle Ruby just a little.

"Since we have company, I thought we'd put on the glad rags and the good dishes."

For the next twenty minutes, everyone was focused on the meatloaf, ham and beans, and biscuits.

"Real food. It's been a while." Glen's face bore the widest and most sincere smile Lee had ever seen on the man.

"So what's the big secret?" Jerome asked after his second helping of meatloaf. He looked around the table suspiciously.

"It's not a secret. Kay had some questions about how our latest customer, Roger Harrington, AKA the Professor, ended up dead and hanging from a deer stand," Lee explained.

"You had some questions too," Kay said with a frown.

"We *both* had some questions," Lee corrected.

"The man fell out of a deer stand. What questions are there?" Jerome asked, afraid that he already knew where this was going.

"Technically, he was hanging from the ladder of the deer stand," Lee clarified.

"Henry told me all about it. Accidents happen. Especially when old guys are out in the woods wandering around on their own."

"It's a little more complicated than that," Kay said.

"Of course it's more complicated, 'cause y'all can't just let a body be a body and bury them, which is what you're being paid to do," Jerome said in exasperation, surprising Lee a bit with his reaction. He'd expected Jerome to be skeptical, but not openly hostile to the idea.

"You're beginning to act like the sheriff," Kay told Jerome, causing him to straighten up in his seat and grit his teeth.

"You don't have any idea…" He took a deep breath and looked around the table. "Okay. Lookin' around, I see a couple of people sittin' at this table who aren't well known for keeping their mouths shut." He gave Lester and Ruby hard looks. Ruby glanced up at the ceiling and Lester stared down at the table. "I need you all to *swear* that what I'm going to tell you will stay in this room for the next week."

"Absolutely!" Ruby said, raising her right hand as if she was taking an oath.

"I promise," Lester said with enthusiasm.

"Henry Booker is going to challenge the sheriff in next year's election."

"That's great!" Lee smiled. "You made it sound like a gloom-and-doom sort of thing."

"It's good and not so good." Jerome shook his head.

"Don't you get it?" Kay asked Lee. "It's going to ignite a civil war within the sheriff's office."

"The lady hit the nail on the head. My next year, assuming I don't get fired first, is gonna be a slog through the jungle. As soon as Henry registers for the race, Sheriff Pratt will start deciding who's on his side and who's a traitor. I'll be a marked man."

"Does Henry have a chance? Isn't he a little young?" Kay asked.

"We were in school together," Lee said.

"That's what I mean," Kay said bluntly.

"A dozen of us got together and kicked it around," Jerome said. "And Henry was the only one with the combination of a spotless record, a degree in criminology, graduating at the top of his academy class and a family with connections. He should have already made sergeant or been moved into investigations, but he's too good, if you get my meaning."

"He's a threat to the inept and lazy," Kay said. "I saw it all the time in the military. If you were too good, the do-nothings higher up would put their foot on your head to keep you down."

"What does this have to do with the guy who was murdered?" Lester looked confused.

"What Jerome's saying is that this isn't a good time to stir things up," Lee said.

"We're already gonna be dodging bullets," Jerome agreed.

"You haven't even heard the evidence," Kay told him. "Bad time or not, if Harrington was killed then someone needs to be brought to justice. Right?"

"The sheriff was reluctant before. Now he won't do anything if he thinks someone on Henry's side wants it."

"That's ridiculous," Kay pronounced.

"I'm just telling you how it is, or how it's gonna be once Henry announces he's runnin' for sheriff. I might not even have a job next week."

"He can't just fire you for no reason," Lester said.

"That's where you're wrong. Deputies work at the pleasure of the sheriff. If he doesn't want me working for him, he can give me two weeks' notice. *Sayonara* and don't let the door hit you in the ass."

"Sounds to me like you don't have much to lose," Glen, who'd been sitting back listening to the discussion, spoke up.

"I guess that's one way of looking at it," Jerome admitted. "All I'm sayin' is the heat's gonna be on, and you can't count on me having much say in what gets done officially." He sighed. "Okay, I surrender. Hit me with your evidence. All I know is you picked the body up in the woods somewhere."

Kay and Glen did most of the talking as everyone gave Jerome the details.

"Some barely visible bruises. That's all you've got?" he asked when they were done.

"Evidence is about what's not there too. If he fell, he should have had more damage to his head and shoulders," Kay explained.

"Probably," Glen added and received a frown from Kay. He shrugged.

"I'm not sure I'd open an investigation with that little to

go on," Jerome said. "Maybe sniff around and see if there's any real proof. Where'd you say the body was?"

Lee told him.

"I took a call a couple of weeks ago about a weird kid out there. A neighbor said the boy kept coming on his property." Jerome pursed his lips. "He was a big kid too, nineteen and six feet tall. If he'd given me a little more lip, he would have found himself taking a ride in the back of my car."

"Weird how?" Kay asked.

"He told me he liked walking around in the woods. I got the feeling he was hiding something, but when I pushed him, he clammed up. Turns out, he's living with his grandfather and works part-time at the Fast Mart."

"That's Cody Morgan. I've met him," Ruby said matter-of-factly. Everyone at the table turned and looked at her. She just smiled back.

"And?" Kay prompted.

"Nothing. He's a little… at loose ends, but I think he has talents." Ruby smiled. "Blueberry cobbler?"

"Yes, please," Glen said.

"Wait, what do you mean by *talents*?" Lee asked.

"I've got ice cream too. I always think a scoop of vanilla ice cream tops off a bowl of cobbler perfectly."

"I'll help," Lester said eagerly, getting up to join Ruby by the refrigerator.

"This meal has made up for all the favors you've gotten out of me in the last couple of years. If the cobbler is half as good as it looks, I may even owe *you* a few." Glen grinned at Lee as Ruby placed a bowl in front of him.

"I still want to know what you meant by talents," Lee said to Ruby as she handed him a bowl.

"Nothing. He just… There's a quality about him. I don't think he even understands it yet. Yang has a girlfriend."

Lee knew that when Ruby abruptly changed subjects it

was impossible to get her back to the original topic, so he let it go.

"It would be cool if he had kittens. I mean, if his girlfriend had kittens," Lester said, sitting back down at the table with his own bowl of cobbler and ice cream.

"I did a card reading for both Yin and Yang when they were younger. They were never meant to have kittens, so I had them neutered. Fate can be cruel," Ruby said.

"We'll need to get the girlfriend fixed if she's going to be hanging around here. Just because Yang can't get her pregnant doesn't mean some other cat won't," Lee said. "And as cute as they are, we don't need kittens."

"She's very aloof, a petite tortoiseshell, but I'll try to find out what her motives are," Ruby assured him.

"If that kid wanders around in the woods regularly, he might have met Professor Harrington," Kay pointed out.

"I ran into him out near McKenzie's property," Jerome said, halfway through his cobbler.

"We've got less than an hour before people start showing up for the viewing." Lee looked up at the clock on the wall. "With the hot weather, we'll take turns standing outside."

"There's a good chance Cody might know something," Kay said, refusing to drop the subject.

Jerome sighed. "I'm gonna have to take you out there, aren't I?"

"Maybe he'll tell us something that convinces me to let it go as an accident." Kay gave Jerome a disingenuous smile.

"Yeah, right. Look, I'm working tonight. I'll take you out there tomorrow after the Wilkins funeral." He knew there wasn't any point in fighting her. Until he'd met Kay, he'd always assumed that his grandmother had been the most stubborn person he'd ever meet, but he'd been wrong.

"I'll be ready. Do you need me tonight?" Kay directed the question to Lee.

"Absolutely. I expect at least two hundred visitors. Tiger Wilkins was big man on campus both in high school and college."

"He didn't go professional?" Glen asked.

"Buggered up his knee his senior year at UF. Came home a hero and took over his father's hardware store. A few years later he opened the Fishin' Chicken restaurant, and the rest is history."

"I saw that place driving in," Glen said.

"There are two locations in the county. They're institutions. Actually pretty darn good biscuits, and the fish and chicken ain't half bad either," Jerome said. "Any time, day or night, you'll find at least one deputy eating there."

"That's a slight exaggeration," Lee said.

"Only slight," Jerome fired back. "We come by our deputy bellies naturally."

"You're fit as a fiddle." Ruby shook her head.

"And if I get fired, I won't have a chance to grow my potbelly." He sighed. "And y'all are just trying to give them reasons for firing me."

"It will all work out," Ruby said with her usual Pollyanna attitude. Jerome just stared at her.

CHAPTER FIVE

The viewing was as well attended as Lee had predicted. After the first hour, he headed out to the parking lot to relieve Jerome.

"I spent an hour last night directing traffic around a fallen tree, and here I am parking cars. I can't believe my destiny is to stand in front of people who can't drive and wave my arms at them," Jerome griped.

"Go inside. You can listen to all the middle-aged guys talking about their glory days on the football field. We've got two more hours to go."

Even with the sun low in the sky, the air was warm and sticky as Lee directed cars. The funeral home parking lot didn't have enough space to accommodate a large viewing, so they had a deal with the shopping center across the street to use it as overflow parking. Whoever was directing traffic would allow older people to park at the funeral home and send the young and healthy across the street.

After fifteen minutes of explaining and apologizing for

the inconvenience, Lee saw Dwayne McKenzie's truck pull into the funeral home. McKenzie's wife, Beth, was sitting next to him as they stopped beside Lee.

"I've got some information for you," McKenzie said. "The Professor's ex-wife finally called me back."

Lee looked at the two cars that had pulled in behind McKenzie.

"Go on and park across the street. I'll wait here for you."

McKenzie nodded and pulled out of the lot. A few minutes later, he came walking up to Lee, hand in hand with his wife.

"Joyce Harrington gave me the name of the professor's parents." McKenzie took a piece of paper out of his pocket. "They live in Boone, North Carolina. From what she said, they aren't in very good health. Beth and Harold Harrington. Their phone number and address are on the paper."

Lee glanced at his watch as the McKenzies went into the funeral home. He wanted to call the Harringtons as soon as he could. He saw Kay standing just inside the front door, greeting everyone and encouraging them to sign the guestbook. Lee gave her a wave and she slipped out the door after greeting the McKenzies.

"What?" Kay asked as soon as she was close enough to be heard.

"I've got contact information for Harrington's parents." He waved the paper that McKenzie had handed him.

Kay snatched it out of his hand and read it.

"I'll give them a call," she said, turning back toward the funeral home.

"Hey! That's what I was going to do," Lee said, feeling like he'd been hoodwinked.

"You've got to be quick to beat your older sister." She waved the paper over her head as she walked away.

Lee wanted to argue but was distracted by another car as

it pulled into the drive.

Inside, Kay moved a tea table next to the door and filled it with the stack of memorial fliers she'd been handing out, then she headed for the privacy of the office.

The voice that answered the Harringtons' phone sounded young.

"Is this Betsy Harrington?" Kay asked doubtfully.

"No, this is Maddie Armstrong. I'm Betsy's granddaughter. Can I help you?"

"Is Betsy there?"

"I'm sorry, who is this?" Maddie asked.

"I'm… well… I'm the owner of the funeral home in Lang, Florida. I've got some rather bad news for the Harringtons."

There was silence on the other end of the phone. Finally, Maddie said, "They aren't able to communicate very well over the phone. Grandpa's hearing is very poor and Grandma is… I doubt she would understand. Maybe you could tell me?"

"You're family, so I guess it would be all right. I'm afraid their son has died."

"Oh no. Not Uncle Roger. That's awful," Maddie said. "What happened?"

"That's a little hard to explain… delicately." Kay gave Maddie the opportunity to say that she didn't want to hear the details.

"I guess you'd better tell me what happened." Maddie didn't sound sure about her decision.

"He was found hanging upside down from the ladder of a deer stand."

"Found? He fell?"

"We're trying to figure out exactly how he came to be hanging… there."

"You're trying to figure it out? You said you owned a

funeral home. Aren't the police trying to figure it out?"

"The sheriff's office thinks it was an accident. Your uncle was climbing the deer stand and fell in such a way that his foot got caught in a rung."

"You don't think that's what happened?"

"I guess it just seemed a little odd to us."

"And you own the funeral home. Do you have Roger?" Maddie still sounded confused.

"Yes. The landowner asked us to take the body until the next of kin could be notified."

"Wow, I don't know how… My mother is sort of taking care of my grandparents. She's gone out to a movie. Can I have her call you back?"

"That would be fine. I'm sorry about your uncle."

"He was a nice guy. Funny, both intentionally and unintentionally. I'll miss him."

"Do you know if he'd had any… problems with anyone lately?" Kay asked, feeling only slightly guilty about the question.

"I haven't seen him since he got divorced about a year ago. That's the last time he came to visit. He called once a week, usually on Sunday afternoons. The calls mostly consisted of him asking his parents how they were and Mom having to tell them who it was."

"It must have been tough," Kay commiserated.

"It's hard. Roger seemed to be in denial about their health. He always acted surprised when Mom answered the phone."

"Y'all are their caretakers?"

"It works out for all of us. My dad passed away four years ago when my grandparents had gotten to the point where they needed someone to help out. Mom does most of the work. I'm in college and help out when I can."

"What about his ex-wife? How well do you know her?"

"Is she under suspicion?" Maddie asked.

"Would you be surprised if she was?"

"I don't know. I wouldn't have believed it two years ago, but after what she put Uncle Roger through with the divorce and all… I guess it's possible."

"So you *do* know her?"

"Just… You know, she came with him when they visited at the holidays, and we went down there to visit them a couple of times for vacation. I liked her. They always seemed to get along. Not like some couples fighting every time they had a couple of drinks. There wasn't any of that. When he told Mom that Joyce was involved with some other guy, we had a hard time believing it. Guess you never know."

"Was he broken up about the divorce?"

"He was at first, but then he started talking about how he was going to be famous. Some ancient document and finding a treasure. I didn't follow what he was going on about. Mom says he's been like that since he was a kid."

"He'd been like what?" Kay asked.

"You know. Excitable. He was always finding some golden ring to chase. She told me that when he was ten, or maybe eleven, he got it into his head that he was going to be a professional football player. It was crazy 'cause anyone could look at him and tell… well, it was clear he wasn't going to be a football player. I mean, none of this family are athletes. Mom says that didn't stop him from devoting a couple of years to intense practice and playing for all the local teams he could convince to take him. Eventually it dawned on him that he didn't have any natural ability. After that, it was stamp collecting. That went on for years."

"Was he the type of person to get into arguments with people?"

"Just the opposite. He was very easygoing. He'd talk to anyone. Usually about his latest passion, whatever that might have been."

"Do you know if Roger made any preparations for his own funeral?"

"I doubt it. Mom might know, but they weren't super close. She didn't see him any more than I did."

"Do you know if he had a lawyer who might have a copy of his will?"

"Gosh, I just don't know. I can have Mom call you."

After hanging up with Maddie, Kay was just about to call the number for Harrington's ex-wife that she'd gotten from Ellie Rutledge when Jerome knocked softly on the doorframe.

"We could use some help," he said with a smile.

"Sorry. I just… Never mind." Calling Joyce Harrington would have to wait.

Two hours later, they finally locked the front door.

"If the viewing was this well attended, what's the funeral going to be like?" Kay asked Lee as he loosened his tie.

"It's going to be one of our biggest funerals to date. You said you called Harrington's parents?" he asked as they walked into the viewing room and started to clean up.

"I talked to Harrington's niece." Kay went on to share what little she'd learned.

"He's fine in the cooler until we get some direction." Lee closed and locked Tiger's coffin.

"I just wish I could shake the feeling that his death wasn't an accident," Kay said, separating the flower arrangements into two groups, one that would go directly to the cemetery and another that would be displayed at the church.

"We can look into it a bit more, but there are limits. Jerome was still grumbling about us stirring up trouble when he left a little while ago. And I hate to be selfish, but with business going so well, I don't know if I want to kick the local bigwigs too hard."

"I won't push it too far. Promise," Kay assured him.

"We'll talk with a few more people before we let it go. Come on, let's finish up here and go to the kitchen. I wouldn't mind another bowl of that cobbler."

"I heard that! Don't eat all of it!" Lester shouted from the hallway. "I'll go close up the embalming room and meet you in the kitchen."

The Wilkins funeral was held at ten the next morning. Four hours later, Kay was helping Lee, Lester and Jerome as they unloaded chairs from the back of Bertha.

"I think everything went well. Just one or two hiccups," Lee said with a grin.

"The fight between the siblings to see whose car would be where in the procession was embarrassing," Kay said.

"I thought the daughter had already agreed that her brother's car would be first, since he's the eldest and has written all the checks for the funeral." Lee shook his head. "I should have known she'd be trouble when she kept calling me up behind her brother's back and trying to change the coffin from the one they'd agreed on. Funerals would be great if the living weren't allowed to attend."

"Dad would be proud of you." Kay smiled and gave him a playful punch in the arm.

"I would have lost the funeral home last year if it hadn't been for your help," Lee said gratefully.

"It was a team effort." She looked around at Jerome and Lester, who were leaning against the black 1976 Lincoln Town Car that they used as the main family car. "And I mean all of you."

"So y'all gonna to be able to hire me on full-time when the sheriff fires me?" Jerome asked.

"He won't fire you." Lester waved the thought away.

"There's going to be hell to pay when he finds out that some of us are supporting Henry."

"I hope we don't get you into more trouble by looking into Professor Harrington's death," Kay said.

"Maybe no one will notice. Besides, with a little luck, it will turn out to be an accident and the sheriff won't have to know anything about it." Jerome eased himself off the car and looked at his watch. "You want to go talk to the boy? I've got a few hours before I have to get ready for my shift."

"Sure. Let me shower and change clothes."

"Let's get the rest of the chairs out of Bertha and we'll call it a day," Lee told Lester and Jerome as Kay hurried off.

Soon, Kay and Jerome were heading out of town in Kay's old Chevy Nova.

"We could have taken my motorcycle," Jerome joked, knowing how much Kay disliked his bike.

"I don't mind driving. Do you think we can find the kid?"

"I think we should start with his grandfather, Bert Morgan. The old man's house is about a mile from McKenzie's property where the Professor was found."

"I was a little surprised you were willing to hunt him up this afternoon."

"The sooner we can put this to rest, the happier I'll be."

Kay took her eyes off the country blacktop and looked over at Jerome. "I think you're lying."

"What are you talking about?" he asked, giving her an irritated look.

"I think you like playing detective, and this is a way for you to take your mind off the office politics and do something interesting."

"I'll admit that taking burglary reports, directing traffic and shaking down druggies isn't that much fun. Still, it's what pays the bills. On the other hand, the crazy stuff you've gotten me into in the past has been… kind of cool." He turned and looked at her. "Though not a worth-losing-my-job-over level of cool."

"I've never wanted to get you in trouble," Kay said.

He smiled. "It's just a side effect of your special brand of crazy. It's all good. All the dirt-poor people I grew up goin' to church with would tell me that one door closing means another will open." He pointed ahead. "The driveway is a quarter mile up on the left."

Bert Morgan's farmhouse was in need of paint and the yard hadn't had much attention, but despite that, it reminded Kay of a Norman Rockwell painting, harkening back to a time when most people earned their living working the soil. Next to the house was a 1965 Ford F-150 bearing all the dents and scrapes of a working truck. Kay parked behind it and looked toward the torn screen door.

Jerome started whistling the theme song to *Green Acres* as he stepped out of the car and walked up to the front door. There was no answer the first time he knocked, though they could hear a ballgame playing inside the house on the TV or radio.

"The old guy doesn't hear too well," Jerome said and knocked louder.

When the door finally opened, the grey-haired man looked closely at them. His eyes were green and sharp under a wrinkled and aged brow.

"You're the deputy that came by when that woman complained about Cody." The words were said without inflection, as a simple statement of fact.

"Yes, sir. Deputy Carter."

"Somebody else complainin' about him?"

"We just want to talk to him. He might be able to help us with another… matter." Jerome had almost slipped up and called it a case.

"He's not here."

"Could we ask you a couple of questions?" Kay asked.

"Guess you just asked one." Bert gave her a small grin. "You a social worker?"

"I'm Kay Lamberton. My brother and I own the Lamberton Funeral Home."

He cocked his head to the side and looked at her inquisitively. "Now you got me wonderin' what's goin' on." Bert stepped back from the doorway. "Come on in."

Once inside the dusty living room, he went over to the small thirteen-inch, black-and-white TV and turned off the game.

"Clear off some of the junk and have a seat," he said, waving to a couch half covered with stacks of newspapers and hunting magazines.

Jerome and Kay each moved some of the magazines and eased down onto the faded flowered print of the couch while Bert dropped down into a chair across from them.

"Where is Cody?" Jerome asked, trying not to sound like a deputy.

"Out walkin' in the woods. That's what he does most of the time when he's not workin'."

"He still have his job at the Fast Mart?"

"Yep."

"Do you know if he ever walks down to the McKenzie place?" Kay asked.

"You mean their hunting property? I don't know. Might. What's the owner of a funeral home doin' askin' me questions about my grandson?"

"She's helping me look into the death of a man on McKenzie's property," Jerome answered.

"I heard about that. The guy lookin' for gold." The old man touched the side of his head. "A little daft, if you ask me."

"You knew him?"

"He came by here about six months ago askin' me all kinds of questions about our farm."

"What kind of questions?" Jerome asked.

"How long it'd been in the family. What parts of the land we'd farmed. Had we ever found any odd rocks or pieces of metal. Stuff like that."

"And he told you he was looking for gold?"

"Said he had some ideas that the Spanish had buried gold around here. Said he just wanted to prove it and that the distribution of any treasure would be between the state and the landowner."

"Did your grandson know him?"

"Yep."

They watched Bert, expecting him to elaborate on the statement. Instead, he just stared back at them.

"Cody met him that day or some other time?" Jerome pushed.

"Cody can tell you himself when he met him. How'd this man die?"

"Probably an accident."

"Man goes around talkin' about gold and ends up dead…" Bert shook his head slowly.

"That's why we're looking into it." Jerome was being careful not to mention the sheriff's office. If he let on that this was an official inquiry and it got back to anyone at work, he'd be hung out to dry.

"Have you heard any of your neighbors talking about Mr. Harrington?" Kay asked.

"You mean the fact he died?"

"That… or about him looking for gold before he died."

"The folks at the feed store always gossip about everyone. Nothin' new about that. Don't think they were very interested in this guy, least not after the first couple months. I think most folks thought that he did too much talkin' about the gold and not enough huntin' for it. Figured he was most likely a bit dotty."

"Did you notice anyone in particular showing an interest in Harrington or the gold?" Jerome asked.

"Look here, I mind my own business. If you want to hear a bunch of gossip, go up to the Creekside Feed Store. They'll fill your ear with every kind of nonsense and rumor goin' about." He paused and looked at Jerome and Kay with eyes that had turned dark and cold. "Listen, I'm not an idiot. If you think this guy was killed, then you're lookin' around for anyone that's gotten into a little trouble or acts a wee bit different than everyone else. What I'll tell you is, if you think my grandson hurt this fellow, then you're as wrong as the man who thinks the sun comes up in the west. Also, if you try and frame that boy for this, I'll do everything in my power to bring y'all to heel. Got it?"

"We're just asking questions. No one is trying to frame anyone," Jerome said as Bert stood up.

"Glad to hear it. I think we're done now."

Jerome and Kay stood.

"If someone was involved in Harrington's death, it's for everyone's good that we find out who it is," Jerome said.

"Guess that's right. Though I doubt it has anything to do with me or my family." The old man was slowly walking them to the front door. "Tell you what. If I hear anything, I'll let you know."

"That's all I'm asking," Jerome said, then hesitantly took one of his cards out of his pocket and gave it to the man. "Call me if you have any additional information. We're going to look for Cody. If we don't find him, would you ask him to give me a call?"

"I can do that." Bert nodded and ushered them out the door.

CHAPTER SIX

"What'd you think?" Jerome asked Kay once they were back in the car.

"His first priority is protecting his family," Kay said.

"When I came by looking for his grandson after the trespassing complaint, he got all puffed up and defensive. I did some background on him and his daughter. Cody's mother has been in trouble with the law since she was in middle school. Drugs mostly, but also a couple of burglary charges, theft of services, bad checks. Point being, he's been around this bush a few times. Since it was just a trespassing issue, I didn't dig any deeper."

"I'll be interested to meet Cody."

"Let's go up to the Fast Mart. Maybe we'll find him there or find someone who knows where he is," Jerome suggested.

Kay nodded and started the car. In the window of the farmhouse, she could see Bert Morgan watching them with a deep frown on his face.

"Might be interesting to know what his financial situation

is," Jerome said as Kay pulled the car onto the main road.

"Everyone could use a little gold."

The Fast Mart was doing a brisk business on a summer's afternoon. Kay parked between a Vega and a Datsun pickup truck. Two men in chambray shirts and jeans were lurking by the payphones and slowly walked away when they saw Jerome get out of the car.

"Former tenants of the county jail," Jerome said as he watched them walk around the side of the building.

"Deputy Clark, you on a date?" the blonde, middle-aged woman working the register asked when she saw him holding the door for Kay. "And you've never even taken me out for a cup of coffee."

"Edna, you know you're too hot for me."

"The weather is the only thing hot around here," Edna laughed as she rang up the purchases of a man in painter's overalls. She handed him his change, then he took his six-pack of Pabst Blue Ribbon and left without meeting Jerome's eyes.

"Is that boy, Cody, around?" Jerome asked.

"Awww, don't tell me he's in trouble."

"Do I look like I'm dressed to arrest? This is a private matter. He's not in any trouble," Jerome assured her.

She stopped ringing up the next customer and looked him square in the face to see if he was telling the truth. Satisfied, she said, "That's good. It's hard to find someone dependable help these days. But I haven't seen him. He's scheduled to work tomorrow morning."

Kay bought a Mountain Dew and a bag of chips and Jerome grabbed a Coke and a bag of peanuts, then they left the store.

"What now?" Kay asked.

"Let's cruise around a bit. Go back past the Morgan place and head toward McKenzie's property."

They listened to the radio as they drove slowly down the road, drinking and eating their snacks. The AM station was playing a mix of summer hits. As "Eye of the Tiger" started, Kay drove past the Morgan property, and she wondered if the old man was still staring out the window.

There was a slight rumble in the distance as dark clouds formed on the horizon. Afternoon thunderstorms were a regular feature of Florida summers. Kay hoped they wouldn't get caught in a storm as she pulled up to the gate of McKenzie's hunting property.

"Gate's locked," Jerome observed, looking at the substantial padlock.

"We can climb over," Kay said, getting out of the car.

"You know I arrest people for trespassing, right?" Jerome reminded her.

"Time you saw things from the other side of the fence. Pun intended." Kay was already at the metal farm gate.

"You're going to be the death of me." Jerome shook his head as he came up behind her. "I should have known I was in trouble when you changed into jeans and tennis shoes." He followed her up and over the gate.

"I just want to see the deer stand."

"This place is hundreds of acres!"

"Lee described it pretty well. This road should lead us to the cabin. There's a lake and we follow the path around it."

"Great." Jerome swatted at a pair of mosquitoes buzzing around his ears. "I didn't bring any bug spray."

"It's not far."

A grumble of thunder rolled across the sky.

"Did I mention that we're probably going to get soaked?"

"The minute I get you off pavement, you turn into a baby," Kay chided him.

"Darn right." He smacked at another bug.

Jerome grumbled for the next fifteen minutes until they

rounded a corner and saw the cabin.

"There," Kay said, pointing to it.

"'Bout time." Jerome looked up and froze, grabbing Kay's arm. "Wait."

"What?" Kay jumped at his touch.

"Hush. I think there's someone here." He tugged at her arm as he sank to his knees with his eyes still glued on the cabin.

"Where?"

"I saw something move across that window," Jerome whispered, pointing to the north side of the building.

They watched the building as dark clouds continued to roll in from the west. A loud crack of thunder caused Kay to jump. A second later, Jerome tapped her arm and pointed.

"See?"

A face looked out of the open window as someone reached up and pulled it closed.

Jerome stood up. "Come on. That's Cody Morgan."

"We're going to just walk up there?"

"This was your idea. Do you want the front door or the back door?"

Kay shrugged. "I guess I'll take the front."

"Let's go." Jerome moved fast across the clearing to the cabin, hoping that Cody wouldn't see them before they reached the doors. He mouthed the words *two minutes* at Kay and disappeared around the side of the cabin.

Kay attempted to compose herself as she looked at her watch. When she was sure she'd given Jerome enough time, she knocked lightly on the front door. Nothing. She knocked again. Still nothing. Then she heard shouting from behind the building.

"I'm not going to hurt you and you won't be in trouble if you just settle down!"

Kay ran to the back of the cabin to find Jerome looking

like a cowboy riding a bucking bronco as he tried to control Cody, who was on his stomach, kicking and twisting as he tried to get loose.

"Cody, we talked to you grandfather." Kay kneeled down beside them as Jerome struggled to hold onto Cody. At the mention of his grandfather, Cody turned his head to look at her.

"You had no right to bother him!" Cody yelled. "I have permission to be here!" He stopped fighting, but every muscle in his body was tense and ready to renew the struggle.

"I always run out the back when I have permission to be at someone's house and hear a knock on the door," Jerome said with heavy sarcasm.

"A guy died here a few days ago. I didn't know who was knocking on the door."

"He has a point," Kay agreed.

"Whose side are you on?" Jerome groused.

"I think you can let him up." Kay was looking at Cody's face, trying to get him to meet her eyes.

"You better be right. I won't be in a good mood if I have to chase him down again."

"Can we talk to you?" she asked the young man.

Slowly, Cody looked at her and nodded.

"No quick moves," Jerome warned him as he released Cody and stood up.

Cody got up and brushed the dirt off his jeans. Now that he was standing up, Kay noticed that he was fully six feet tall, if not a little taller, with broad shoulders but still the slim waist and legs of a boy.

"What do you know about the man who died here?" Jerome asked.

"Why aren't you wearing a uniform?" Cody asked, looking closely at Kay and Jerome.

"I wasn't planning on doing any work when I came out here," Jerome told him.

"How well did you know Professor Harrington?" Kay asked quickly, not wanting them to get into another fight.

"A little. We talked a lot," Cody answered.

"What'd you talk about?"

"The gold. A lot about that. He told me all about the manuscript he'd found, and how finding the gold was going to make him famous as a professor."

"What else?"

Cody looked down at his feet and shrugged his shoulders.

"What did you tell *him*?" From Cody's sudden shyness, Kay figured he had confided in Harrington.

"I guess I told him about some of the stuff that's bothering me," Cody admitted.

"You were friends?"

Cody looked up at her. "Yeah."

"I'm sorry you lost your friend," Kay told him. "I'm Kay Lamberton. My brother and I own the funeral home in town. We have Mr. Harrington in our care. If we host the funeral for him, I'll make sure that you can attend."

Cody's face showed a mix of emotions that were hard to read. The most prominent seemed to be gratitude.

"Do you know what happened to him?" Jerome's voice was supportive.

"I heard things. Jerry is an EMT who comes into the Fast Mart. He said that the Professor was found hanging upside down. I don't understand how that could happen. When I asked Jerry, he said he didn't actually see the... body. It was just what he'd heard."

"Do you want to see where it happened?" Kay asked.

"I don't think that's a good idea," Jerome said, locking eyes with Kay.

"I want to know what happened to him," Cody insisted.

"We'll be right back." Jerome waved Kay over to a spot far enough away not to be heard, but where he could still keep an eye on Cody.

"What?" Kay asked.

"If this guy was murdered then there's a possibility that the kid had something to do with it. Or he might be a key witness. We don't want to give him too much information about the crime."

"If it's a crime," Kay reminded him, frustrating Jerome by playing both sides of the question.

"I'm just saying that if investigators get involved at some point, they aren't going to be happy if we gave out a bunch of details about the crime scene," Jerome argued.

"Sounds like some EMTs are already talking about it," Kay pointed out. "Besides, he could come out here any time without anyone being the wiser."

Jerome looked thoughtful. "Guess you have a point. Okay, here's the deal. Don't tell him anything specific, like which foot was hooked in the ladder. Also, let's see if he can lead us to the deer stand. Agreed?"

Kay nodded.

"Do you know where the deer stand is?" she asked when they walked back to Cody.

"Which one?" he asked.

"How many are there?"

"Eight. Three permanent ones and five portable ones."

"Which one is closest?"

"There's a big one on the other side of the pond."

Kay and Jerome looked at each other and Jerome said, "We'll follow you."

Cody walked confidently down the path behind the cabin and around the pond, while dragonflies zipped back and forth around their heads, catching mosquitoes in the afternoon sunlight.

As they walked, Kay thought about how Cody had acted. He seemed sincere in his grief for his friend, though she knew psychopaths could be very good at mimicking emotions. It also seemed odd that they'd found him out there alone in the cabin.

Soon they were standing at the base of the deer stand, where the grass still looked trampled by all the activity on Tuesday. All three of them stared up at the ladder.

"How did it happen?" Cody's voice was barely audible.

"We aren't sure," Jerome said, turning to look at the him.

Kay had imagined that she would be able to tell which rung Harrington's foot had hung up on, but the wooden ladder was too scarred and worn by years out in the elements and the tread of many hunting boots.

"Would Harrington have climbed up there?" Jerome asked, pointing to the platform at the top of the ladder.

"It's possible," Cody said. "He went everywhere looking for the treasure. He hiked all over the place."

"Did you ever go looking for the treasure with him?"

"I guess, a couple of times. He asked me about stuff around here."

"What kind of stuff?"

"Like sinkholes, rocks or really big trees. One time I told him about a place where there are a bunch of big limestone rocks way back in the woods, so we hiked out there."

"It's on McKenzie's property?" Jerome gave Cody a hard look.

"No. It's about a mile from here behind a bunch of farmland."

"Trespassing."

"This was before Mrs. Canfield called the cops." Cody looked down at his feet. "I wasn't hurting anything."

"We had that talk. You can't go on other peoples' property unless they've given you permission. What did I tell you would happen if you did?" Jerome asked seriously.

"Someone will shoot me."

"Exactly. Don't do it."

"I think he gets it." Kay didn't want to shut Cody down. "Did the Professor ever suggest that anyone had threatened him or that he was scared of anyone?"

"No. I guess a few people had told him not to come on their property." Cody looked at Jerome before going on. "But that's all. I mean, some folks made fun of him. Said there isn't any gold out here."

"Did anyone else seem interested in the treasure?" Kay asked.

"You think he was killed." Cody's eyes went wide, full of anxiety. "He was hanging from the ladder. It would take a big guy to do that."

Kay was sure they were all thinking the same thing. Cody was a big guy.

"I…" Cody's mouth moved, but no words came out. He started breathing rapidly.

"You don't have to worry. No one thinks you did it." Kay wasn't sure if she was telling the truth or not. Jerome was still watching the kid closely, and her own inner voice told her there was room for doubt.

"I didn't do anything!"

"Breathe deep. No one is accusing you of hurting anyone," Jerome told him. "There's a real possibility that this was just an accident. We came out here to look around, that's all."

"Are Mr. Harrington's personal items still in the cabin?" Kay thought changing the subject was a good idea.

"I didn't touch anything!" Cody looked ready to run.

"Walk back to the cabin with us. We just want to look around," Kay promised. She felt a little frustrated with his paranoia. Physically, Cody was almost a man, but his emotions and reactions were those of a thirteen-year-old.

"I didn't do anything," he mumbled, but he started walking back down the path.

Kay glanced at Jerome, and he just shook his head as if to say: *This boy has issues.*

They entered the cabin quietly. On their way out to the property, Kay and Jerome had discussed whether they should even look inside the cabin. Kay had been worried about disturbing evidence, but Jerome had pointed out that the crime, if there was one, had taken place *outside* the cabin. If the killer wanted to take any of Harrington's items, then they'd had plenty of time to do so. Looking around and assessing what Harrington had left behind was a better plan than letting others come and go while they waited for an investigation by the sheriff's office that might never happen.

The small building consisted of a large central room that included a kitchen along one side and a fireplace on the other. Four smaller rooms—two bedrooms on the east side and a bedroom and bath on the west side—completed the floorplan. All the furnishings were what you would expect in a cabin used by hunters. The couch facing the fireplace was overstuffed and worn, with the slight odor of beer and cigars. Two of the bedrooms held bunkbeds, and the third had a queen-sized bed on a simple frame. Cody led them into that room.

"He slept here."

Jerome and Kay looked around the room. Harrington's clothes and other personal belongings were scattered around the bed and a small dresser.

"Not a neat freak," Kay said, noticing the dirty clothes tossed in a cardboard box in the corner of the room.

After a quick look around, Jerome went back to the front door and began a methodical, room-by-room search. Then he got down on his hands and knees and looked under the queen bed, where he found a green Samsonite suitcase that looked like it had been tossed around by every bored baggage handler in the United States. He flipped up the latches.

"Bingo!" Jerome said as he looked at the papers and journal inside.

"These must be the records of his search for the treasure," Kay said, thumbing through the journal that bore meticulous notes about his hunt for clues. Each entry included coordinates and descriptions of what he'd found or, in most cases, hadn't found. Kay noticed several sketches of rocks, trees and other natural landmarks. The last couple of pages were filled with drawings of rocks with numbers beside them. Some of the numbers looked like measurements.

Also under the bed, Jerome found a cardboard box full of artifacts—mostly arrowheads and pieces of pottery, but there were a few rusted items that defied classification. Each item had an identification number taped to it.

"He worked at this." Jerome shook his head at the sheer amount of effort it all represented.

"I think it's clear that he believed in his quest," Kay observed.

"What's going to happen to all of that?" Cody had been watching the search from the doorway. His question caused both Jerome and Kay to turn and look at him.

"It belongs to his next of kin," Kay said.

"Who's that?"

"His parents, or possibly his sister." Jerome didn't like the boy's interest in Harrington's possessions, though he had to admit that it didn't look like he'd taken anything yet, though he'd certainly had the opportunity.

"Did he ever mention his family?" Kay asked.

Cody looked embarrassed and didn't meet her eyes.

"What did he say?" Kay pressed.

"A lot of stuff about his ex-wife," Cody admitted.

"Like what?"

"It's kind of embarrassing."

"It's okay. Just tell us what he said," Jerome encouraged.

"It might be important," Kay added.

"Just that she cheated on him with this other guy. He said a lot, a whole lot about the other guy." Cody's face turned red at the memory.

"Can you tell us some of the things he said?" Kay asked.

"He said the guy was a pig, a rutting pig that didn't deserve to be a professor of anything, let alone classical Spain. There was other stuff about the guy's, you know, anatomy. He was still really mad about the affair that his wife had had behind his back."

"What did he say about his ex-wife?"

"That she had been fooled by the... gross baboon. And that she had the morals of a rutting goat."

Kay fought the urge to chuckle. "Do you know if he still had contact with her?"

"I think he called his ex-wife sometimes. A couple of times he talked about her wanting him to go back to work so he could pay her alimony. That made him laugh. He said that he didn't want to keep any of the gold when he found it because his ex-wife and the bloated boar would get their hands on it."

Kay was going to ask Cody another question when there was a pounding on the door that caused all three of them to jump. Jerome's hand went to the .38 Colt Police Positive revolver he had holstered in the small of his back.

"Open up!" shouted a stern voice from the front door. "I own this property and I'm armed."

"It's okay, Mr. McKenzie! It's Deputy Jerome Carter, Kay Lamberton and Cody Morgan," Jerome yelled. "I'm going to open the door. You okay with that?"

"Yes."

Jerome walked to the front door and stepped to the side of the door jamb before carefully turning the doorknob, half expecting the door to be riddled with bullets.

Dwayne McKenzie was standing outside with a shotgun held in both hands, pointed safely at the ground. Sweat on his face glistened in the summer sun.

"What are you all doing out here?" he asked.

"Sorry. We just wanted to take a look at the ladder where Harrington died," Kay told him.

"Is that part of the services your funeral home provides?" There was still an edge to his voice. "Neighbor called me up and said a strange car was parked outside my gate."

"You should have called the sheriff's office," Jerome said, though he was secretly glad that McKenzie hadn't followed his advice.

"My family doesn't call the law if we can deal with it ourselves. Fifty years ago, my grandfather was the sheriff. You goin' to invite me into my own cabin?"

"You know Cody?" Jerome said, stepping back from the doorway.

"Sure. He's the only one of the three of you that has my permission to be here." This time McKenzie's voice was more relaxed.

"There's the matter of Harrington's possessions," Jerome said.

"I thought about that. I figured I'd box them up and send them to his family or give them to 'em at the funeral."

"According to his niece, both his parents are in poor health. Harrington's sister is supposed to call me back," Kay told him.

"I'll box it up then."

"If you don't mind, I'd like to take the items," Kay said.

"Of course, I'll send them to his family."

"What's going on?" McKenzie looked between Jerome and Kay.

"There isn't an official investigation, but we're checking into a few things," Kay said, looking over at Jerome, who was staring up at the ceiling.

"If there's something fishy about his death, why isn't there an official investigation?" McKenzie looked at Jerome.

"The sheriff isn't always willing to open an investigation if he doesn't see a… benefit in it." Jerome gave McKenzie a significant look, hoping that the man would pick up what he was putting down.

"I've noticed." McKenzie nodded. "I don't like the idea that someone was killed on my place. Let me look at what Harrington left behind."

"Most of his stuff is in the bedroom," Jerome said.

They followed McKenzie back to the room where Harrington's suitcase was still open on the bed.

"I think the man could have talked the paint off the walls." McKenzie was casually looking through the suitcase. "I'm not sure I ever saw anyone more obsessed with a single subject."

"He was kinda like Indiana Jones." Cody stepped up beside McKenzie.

Kay watched the two of them interact and noticed that Jerome was eyeing them as intently as she was.

McKenzie picked up Harrington's journal and slowly turned the pages. "He's made detailed notes on his search. He's got coordinates with a lot of the entries." He turned more pages. "I could plot out these places."

"You know your longitudes and latitudes?" Jerome asked. He'd had an orienteering class as part of a search-and-rescue seminar. It hadn't come naturally to him.

"I was with the engineers in the Army. My job was

mapping coordinates. I should be able to cross-reference what I know about the land around here with the coordinates he's recorded. Of course, that assumes that he knew what he was doing."

"He always had a knapsack with a bunch of maps." As soon as Cody said this, the others turned and looked at him.

"Where's the backpack?" Kay asked.

"I didn't see one when we found the body," McKenzie said.

"Let's look for it," Jerome said. "If you find it, don't touch it until I get a look at it."

Kay and Cody looked around the inside of the cabin while Jerome and McKenzie searched outside, including a gardening shed and a pole barn that housed a tractor and other maintenance equipment.

"Nope," Jerome said in response to Kay's frustrated look when they met back up inside the cabin.

"We didn't find it either. So who took it?"

"He could have left it somewhere." Jerome turned to McKenzie. "Did he have a car?"

McKenzie snapped his fingers. "He did. An old beat-up Land Cruiser."

"It was always breaking down. I think it's at a shop in Gainesville that does foreign cars," Cody added.

"The bag could be in the Land Cruiser," Jerome suggested.

"I saw him with it after the car was towed away," Cody said.

"He moved out of his apartment in Gainesville and was living here, but he could have a storage unit in Gainesville," McKenzie said.

"That's something to check out." Jerome sounded doubtful.

"He had the backpack with him all the time," Cody said.

"Now that I think about it, Cody's right. Whenever I saw him, he had the backpack nearby. I never thought much about it," McKenzie said.

"If that's the case, then someone took it," Jerome said.

"Let me check out these coordinates. Maybe he stashed some stuff somewhere other than here," McKenzie said.

"Maybe he did if he got wind that someone might steal his maps," Kay suggested. She looked at Cody and the expression on his face made it clear he didn't believe it.

"You shouldn't stay out here by yourself," Jerome told Cody. "If someone did attack Harrington, anyone out here alone could be in danger."

"I'll keep the gate locked and I'll tell the guys that hunt out here to stay away until we have some answers," McKenzie promised. "This time of year, they're just working on the feed plots and keeping the place mowed. Anything it needs, I'll take care of."

"That warning was for you too," Jerome said.

"I'll keep my eye out. A friend of mine is a helluva tracker. I might get him to come out with me and look for signs of anyone else stalking around through the woods."

"I'd like to come along too," Cody said with a slightly odd inflection that made Kay wonder what he thought they would find.

"If I can set it up, I'll let you know. Come on, if you want me to drive you home," McKenzie offered. "And I'll take you two back to your car."

When they were on their way back to the funeral home, Kay asked Jerome what he thought of Cody Morgan and Dwayne McKenzie.

"They're both hiding things. Trouble is figuring out whether they're hiding things that matter or if it's just the usual stuff people don't want others to find out about."

"Should you have let McKenzie keep the journal?"

"There's not an official police investigation, and it was on his property. Not much I could do to stop him."

"What if he just wants to use it to find Harrington's gold?"

"Again, not much I can do to stop him."

"Frustrating."

"Welcome to my world." Jerome heaved a sigh.

"I hope Henry Booker wins the election. A new sheriff would help."

"There's about a one-in-a-thousand chance of that happening."

"But Sheriff Pratt is awful."

"Don't underestimate his ability to schmooze. He knows just who to sweettalk and who to lock up to get reelected."

"He wouldn't really fire you for backing Henry Booker, would he?"

"He will if I give him an excuse."

Kay pulled into the funeral home's parking lot and Jerome hopped on his Kawasaki motorcycle just as the rain began to fall.

"You're going to get wet," Kay told him, and he just shrugged.

"Let me know if you hear anything back from McKenzie," he said and roared off.

CHAPTER SEVEN

While Kay and Jerome headed out to find Cody Morgan, Lee and Lester finished putting up the funeral gear. Lee gave his apprentice the afternoon off, but he knew Lester would be back for dinner.

Lee had just decided to head over to the appliance store to visit Alison when he heard the phone ring. He picked up the extension in the hallway.

"Hi, this is Tess Armstrong. Roger Harrington is… was my brother." The woman sounded nervous and emotionally on edge.

"I'm so sorry for your family's loss," Lee told her.

"I don't understand… What happened?"

Lee explained what they knew about Harrington's death.

"Rog was always a little strange. I don't know how I'm going to explain this to our parents." There was a tremor in her voice. "I don't know what to do now. Is the funeral going to cost much?"

"It depends on what you'd like us to do. Did Roger ever

express any opinions about how he should be buried?"

"Not that I know of. Joyce might know, but they had such a contentious divorce that I don't know if she'd even care. I can't afford much. I quit work to take care of my parents and all they get is Social Security. Even the house is heavily mortgaged."

"Do you know if Roger had a lawyer? Maybe some insurance?"

"He did hire a lawyer for the divorce. I don't know about insurance, but maybe Joyce would. I've mostly seen my brother at the holidays over the past few years. We weren't that close."

For Lee, this is the worst part of the funeral home business: having family members who wanted to do the right thing by the deceased, but who simply didn't have the money for a proper funeral.

"It would probably be cheaper to have your brother buried down here. That would eliminate the cost of shipping his body. Of course, cremation is the least expensive of your options," Lee explained gently.

"I don't know. Do I have time to think about it?"

"Of course. If you want, I can send you some cost estimates for different options."

"Yes, that would be helpful."

After making arrangements for Lee to send her a quote via fax, Tess hung up, still sounding overwhelmed.

Lee considered working on the numbers right away but decided to put it off until later and walked down the street to Alison's shop. Even the short walk left him sweating, so it was a relief to open the door to a wave of cool air.

The little bell above the door jangled when he entered, and Alison looked up from the cash register where she was checking out a customer. Her face blossomed into a cheery smile that made Lee's heart swell. Over the last couple of months, he'd tried to understand his feelings for Alison. He was pretty sure that he'd moved on from infatuation to something close to real, actual love, but he couldn't figure out was why he wasn't working harder at the relationship. He felt an internal reluctance that he couldn't wrap his mind around. There were two voices inside his brain, one telling him to live in the moment while the other one sounded like the robot on *Lost In Space*, warning him about the dangers of falling in love.

The customer left and Alison gave Lee her full attention. "This morning was amazing. I won't know until I clear out the register tonight, but I think it was the best day yet." She held up her hand with her fingers crossed.

"You're incredible."

"I'm really glad that your funeral home is doing so well now. If y'all were still on the edge of a financial cliff, I couldn't brag about the store."

Lee gave her a light kiss. "I hope I could be proud of you no matter how well I was doing."

They spent a few minutes chatting, then Alison asked, "Does Kay still think that guy was killed?"

"More than ever. She's out now with Jerome trying to find a kid who's been hanging around the McKenzie property." Lee went on to tell her about everything else they'd learned.

"The ex-wife. It's always the ex," Alison told him before going over to help a woman pick out a stereo for her son's birthday.

Lee remembered that Kay had said she had a phone number for the ex-Mrs. Harrington. He thought it would be interesting to talk with her. Alison was right that murder was often the bitter fruit of love.

He waved to Alison as she continued her sale, then headed back to the funeral home. He found Joyce

Harrington's number on a note on Kay's desk and gave her a call.

"Yes?" came a wary woman's voice from the other end of the line.

"I'm trying to get ahold of Joyce Harrington."

"Who is this?" she asked suspiciously.

"I'm a mortician. We have Mr. Harrington's body and I need to speak with her." Lee didn't want to assume that the woman was Joyce.

"What do you want?"

"Are you Joyce?"

"Yes, yes, yes. Now what is it you want of me?"

"I've talked with his niece, but his family isn't really in a position to assist with the funeral arrangements, so I wanted to speak to someone else who knew him."

"Are you handling the funeral?"

"I believe so. We're still waiting for the final word from the family." After his talk with Tess, Lee wasn't even sure there would be a funeral, but it still provided an excuse for calling Joyce.

"So ask away."

Taken aback by her brusque manner, Lee decided to start with questions that would be helpful for the hypothetical funeral. "What type of music did he like?"

"He was a folk music guy. I used to get so tired of him playing old folk songs and sea shanties." Lee was surprised to hear a slight wistfulness in her voice.

He asked several more questions about Harrington's preference in dress, flowers and religious texts. Finally, after about ten minutes, Joyce started to sound more relaxed. Lee was just getting ready to shift the conversation to possible enemies that the Professor might have had when Joyce suddenly started to cry.

"I feel awful," Joyce moaned.

"You'll be at the funeral?" Lee asked, feeling a little awkward with the turn of the conversation.

"I couldn't. No, I just couldn't."

"Funerals can help people express their grief," he said, slipping into his mortician's voice.

"I… I feel… No, I really couldn't."

"I'll keep you informed of the arrangements in case you change your mind."

"Of course. Thank you."

Not wanting to lose the opportunity, Lee asked, "Do you know anything about his hunt for Spanish gold?"

The words were barely out of his mouth before she burst into more tears.

"Can you tell me anything about that?" Lee knew he'd hit a nerve.

"Why are you asking these questions?" she wailed. "I thought you were a mortician. Now you sound like a police officer."

Before Lee could say anything else, she slammed the receiver down, leaving a ringing in Lee's ear. He looked at the phone, wondering why she had sounded so… upset… angry… or maybe guilty.

He kept coming back to guilty. St. Augustine was only a couple of hours away. A person could easily make the round trip in half a day. He thought again about what Alison had said about ex-wives.

When Kay came into the house, she was greeted by the smell of meat in the oven and Ruby smiling as she stirred a boiling pot of macaroni.

"Brisket and mac-and-cheese tonight. I thought everyone could use a little downhome comfort," Ruby told her.

"Biscuits?"

"You know it."

"Sounds good to me." Kay nodded and went to the office, where she found Lee waiting for her.

"What did you find out?" he asked.

Kay filled him in on the afternoon's events, then he told her about his odd phone call with Joyce Harrington.

"The gravy's getting thicker." Kay shook her head.

"Grandma used to say that." Lee smiled. "I can hear her voice."

"You were only eleven when she passed away."

"I wish I'd gotten to spend more time with her."

"And Mom and Dad," Kay said wistfully.

"Life is short and nothing is guaranteed. That's the one thing you learn handling funerals day in and day out." Lee shook himself. There had been times after his dad died when he'd felt despair, an overwhelming darkness that lurked just around the corners of the funeral home. At first, he couldn't decide if the memories of his parents made that darkness stronger or helped keep it at bay. After a while, he figured out that it wasn't the memories, but how he thought about them. If he only saw loss, then the darkness grew, but if he could think of them as shiny moments of happiness preserved in time, then he was able to take power away from the despair that threatened to wash over him.

"Are we closer to deciding if the death was a murder?" Kay asked.

"All I know is that we have a bunch of good suspects," Lee said.

"Cody Morgan, Dwayne McKenzie, the ex-wife and anyone who might have wanted to find Harrington's gold."

"Joyce Harrington was certainly putting off some weird vibes today."

"I'd have to say that Cody was too."

"You also mentioned McKenzie. What motive does he

have?" Lee asked.

"If the gold is on his property, I think that would be enough." Kay tapped a copy of the *Gainesville Sun* newspaper that was on the corner of her desk. Among the front-page articles was one on the collapse of the family farm. "We need to look into his finances. Is his business as healthy as he makes it look?"

"Good point. I wonder if Harrington had any life insurance."

"The ex could still be listed as the beneficiary," Kay agreed.

"Or his parents, in which case his sister could have a motive." Lee shook his head. "I would put that one *way* down on the list. Tess Armstrong didn't sound like she could hurt anyone."

"She would be easy to rule in or out based on her alibi. It would take more than a full day to drive down here, kill Harrington and drive back to North Carolina."

"What about Cody? What's his motive?" Lee asked.

"He was definitely hiding something. The gold's as good a possibility as anything right now."

"Gold is a viable motive for any suspect," Lee agreed.

The phone rang. Kay picked it up and, after a few words, passed it to Lee.

"There's a body at the nursing home," he told Kay.

"A mortician's work is never done," she said to his back as he hurried out the door.

Lee spent the rest of the weekend handling the details for two new bodies and walking Tess Armstrong through the quote he'd sent her for Harrington's funeral options. By Monday, he was just waiting on the family to decide if they were going to go with the cheapest burial or just cremation.

He was a little surprised that Tess hadn't seemed more interested in how her brother had died, but when he'd brought up the possibility of murder, it just seemed to overwhelm her. On the other hand, he'd learned that family members could have very different reactions to a loved one's death, and nothing surprised him anymore.

He was heading to the kitchen for coffee when the phone rang and he picked up the hall extension. It was Jerome.

"We've got trouble," he said ominously.

"What?"

"Dwayne McKenzie is missing, and Wade Sutton is the investigator assigned to the case."

Lee winced. "That's not good."

"No kidding. And there's more. Dwayne's wife said that Kay and I were two of the last people to talk to McKenzie."

"Let me guess. Sutton is on the warpath."

The Lambertons had had previous run-ins with Deputy Sutton and they'd never gone well. Sutton, who everyone suspected had only been made a detective because he was the sheriff's brother-in-law, was at best incompetent and at worse a walking, talking trainwreck. Kay in particular couldn't stand him.

"You got it. He's already told the sheriff."

"We need to talk about this."

"I'll be there in fifteen minutes." Jerome hung up before Lee had a chance say another word.

CHAPTER EIGHT

Jerome banged through the door into the kitchen where Lee was sitting at the table with a slice of apple pie.

"I told Kay you were coming. She'll be here in a minute."

"Pie?" Ruby asked, already holding a bowl with a slice in it out to Jerome. "Ice cream is in the freezer."

By the time Jerome was having his first bite of pie, Kay came into the kitchen. She waved away Ruby's offer of pie and sat down across from him.

"What's happened to McKenzie?" she asked.

"Just gone. We got the call this morning. His wife hasn't seen him since Sunday morning. Like I told Lee, the really bad news is that the sheriff assigned Wade Sutton to look into it."

Kay groaned. "Not that idiot."

"It's going to get worse before it gets better. He found out that we were some of the last people to see McKenzie on Saturday, so he's fixated on us. I've already been interviewed by him. I'm just glad he hasn't learned that

Henry's going to run for sheriff. That would really put the fire under his ass."

"That's right. He's the sheriff's wife's nephew or something like that," Lee said.

"And he knows that everyone else in the department knows he's a boob. If Henry gets elected, Sutton's out of investigations and back on the street... or maybe even out of the department altogether." Jerome sighed. "And he knows about Harrington's journal. McKenzie's wife told him about it."

"Where's the journal now?" Kay asked.

Jerome shrugged. "McKenzie must have had it with him, and they haven't even found his truck yet. With Wade the blond Neanderthal on the case, I'm surprised they found McKenzie's *house*."

"So now what?" Lee asked.

"Sutton is coming over here. To be honest, I wasn't sure I'd beat him." Jerome got up and put his bowl in the sink.

"What can we tell him?" Lee frowned.

"He's already forming a theory where we conspired to steal the gold."

"What sense does that make?" Kay was disgusted. "We're the ones saying that Harrington was murdered. We gave the journal to McKenzie."

"You have to think like Sutton. He's talked to Cody already and figured out that McKenzie caught us burglarizing the cabin and that McKenzie took the journal away from us. That's our motive for getting rid of McKenzie."

"That's crazy," Lee said.

"Think who you're dealing with."

"Great," Kay said with a heavy dose of sarcasm. There wasn't anyone in the county that she despised more than Wade Sutton. Each of their encounters had turned into a personal grudge match. So far, the score was a shutout in

Kay's favor, which had only fueled Sutton's disdain for her and Lee.

"He's here," Ruby said, hearing a car door slam in the front drive.

"I parked my motorcycle out back by the hearses. Don't tell him I'm here," Jerome said over his shoulder as he hurried out of the kitchen.

"I'll answer the door," Lee told Kay. "You'll have to talk to him. Just try and keep it civil."

"I'll try." Kay's teeth were clenched, and her hands were gripped into fists. Lee shook his head and went to door.

"Where's your sister?" Sutton demanded without preamble. His blond mustache sat on his upper lip like a drooping caterpillar. Lee had always found it a little creepy.

"Would you like to speak with her?" he asked, keeping his voice calm.

"You know I do. I'm sure Deputy Know-it-all has already called you."

"I'm sure no one has ever called *you* Deputy Know-it-all." The words were out of Lee's mouth before he could stop himself.

"You're all a bunch of smartasses. One of the most important men in the county is missing and your sister is smack in the middle of the investigation. Where is she?" As he spoke, Sutton tried to look around Lee and into the house.

"She's in the kitchen."

As soon as Sutton crossed the threshold, Ruby shoved a plate with a piece of pie at him.

"Have some pie."

With the plate in front of his face, Sutton looked very confused. His eyes darted from his assailant, Ruby, to his desired prey, Kay, who kept her face neutral as he struggled to figure out what to do. As though they were beyond his control, his hands slowly reached out and took the plate.

"Apple pie in the summer seems so natural," Ruby said. "Ice cream?"

She winked at Sutton, utterly confusing him. "I don't..."

"Sit down," Ruby instructed, and he slowly moved to the table and eased himself into a chair. "Now, about that ice cream..."

"No! No ice cream," he almost shouted as he tried to regain the initiative.

"To each his own," Ruby said.

"You're the person I want to talk to." Sutton stared at Kay.

"So talk."

He looked at the apple pie as though he didn't know what to do with it.

"Nothing wrong with eating and talking," Ruby said, patting him on the shoulder like he was a little kid. His whole body flinched at her touch, and Lee thought for a moment that Sutton might hit her. Instead, he reluctantly cut the end off the wedge of pie with his fork.

"Dwayne McKenzie is missing." He pointed the fork with the pie on it at Kay before putting it in his mouth. "What did you and Carter talk to him about?"

"When did he go missing?"

"I'm asking the questions." Sutton tried to make it a growl, but the second forkful of pie in his mouth made it come out more as a mumble.

"I'm just trying to get a clear picture of what's happened. The information will make it easier to give you helpful answers," Kay said sweetly.

"Make up lies, you mean. It's a simple question. What did you talk about?"

"We were there to look over Mr. Harrington's possessions. We have his body in our cooler and wanted to be prepared to embalm him and dress him for the funeral." Kay considered this a white lie.

"Did you take any clothes when you left?"

"No."

"But isn't that what you went there for?"

"None of the clothes he had with him were appropriate. They were everyday clothes."

"You still haven't told me what you talked about." He took another bite of pie and Kay tried not to shudder as she watched his mustache go up and down as he chewed.

"We talked about the funeral. We talked about Mr. Harrington's belongings. Finally, we talked about whether or not Mr. Harrington had been murdered and who did it." Kay watched him closely to see his reaction to her last comment.

"I thought Harrington's death was an accident." Sutton frowned.

"Undecided," Kay said. "At least as far as I'm concerned." She restrained herself from adding that she wasn't as willing as the sheriff's office to let murderers run free and mentally patted herself on the back for showing some restraint.

"Who are you to decide who's been murdered and who hasn't?"

"Lee made some observations when he saw the body that left him wondering what happened to the man. We like to have answers when the next of kin ask us questions, so we thought we should do a little digging."

Sutton took the last bite of his pie and squinted at Kay. She could see the rusty gears in his head turning as he tried to figure out if that was a good enough answer.

"McKenzie took a journal from you."

"What? No. It was Harrington's journal, and Mr. McKenzie thought he could plot out the coordinates that Harrington had noted."

"What kind of coordinates?"

"You know, like the kind on maps." Kay gritted her teeth to keep from adding: *dumbass.*

"Oh, so he was planning on roaming around in the woods." Sutton nodded, as if that might solve the question of what had happened to McKenzie.

"I don't know what he was planning to do. He said that he recognized some of the locations described in the notebook. Others he wasn't sure about."

Sutton seemed to think about this for a few minutes. Lee and Kay looked at each other and rolled their eyes.

"Are you searching the woods for him?" Lee asked.

"Nah, we haven't found his truck. Until we find the truck, we won't know where to start looking. Of course, he might have just driven off somewhere."

"When was the last time his wife saw him?"

"When he got up Sunday morning. She stayed in bed for another half hour. When she got out of the bathroom, she heard his truck drive off and she hasn't seen him since." Sutton frowned and his face turned a light shade of red, clashing with his blond hair. "Wait, I told you I was going to be the one asking the questions."

"We need to know what happened if we're going to help you find him," Lee said.

"I don't need your help."

"Then why are you here? Did you just come for the pie?" Kay smirked.

Sutton shoved the empty plate across the table and shook his finger at her. "Don't get that attitude with me."

"Romans associated blond hair with prostitutes," Ruby said softly. She'd been leaning against the counter behind Sutton. He turned and looked at her. It was obvious that he'd forgotten she was there. "Of course, these days people make those awful jokes about blonds and their intelligence."

"Who the hell are you?" Sutton demanded.

"You do have a short memory. I'm the one who gave you the pie. Ruby Bowen, by name, dear. You really should do your research before walking into a house and insinuating things."

"Why are you here?" He scowled at her.

"I'm the cook who made that apple pie that you scoffed down without so much as a *thank you, ma'am*. A better question is: How did your parents raise you?"

"What?" he asked angrily.

"Manners. It wouldn't hurt you to be polite."

"I'm... Never mind. Get out of here!"

"This is my kitchen," was all she said. But the two steps she took toward him and the hand reaching for the cast-iron skillet were what made his eyes go wide as he leaned away from her.

"Are you done asking questions?" Lee asked him.

Without taking his eyes off Ruby, Sutton turned his head just enough so he could see Lee.

"I had a few more. Is she threatening me?"

"We can go into the hall." Lee waved his hand toward the door. "You've riled her up and I've always found it's the better part of valor to retreat when she gets her dander up."

Sutton stood up slowly, keeping his eyes on Ruby. "Crazy—" he muttered.

"I wouldn't complete that thought unless you want her to resize your head with that skillet," Kay warned him.

"You let that woman cook your food?" he asked once they were standing in the hall.

"And the food is very good. She doesn't tolerate foo... people much," Lee finished carefully.

"You can have her and her food."

"You seemed to like the apple pie," Kay observed.

Sutton gave her the side-eye. "What kind of mood was

McKenzie in when he left the cabin?"

"He drove us back to our car and didn't appear to be upset about anything. He seemed to be very interested in the journal." Kay recalled their last moments with McKenzie, trying to think if there had been anything odd that she had missed.

"What about the kid?" Sutton pulled his pocket notebook out and flipped through it. "Cody Morgan."

"What about him?" Kay asked innocently.

"Don't play stupid," Sutton growled. His feathers were still ruffled from his encounter with Ruby. "Was he acting suspicious?"

"No."

"What was he doing there? Doesn't he live with his grandfather?"

"He's a kid who's gone through some tough times," Kay said.

"Yeah, his mom has been in the county jail more than once."

"So can't you understand why he might like being out in the woods?"

"Why at McKenzie's place?"

"I don't know. It's close to his grandfather's house. McKenzie is a nice guy. Also, I think Cody got to know Professor Harrington. They were friends."

"That kid was friends with an old guy like Harrington?" Sutton snorted in derision.

"Maybe Harrington was a mentor to the kid." Kay was surprised that she felt the need to defend Cody. In truth, she thought he was a bit strange.

"Mentor, ha! From what McKenzie's wife tells me, Harrington was crazy and this kid isn't much better."

"If you have all the answers, then why are you asking us questions?" Kay said, exasperated with Sutton's stupidity.

"You wouldn't know," he replied nonsensically. "You all stay away from this investigation and stop digging into stuff that's none of your business." He glared with what he thought was a menacing expression, though it looked more like the expression of a spoiled seven-year-old who was about to throw a tantrum.

Lee held his hand out to the door. "Always a pleasure to see you, Deputy Sutton."

Sutton just glared as he jerked the door open and stomped out.

CHAPTER NINE

"That went well." Jerome came out of the office shaking his head.

"How much did you hear?" Kay asked.

"Oh, I heard every word. I only wish I could have seen his face when Ruby went after him."

"She came close to knocking him in the head with a frying pan," Lee said, relishing the memory.

"I guess y'all are going to double down on the investigation now." It wasn't a question. Jerome knew that Wade Sutton strutting around was a sure way to get Kay to plant her feet.

"You know it," she assured him.

"So where is Dwayne McKenzie?" Lee asked.

"Wade Sutton sure as hell isn't going to find him," Jerome said.

"Why'd the sheriff put that idiot in charge of the investigation?"

"He probably doesn't think McKenzie is really missing.

My guess would be that when Mrs. McKenzie made the report, Pratt dismissed her as a woman looking for a husband who doesn't want to be found."

"So not finding him is actually doing McKenzie a favor. That's twisted thinking," Lee said.

"It also means the sheriff doesn't have to do any work," Kay added.

"Now you're getting it. The less they do, the happier they are. That's why you irritate Pratt so much. As far as the sheriff is concerned, you just stir up trouble."

"He'd rather have a killer on the loose than—" Before Kay could finish her thought, the phone rang.

Lee answered it in the kitchen, only a little surprised to hear Chester Madison's voice on the other end. Madison was the owner of Granite Insurance Company and had employed the Lambertons on more than one occasion to do more digging into suspicious deaths. The first time had involved the murder of a friend of Kay's who'd been one of the insurance company's best agents.

"I heard it through the grapevine that Dwayne McKenzie is missing?" Madison said without much preamble.

"Let me guess: You have a policy on him," Lee said.

"More than that. We have a policy on both him and his business. If his business suffers because of his absence, then we could be liable for those losses too."

"So you want us to find him?"

"And preferably alive."

"His disappearance appears to be tangled up with an unexplained death." Lee told him all about Roger Harrington.

"Our exposure with McKenzie is... considerable. Do you have any ideas at this point?" Madison asked.

Lee waved for Kay to pick up the extension in the office.

"Mr. Madison, this is Kay. Coincidences happen, but it's

best not to count on them. If McKenzie isn't partying in Gainesville, then something bad has probably happened to him and it's more than likely related to Harrington's death."

"And this is all about some Spanish gold?" Madison sounded skeptical.

"If there *is* any gold, then it would be a powerful motive. And I'm not qualified to say whether Harrington's information is correct or not," Kay said.

"Lee, you mentioned that he had an ex-wife. Do you think she'd know anything?" Madison asked.

"I talked to her briefly, but her emotions were all over the place. I couldn't tell what she knows."

"What sort of person was Harrington?"

"By all accounts, he was just a nice guy who talked a lot."

"Being talkative is not a quality that a treasure hunter should cultivate," Madison said astutely.

"Exactly. And it's the gold and the garrulousness that opens the suspect list up to everyone in the county and then some," Lee said.

"I see. Of course, this all presupposes that Harrington was murdered."

"I think he was tortured," Kay interjected.

"Lee was saying that before you came on the line. That increases the likelihood that this was all about the gold."

They talked for a few more minutes before Madison wrapped it up with, "Keep me informed, and consider yourselves on the payroll until the disappearance of Dwayne McKenzie is solved."

"At least you're going to be paid for sticking your nose in this mess," Jerome said once Lee joined him and Kay in the office.

"We'll pass some of the money along to you," Kay promised.

"Only fair since I'm the one who's going to be out of a

job because of you meddling kids."

"Where do we go from here?" Kay asked.

"I think the ex-wife is hiding something," Lee said.

"We could take a road trip tomorrow." Kay couldn't keep the excitement out of her voice.

Lee nodded. "I can get away for half a day."

Just then, they heard Lester come in the back door and knew he was heading for the kitchen and his own piece of pie.

"Let's go tell him he's going to be in charge tomorrow," Lee said.

Lester was thrilled at the prospect of taking on more responsibility.

As Kay watched him shovel pie into his mouth, she wondered aloud, "Is it possible that McKenzie *is* off somewhere, living it up with a pile of gold?"

"I don't think so," Ruby said as if she were getting information from the other side of the veil. "He's been taken."

"That sounds ominous." Kay was always skeptical of Ruby's premonitions, though even she had to admit that they had been proven right more than once.

"I'd like to know more about the search and what's going on," Lee said.

"Beth McKenzie has the farm employees and neighbors all out searching," Jerome told them.

"Let's drive out there." The confrontation with Wade Sutton had energized Kay.

"I'll stay here and watch the place with Lester. There will probably be a deputy or two out there already and it wouldn't be good for me to be seen with you." Jerome paused and then added, "No offense."

"None taken." Kay smiled.

"Besides, I got off four hours ago and haven't gotten any

sleep, so I'll probably take a nap on the couch."

Lee looked down at the suit he was wearing. "I'd better change first."

Half an hour later, Lee and Kay were standing at the back door as Ruby handed each of them a paper bag.

"I packed you chicken-salad sandwiches, chips and an apple," she told them. "You might want to take a raincoat too. I saw Yin looking off to the west a few minutes ago."

"Yin's a meteorologist now?" Kay raised her eyebrows and looked at the cat, who was sitting on the back stoop.

"I'm just saying Yin is more in tune with the elements while Yang is more in touch with the cosmic realm." Ruby left no doubt whose fault it would be if they got soaked.

Kay and Lee dutifully took their raincoats off the hooks by the back door. It was Florida in the summertime, so betting on rain was never a long shot.

"We'll take your car. I don't think it would inspire confidence to show up at a search for a missing person in a hearse... or even one of the family cars," Lee said.

"Point taken. If we're taking my car, then I get to drive." Kay pulled her keys out of the pocket of her jeans.

There were more than thirty cars and trucks parked around the house at the McKenzie farm. Lee thought the ranch-style home was quite modest considering how much land Dwayne McKenzie owned.

There were a lot of people milling about in the yard, some with dogs, some on horses and others riding small motorbikes. Kay and Lee exchanged nods with a few of the folks they recognized as they made their way up to the house.

"Is Beth around?" Lee asked a teenager who was standing by the front door.

"Aunt Beth is out back with a deputy."

As they rounded the house they saw a petite older woman in jeans and a blue blouse standing inches away from a deputy who must have been double her weight. Lee recognized the middle-aged deputy as Dan Archer, a good-natured officer who tried to straddle the fence of working for Sheriff Pratt *and* the community.

"We need more support from you!" Beth McKenzie was close to shouting. "Where's that useless sheriff of yours?"

The deputy looked embarrassed. "We have half our men driving around the county looking for your husband's truck."

"Driving around! I've got our employees and friends sweating their behinds off traipsing through the woods, and y'all are just driving around in your air-conditioned cars."

"Now be fair, Mrs. McKenzie. Your husband is probably wherever his truck is."

"Unless someone stole it, you dimwit." Her fists were clenched. Something about her reminded Lee of Barbara Stanwyck in the episodes of *Big Valley* that he'd watched as a kid.

"We've requested the civil air patrol's help," Archer offered.

"Guess that won't cost the sheriff anything. Go on, get out of here." Beth waved her hands at him.

Gratefully, he started to walk away.

"And if you *do* manage to stumble upon the truck, I better be the first person who hears about it." There was menace in her voice.

"Yes, ma'am," Archer said obediently.

No sooner had she dispatched him than her eyes locked on Lee and Kay.

"You're the Lambertons," she declared, walking over to them.

"Yes. I'm Kay, and you've met my brother, Lee."

"You're the one I want to talk to."

"We wanted to talk to you too," Kay said, and Beth gave her an appraising look.

"You saw Dwayne at the cabin. What did he say?" Beth's eyes bore into Kay as she asked the question.

Kay told her everything she could remember from that afternoon.

"That's what Dwayne said. Not that I was listening very well. I… Well, after thirty-five years of marriage, you don't exactly hang on every word." She looked past Kay and Lee as though she could see Dwayne walking away from her.

"Do you think this has anything to do with Professor Harrington's murder?" Lee asked.

"That was going to be my next question for you," Beth responded. "This Harrington guy is found dead on our property, then a few days later my husband goes missing. So, yes, I believe it's connected. Was that fellow killed?"

This time it was Lee who explained what they knew.

"I keep thinking back to Saturday, and it seems that Dwayne was worried. But am I just thinking that because he's gone?"

"We heard that he drove off Sunday morning. Was that normal for him?" Kay asked.

"Yes and no. He doesn't go to church with me every Sunday, but he usually tells me where he's going when he leaves. *Usually*, that's the key word. If there's work he wants to get done, his mind just fixates on that and he's got to do it before he thinks about anything else. That's what I thought had happened on Sunday. I figured he'd remembered a water trough that needed filling or a cow he wanted to check on. Could have been a hundred different things."

"Did he take anything with him?"

"You mean besides his truck? I think he took that man's journal with him. Dwayne showed it to me Saturday night, and I saw him flipping through it most of the evening. After I realized he was gone, I went looking for it. The journal isn't in the house."

"What about any medicines he needed, his wallet, stuff like that?"

"Now you sound like that fool of an investigator. Dwayne didn't run away. Now, if he did, he had everything he'd need in that truck. It was his office. Sometimes he even slept in it when he was hunting or traveling. Gun, maps, a jug of water, first aid kit." She shook her head.

"How many people you got searching?" Lee asked.

"A couple dozen folks from church, along with our farmworkers and a few of our neighbors."

"Would you like us to set up some of our tents for shade or to keep people dry if it rains?" Lee offered. As if on cue, they heard a grumble of thunder in the distance.

"That would be fine. We've got a few groups out searching now."

"Any at your hunting property?" Kay asked.

"That was the first place I thought about. Our daughter took some of her friends and their horses over there to ride the trails and look for him."

"Can you think of anyone he's been in an argument with?"

"Dwayne? Not likely. Everyone got along with him. If he didn't like someone, he just avoided them."

"What about employees and family?"

"We haven't had trouble with an employee in a couple of years. We hire some that don't work out, but it's mostly 'cause the work's too hard for them so they up and quit. Family? No. We're close. I'm sure this has something to do with that man and his treasure-hunting. It bothered me the first time Dwayne told me about him. The thought of free money is dangerous. People would rather squabble over a bag of money than go out and earn their own."

"Tell us where you want the tents," Lee told her, then he headed back to the funeral home, leaving Kay behind to help.

Lee was back an hour later in a borrowed pickup with two funeral tents, some tables and supplies for making coffee and tea.

"I hate to agree with the sheriff's office, but finding the truck is going to be their best bet," Lee told Kay as they unloaded the truck.

"Is there any possibility that someone carjacked him?" she asked.

"If so, why would they take him with them?"

"They might have dumped his body in a lake or sinkhole."

"Maybe he used the journal to find Harrington's gold," Lee suggested.

"And ran off with it?" Kay sounded doubtful.

"He wouldn't be the first person to do a runner when he had the chance." Lee waved his arm around. "Lot of responsibility here. The kind that can wear a man down."

"Did he look worn down to you?" Kay asked.

"No," Lee admitted.

"Me either. But if his disappearance is connected to Harrington's death, then wouldn't it mean that it's all about the gold?"

"There wasn't much else that connected the two of them."

"Unless the motive for Harrington's murder was something other than gold, and somehow McKenzie figured out who the murderer was, so the murderer had to kill him too." Kay paused as she handed Lee a coffee pot. "Sounds too convoluted."

"We're missing too many pieces of the puzzle. I think we

need to go talk to the ex-Mrs. Harrington."

"You go tomorrow. I think I need to stay here." Kay looked around at the people coming and going. "I want to search for McKenzie and talk to everyone I can. There's a chance that the person who abducted him will participate in the search."

"The criminal returning to the scene of the crime?"

"Being involved in the search would be a good way for the murderer to keep in touch with what's going on. Maybe even direct the investigation away from themselves."

"Makes sense. If that's the situation, then you need to be careful," Lee told her.

"Don't worry. I'm not going to stick my neck out too far."

"Maybe the search will find McKenzie before that." Lee tried to sound hopeful. A cool gust of wind and a clap of thunder announced the imminent approach of the storm that had been building in the west. Within minutes, twenty people were gathered beneath the funeral tents.

After the storm, the searchers headed back out, but to Lee the mood of the searchers seemed particularly melancholy. The storm seemed to have washed away any optimism that they would find Dwayne McKenzie alive and well.

CHAPTER TEN

On Tuesday, Lee and Kay were up with the dawn.

Ruby was already in the kitchen, making up a huge batch of egg-and-sausage biscuits for Kay to take to the McKenzie place. As she handed him a biscuit, Lee handed her a list of instructions for Lester while he was holding down the fort.

"See if you can talk to some of the neighbors around McKenzie's hunting property. They might know more about Professor Harrington. Cody said that Harrington talked to a lot of them and walked their property searching for the gold," Lee told Kay as they were both getting into their cars.

"And if McKenzie was trying to follow Harrington's coordinates, he might have gone onto the neighboring properties. That's not bad thinking, Watson," Kay said, nodding.

"I thought we'd settled who's Watson and who's Sherlock."

"We had, Watson. Aren't you worried that it'll be a little early for popping in on the ex-Mrs. Harrington?"

"I called the college and found out she has office hours this morning. It'll take about an hour and a half to get there, so I should time it just right."

They wished each other good hunting and drove off in opposite directions.

The trip to St. Augustine was along back roads through rural scenery where people lived their lives by the lyrics of country songs. As he drove, Lee tried to come up with questions for Joyce Harrington and then imagined what her answers might be. It was difficult since he'd never even met the woman. For that matter, he hadn't met Roger Harrington until he was hanging dead from a deer stand.

The campus of Flagler College was quiet. Lee easily found a parking spot for the black Lincoln Town Car and walked to the language arts building. A brief perusal of the directory informed him that Joyce Harrington's office was on the second floor.

Her office door was covered with various notices, including several for Spanish tutors and summer tours of Spain. Lee knocked lightly.

"Come in," a woman's voice called.

When he opened the door, Joyce Harrington looked puzzled to see him. She was in her early fifties and attractive, with black hair down to her shoulders. A pile of papers was spread out on her desk, and she held a pen in her right hand.

"If you want to add my class, you'll need to wait until the drop/add period in three weeks." She sounded like she expected that to end the matter.

"I'm not a student."

Joyce put down the pen she'd been holding and looked at him. Lee could see a darkness cross her eyes. Fear. *What is she scared of?* he wondered.

"Then who are you?"

"I'm Lee Lamberton. We talked on the phone a couple of

days ago."

The look on her face was that of a trapped animal. "You… You need to make an appointment," she stammered.

"I'm sorry about surprising you, but I was in Jacksonville on business and thought I would take the opportunity to stop down here and talk to you in person," Lee lied.

"I can't do that." She looked at the phone on her desk. He couldn't tell if she was hoping it would ring, or if she was thinking about grabbing it and calling for help.

"Please. Just a few questions."

"I have nothing to talk to you about. I answered all your questions on the phone!" Her voice was high and thready.

"I only want to ask you a few more questions about Mr. Harrington." Lee was trying his best to sound non-threatening.

"I don't know what I can tell you." He could tell she was on the edge of hysteria.

"Y'all had been together for a number of years, right?"

"So?"

"Who would know him better than you?"

"What do you want?"

"May I sit down?" Lee thought that sitting would be a good way to get his nose under the tent, and that he might seem less threatening.

"I… Of course." Joyce seemed unable to fight her own innate hospitality. She waved to an institutional metal chair on the other side of her desk.

"Thank you." Once he was seated, Lee asked, "Do you know of anyone who might have wanted to hurt your ex-husband?"

"No, he was a nice and gentle man." Joyce sounded surprised by the question and her answer seemed sincere.

"Why did you separate?"

"What does this have to do with his funeral?" Joyce asked, clearly confused.

"You said on the phone that you wouldn't be able to make the funeral. So we wanted to get your perspective and background on Mr. Harrington. This helps us when we're reviewing the obituary, eulogies and other remembrances. If someone submits something that is…well, far off the mark, then we want to be able to correct the record." This was all nonsense. In reality, they took whatever a family gave them and ran with it. If other members of the family didn't like it, then they could hash it out on their own time.

"I guess that makes sense."

Lee thought he knew how conmen must feel when they were reeling in a mark. Despite the somewhat sleezy feeling it gave him, he asked, "So what was it that caused you all to break up after…?"

"Twenty-two years." Joyce tossed up her hands. "I don't know. He was a great guy to be around… for an hour or two. The problem was that after twenty-two years of being around him every day… it got old. I mean his enthusiasm was too much. I love the Spanish language. I enjoy the culture and the history of Spain, but I can let it go. Not Roger. Every day, he had a new and exciting fact that he had to share. Like he'd discover some courtesan from the reign of… oh, I don't know… pick a Spanish ruler. The courtesan would be so fascinating that he would spend months and months researching her. He'd constantly be telling me something new he'd learned about her." She paused and took a deep breath. "Trust me, it gets exhausting."

Lee noticed that her hands were shaking.

"What about this Spanish gold?"

As soon as he said it, he saw her body tense and she got a wild look in her eyes.

"I don't know anything about that."

"He never told you about the Spanish gold he was hunting?" Lee couldn't keep the incredulity out of his voice.

Joyce looked down at her desk as though carefully considering her answer. "Yes, he talked about it. Like I said, he talked constantly about whatever his latest big thing was. Our marriage was already shaky at that point. I just wasn't listening to him."

"My sister talked to a friend of yours who said that you moved over here to be with a male friend."

"That's enough!" Joyce stood up. Her face was bright red as she began to hyperventilate. "I… You need to get out of my office." Her arm flew out and pointed to the door. "You clearly aren't here as a mortician."

"You're right." Lee continued to sit in the chair and looked at her steadily. "We have reason to believe that your ex-husband was murdered."

The words had an instant effect on her. Joyce stiffened and fell back into her chair. "What?"

"We think someone killed him. Now another man is missing."

Joyce's mouth was opening and closing as her mind tried to grasp what Lee had said. "Why? Why would someone kill Roger?"

"That's what we're trying to find out."

"I thought you were a funeral director." Joyce eyed him suspiciously from her side of the desk.

"I picked up Mr. Harrington's body and we have it in our care. However, as we looked at the scene and the body, it became clear to us that he was probably killed. The questions are why and who."

"This is crazy."

"We need your help."

Joyce stood up again and headed for the door. "I've got to go… freshen up. You can wait here."

Lee looked around, wondering what her reaction meant. *Maybe she just has a small bladder*, he thought. After just a few minutes, she was back.

"Sorry." She looked more in control.

"I didn't mean to upset you."

"No. I'm fine." Her eyes darted toward the door for a second before meeting his. "It was just shocking to hear that anyone thinks Roger might have been killed. As I said, he was a good man."

"When did he become obsessed with this Spanish gold?"

"I'd rather not talk about that." Her eyes flew to the door again.

"If it's connected to his death, it might be important."

"I doubt it's connected." She took a deep breath and let it out. "Okay. The… gold thing became his focus about two months before we separated. About a year ago."

"How did it start?"

"He found a manuscript. Look, I don't know much about it, so there's no point in asking me any questions about the… gold or anything else related to it. I never had an interest in any of that stuff." Lee noticed that her hands were nervously touching objects on her desk as she spoke.

"You said that you were… bored with your husband. This isn't an accusation… but is that why you became involved with another man?" Lee worked hard to sound sympathetic as he spoke.

"I'm not embarrassed by anything that Hugo and I have done. We're going to be married in the fall." She lifted her chin slightly.

"Congratulations on your upcoming marriage. Does Hugo teach here?"

"If you must know, yes. He is a world-renowned expert in Spanish antiquities."

"Hugo…?"

There was a flash of irritation in her eyes. "Valero. Hugo Valero. Look, I don't know why I'm answering all these questions. You're a mortician, for Pete's sake."

"You're doing it because you don't want me to tell the investigators that you were uncooperative." Lee decided to switch it up and use more stick and less carrot.

Her mouth opened and closed like a fish out of water.

"Mr. Harrington was probably killed last Monday afternoon. Do you know where you were at that time?"

"Are you planning to become a detective? You're certainly well versed in the techniques. All right, let me think. Hugo and I had rented a bungalow at the beach for a few days. We just hung out at the house and cooked most of our meals there. We didn't really go anywhere, so I don't have an alibi. Happy now?" She seemed less nervous and more angry. "I've answered your questions. Now I have a few of my own."

"Of course."

"How did he die?"

"He was found hanging by his foot on a ladder attached to a deer stand."

From her expression, Joyce clearly hadn't been expecting that sort of answer. "Where?"

"On a hunting property. He had been staying in a cabin nearby."

"Hunting for gold." Her voice trembled.

"Yes."

"What did he die of?"

"Positional asphyxiation."

"What's that?"

"He died from hanging upside down too long. From what I understand, it can put pressure on your lungs and make it difficult to breath. It can also lead to a stroke or heart attack."

"Oh." She seemed to think about this, then said in a voice so quiet he could barely hear her, "I think I want to be alone now."

Lee stood up. "I'm sorry for your loss."

Joyce looked at him. "If there's a memorial service, let me know."

He nodded and left her office. When he was three doors down the hall, he thought he saw movement out of the corner of his eye. The door on his right closed soundlessly as he passed it.

He thought about Joyce's sudden bathroom break and turned and stopped at the next hallway. He leaned against the wall and listened for sounds from the direction of Joyce's office. Sure enough, he heard footsteps, then a door opening and closing. Quickly, he went back down the hall to her office and pressed his ear as close to the door as he dared.

"Do you think he suspects anything?" asked a deep baritone voice with a light Spanish accent.

"I don't know." Joyce sounded unnerved. "How did we get ourselves into this mess?"

"Love, my dear."

"Look what it's brought us to."

"We did what we thought was right."

"Did we? I thought we did it to get what we wanted."

"You have to let it go. If we get caught now…"

"It would ruin you," she said.

"And you."

"I need a drink."

Lee heard them moving toward the door. He ran down the hall and around the corner as quickly and silently as he could. He saw an exit sign and followed it down a staircase and out the door to his car. His mind was racing. *Did I just hear Hugo and Joyce confess to murdering Roger Harrington?*

On the drive back to Lang, Lee ran the conversation

between Hugo and Joyce over and over in his head, trying to remember the exact words and the intonation. By the time he pulled into the driveway of the funeral home, he thought he had most of the conversation memorized. He went straight to the office to write it all down.

CHAPTER ELEVEN

When Kay arrived at the McKenzie property, she found they had put the Lamberton Funeral Home tents to good use. The tables underneath were loaded down with snacks, first-aid supplies and photos of Dwayne McKenzie and his truck. A volunteer sign-up table had been set up at the first tent.

"Are you here to help with the search?" asked a blue-haired woman as Kay walked up to the table. The woman was the epitome of what Kay's father would have referred to as a *church lady*.

"Yes."

"I recognize you!" the woman said enthusiastically. "Yes, you were at Miss Lottie's funeral." She narrowed her eyes. "Wait, you're one of the Lamberton children. That's right!"

"I'm Kay."

"Of course. I'm Mrs. Cutter. Your father buried my father and mother. It was a shame about your dad."

"Thank you."

"And this is so horrible about Dwayne. We all go to the

same church. Some folks are saying horrible things about him, but don't believe them. He's a good man. I know he'd never run off and leave his family. I've never even seen him look at another woman. Not like some men." She shook her head.

"What can I do?" Kay asked.

"It's early yet. More people will be showing up. Beth said that as soon as we get enough folks, we'll start giving out assignments. Go ahead and sign in." She handed Kay a clipboard. "Beside your name, put down any special skills that might help in the search."

"Special skills?"

"Like horseback riding, tracking, cooking, mechanics, that sort of thing."

"It sounds like they're planning on being here awhile."

Mrs. Cutter's face turned sorrowful. "It's not going to be easy. They've already covered the likely places and haven't even found Dwayne's truck."

Kay filled out the sheet. For special skills, she put down nursing.

Mrs. Cutter raised her eyebrows as she reviewed Kay's sheet. "A nurse! You'll be in demand. Yesterday we had several bad scrapes and a sprained ankle."

Now that the sun was well above the trees, more people were showing up. A man in an orange vest was parking cars and Mrs. Cutter had pulled out a couple more clipboards for people to use.

Kay drifted over to a live oak tree to watch all the volunteers milling about. She knew that if someone had kidnapped or killed Dwayne McKenzie, there was a good chance that they might show up to help with the search. She heard a motorcycle and looked toward the front gate.

Jerome was wearing jeans and a blue T-shirt as he got off his bike and put down the kickstand.

"What are you doing here?" Kay asked when he walked up to her.

"Ruby called and told me I needed to come watch over you." He shook his head. "It's been two weeks since I had a full eight hours of sleep."

"I didn't ask you to come here."

"I'd feel bad if you got yourself murdered."

"You need to go sign in." She pointed to Mrs. Cutter's tent, which was now manned by a young woman who looked barely old enough to be a Girl Scout.

As Jerome was waiting in line by the tent, a young man wearing a T-shirt that marked him as a member of the Lang Volunteer Fire Department yelled that they would be sending out search teams in the next half hour.

"Notice anything odd?" Kay asked Jerome, who looked around and shook his head. "A bunch of these people don't look worried. They look… excited."

"Folks like to be involved in things. Doesn't matter whether it's something good or something bad. Some folks just have to stick their noses in. At least here they might be able to do some good. It's a hell of a turnout for a Wednesday morning. Next time the sheriff's office needs volunteers, they should mention lost gold."

"That's just it. I'm afraid that's the only reason most of these people are here." Kay frowned as she watched a group of college-aged kids laughing and shoving each other. She edged closer to them so she could hear what they were saying.

"I heard there was eleven million dollars' worth of gold out here somewhere," said a boy with glasses and a preppy haircut.

"It's Spanish gold and Aztec jewels. The value of the gold might be eleven million, but the value of the artifacts could be… who knows," said another boy in a polo shirt and slacks, his eyes burning with excitement.

The girls in the group were nodding and smiling like they were going to the mall with their father's credit card. Disgusted, Kay walked back to Jerome.

"They *are* just here for the gold."

"Ha! That figures." Jerome looked intently at everyone in the crowd. "I wish we had a better idea who we're looking for."

The fireman yelled for everyone's attention and began calling out names and placing people in different groups. Each group had a person who was the designated leader. Though Kay and Jerome were initially separated, he had a quick word with the fireman and soon came back to her side.

"Fixed that," he said with a grin.

"I don't need a babysitter." Kay was both a bit miffed and grateful to have him there.

"We'll see. Maybe I want to be with the group that has a qualified nurse." He nudged her arm.

"Hopefully no one will need a nurse."

"You're the nurse?" asked a gruff older man with a receding hairline. He had been assigned as the leader of their group of twenty.

"I am."

"They gave us a first-aid kit." He held out a khaki military rucksack with a red cross in a white circle. "You ought to take it."

Kay grabbed the bag and took a quick inventory of the contents.

"I'm Joe," the man introduced himself. "We're going over to McKenzie's hunting property."

"What are the odds he'll be there?" Kay whispered to Jerome.

"The last body was there," Jerome whispered back, and Kay elbowed him in the side.

"We don't have a bus, so everyone needs to take their own car. Anyone who needs directions, see me," Joe shouted.

"Ride with me?" Kay asked Jerome. He looked over at his motorcycle and nodded.

Joe had unlocked the gate to the hunting property by the time most cars started pulling in. At the cabin, he split the group into ten pairs and used a map to indicate which trails each pair should follow.

"They had horses out here yesterday, but Mrs. McKenzie wants us to go over the ground again looking closely for clues, like pieces of clothing or equipment. The riders were just going along calling out for Dwayne. Be careful. It's muddy after the rain. I've got insect repellant for anyone that needs it, and keep a sharp eye out for snakes. That sound you hear won't be a baby's rattle."

Two hours later, hot, sweaty and covered in bug bites, Jerome and Kay came back to the cabin.

"A few beer cans and some other trash. All of it looks like it's been there longer than a week," Jerome told Joe.

"We'd like to go talk to some of the neighbors," Kay said.

"I guess that can't hurt," Joe said. He picked up an OD green military walkie talkie. "Do you know how to use this?"

Kay reached past Jerome and took the radio. She checked the frequency, pressed the switch and made a few more adjustments.

"Guess you do," Joe said. "That's just in case someone gets hurt and we need you to come back."

"Which way?" Kay asked Jerome as she pulled her car out of the gate.

"Go left. That's toward Cody's grandfather's farm. We ought to check out the houses in between. We can ask a few questions about the kid while we're talking to the neighbors."

The first house they came to was a small shotgun-style cabin. The yard was filled with old car and mower parts. A sign on the porch read: *Mac Mower Repair—small engines repaired, parts plus reasonable labor.*

"I forgot Mac lived here," Jerome said.

"You know him?"

"His family has lived within a mile of this place for a hundred years. Pull in."

When they got out of the car, they could hear the sound of an engine behind the house. It would start, run for a minute and then stop.

"He's around in the shop. When I was a kid, he helped me fix my mowers so I could cut grass for cash."

"When was this?" Kay had never heard about this part of Jerome's life.

"From the time I was big enough to push a mower until I got out of high school and went to the law enforcement academy."

"Hard to believe you worked for a living," Kay joked.

"Woman, please." Jerome laughed and showed her the palms of his hands. "I've had these calluses since I was twelve."

Outside the shed behind the house, an elderly black man was studying an old yellow push mower.

"Mac!" Jerome shouted.

Mac looked startled and Kay soon figured out he was a bit hard of hearing.

"Roamin' Jerome! What you doin' out here, son?" The man put his hands on his hips and gave Jerome and Kay a big smile. His denim overalls had a few grease stains and looked like they'd been neatly mended more than once.

"We wanted to ask you a few questions about your neighbors," Jerome said, his voice pitched louder than normal.

"You aren't wearin' your sheriff's star. What's this about, before I go stickin' my hand in a hornet's nest?"

"Nothing like that. This is unofficial. A man died last week on the McKenzie hunting property and now Mr. McKenzie has gone missing."

"So why are you here unofficially? That all sounds like deputy dawg business to me."

"It's a long story. This is Kay Lamberton." Jerome stepped back and gestured toward Kay.

The old man gave her an appraising look.

"I knew your father. I was the grounds keeper at the Eastside Cemetery, as well as the First Baptist Church's graveyard. He was a good man. Grieved me to hear he'd passed."

"Thank you. I've sort of dragged Jerome into this. We're taking care of the body of Roger Harrington, the man who was found dead at McKenzie's place, and some questions came up."

"I work part-time for the funeral home," Jerome added.

Mac still looked skeptical, but he nodded. "Go ahead then. Ask away."

"Did you know Mr. Harrington?" Jerome got a blank look from Mac and added, "Folks called him the Professor."

"Oh, yeah, him. We talked a couple times. He was real interested when he learned my family had been around here for over a hundred years."

"What did you talk about?" Jerome asked.

"Mostly landmarks like ponds, creeks, big ol' trees, rocks, that kind of thing." He paused and thought for a moment. "Oh yeah, and where people had farmed and if anyone had ever found anything strange like bones or pieces of metal. He told me there was a fortune in gold buried around here. I told him he was crazy. If there was gold within fifty miles of here, my family would have dug it up for sure."

"You don't think there's any buried treasure around here?" Kay asked.

"Pleaaasee! When I was a kid, my brother and me hunted squirrels and birds over every inch of ground around here. When we weren't huntin', we were fishin'. I still know every fishin' hole around here. If there was something to find, we'd have found it. See in there?" He pointed back toward his workshop.

Kay looked at the shed, which was big enough to park four cars. It was full of engine parts and tools, and dozens upon dozens of deer antlers hung from the rafters.

"See all them antlers?" Mac asked her. "Those are all the shed antlers I've found over the years. Now do you think I keep my eyes to the ground?"

"Yes, sir, I think you do," Kay acknowledged.

"Did Mr. Harrington ever mention any problems he was having with other people? Maybe someone following him? Or a landowner who wasn't happy with him?" Jerome asked.

"A couple folks shooed him off their place, that's a fact."

"How'd he take it?"

"His feathers weren't too ruffled."

"What was everyone saying about him?"

"Ha! That's easy. They all said he was nuts." Mac paused and a smile crossed his face. "Funny that. After they met him, I bet every one of them looked on their property for that gold. I got four acres here and I took a turn around the place." He laughed at himself.

"Do you remember the people who didn't want him on their property?"

"Mostly the usual suspects. Drive down the road and see the ones with the 'no trespassing' signs and the locked gates. Now don't get me wrong. I lock up my property too. There are potheads and drunks that think everyone's property is theirs. I caught Gizzard walkin' off with one of my lawnmowers a couple years ago. I yelled at him and the old drunk just gave me the finger and walked off laughin'." Kay could see a flash of anger in the old man's eyes.

"What did the Professor say about the people who wouldn't let him search their property? Did he think they were hiding something?" Kay asked.

"It sure enough ate at him." Mac chuckled. "The Professor said it was like a woman teasin' him. If they told him he couldn't, then he *really* wanted to look around their place. I asked him what he would do, and he winked and said most folks sleep at night."

"You think he trespassed on people's property at night?" Jerome asked.

"*Trespass* is a lawful word. I think the professor would say he was just goin' for a moonlight walk."

"People could get angry finding someone walking on their property after they told him not to," Jerome pointed out.

"I said the same thing. But the Professor said that the gold would be worth millions and millions of dollars. Said nobody's going to be mad at him if he makes them rich. 'Spect he was right about that."

"Can you think of anyone that didn't like him?"

"Naw, not really. Sure, there were a few that would cross the street when they saw him or not answer the door if they knew it was him knockin'. They didn't hate him; they just had grown weary of listenin' to him talk about that ol' gold."

"What about Cody Morgan?" Jerome asked directly.

"That boy?" Mac looked surprised at the question. "He's got some trouble in his life. Comes by sometimes and sits and watches me work. Helps out a little. From what I gathered, he and the Professor were... I guess I'd say friends. They were a good match. The Professor loved to talk, and Cody liked to hear stories."

"Did Cody believe the professor's stories?" Kay hadn't been able to get a handle on Cody's motivations when she'd met him.

"Yep. That boy's a believer. I've tried to joke around with him, tellin' him some of the crazy stories my pappy told me. Doesn't work 'cause he believes every word. You could take him on a snipe hunt without hardly tryin' and even after you explained to him that it was a joke at his expense, I think he'd tell you he saw one."

"You ever seen Cody be violent?" Jerome asked.

"No, sir. He's a quiet one."

"Sometimes it's the quiet ones you have to watch out for."

"That's true enough," Mac agreed.

"What have you heard about Dwayne McKenzie's disappearance?"

Jerome's question caused Mac's face to lose its good humor. "I know there's some people with darkness in their hearts. Mr. McKenzie is a good man and since I heard he'd gone missin', I've been prayin'."

"What do you think happened to him?"

"He's one of those men whose family always comes first, right after God and just before his friends and neighbors. If he's not here, then something real bad has happened to him."

"Any ideas what that could be?" Jerome continued to press the old man.

"You remember Mr. Stern. I'm afraid it's like that."

"Who was Mr. Stern?" Kay asked, confused.

Jerome explained. "Mr. Stern ran the Red Creek Corner grocery store back in the early sixties. One day a customer came in and there wasn't anyone in the store. Mr. Stern's house was within sight of the store so the customer, who knew Stern would never leave the store open without anyone to watch it, went up to the house. One of Mr. Stern's children answered the door and said his father should be at the store. Long story short, two men had come in and robbed the store, but they were so angry that there wasn't any money, they decided to take Mr. Stern and force him to take them to his house."

"Stern never had much money at the store except on Saturday," Mac said, taking up the story. "See, he gave credit to most folks during the week, and they'd come in and pay on Saturday. Everyone 'round here knew that, so we all knew they weren't local."

"You said the house was within sight of the store. But wasn't Mr. Stern's son at home when the customer went to check on him?" Kay wondered if she'd missed something.

Jerome shook his head. "Mr. Stern wasn't about to take them to his house. He would have known they weren't locals, so he told them that he lived out by the old sawmill. There was a house out there that no one lived in."

"So they killed him?"

Jerome nodded sadly. "After what must have been one hell of a fight. There are pictures of the interior of the house at the sheriff's office. They're on the wall in the locker room. They caught the two guys up in Lake City two days later when a motel clerk reported two men who looked like they'd been hit by a truck had checked in."

"For Dwayne McKenzie's sake, I sure hope you're wrong," Kay told Mac.

"Me too, ma'am. Me too."

Kay and Jerome thanked the old man for his time and let him get back to work.

"Next house down?" Kay asked as she started the car.

"Yep. We'll keep going until we get to Mr. Morgan's house, then turn around and do the houses on the other side of the road."

"Why do they keep pictures of the Stern crime scene in the locker room at the sheriff's office?" Kay had thought this was odd.

"The field training officers always make a point of taking the recruits by those pictures and showing them what they might walk into one day. If you aren't prepared… well, you aren't prepared, and that can cost you time when you don't have it."

"That makes sense."

"The other thing they tell them is to fight like Stern. He went down, but he left enough of a mark that they caught the bastards who killed him."

"I can see that too."

Most of the houses they stopped at were empty, which wasn't a surprise during the middle of the week. They did manage to talk to a few people who admitted to knowing Professor Harrington and Cody Morgan, but they didn't have strong opinions about anything one way or the other. No one they talked to had seen or heard anything from Dwayne McKenzie since Saturday.

CHAPTER TWELVE

The next occupied home they came to was a newish singlewide trailer. A young woman wearing jeans and a tank top answered the door, holding a squirming one-year-old in her arms.

"Whatcha want?" She brushed at a strand of sweaty auburn hair hanging down over her forehead.

"We're helping with the search for Mr. McKenzie," Jerome said. When he saw her bored expression, he decided to up the ante. "I'm Deputy Carter."

The badge captured her attention. "We don't know nothin' about him."

The baby flipped around to look at Jerome and Kay.

"He's adorable. What's his name?" Kay asked, noticing the tension in the woman's face.

"This is Christopher." The woman couldn't help but smile when Christopher cooed as if he understood she was talking about him. She bounced him gently on her hip, causing him to laugh. "He just started to talk."

"Could we come in and ask a few questions? There was another death up the road and we're looking into that too. We just want to make sure the area is safe," Kay assured her.

"I guess. You'll have to excuse the mess. Christopher is my first. Momma says it gets easier. I sure hope she's right."

"I'm Kay," she said as they followed the woman into the living room.

"I'm June Mercer."

Despite June's apology, the room was clean and neat, with a beautiful large quilt on the floor covered with toys. There were no walls separating the kitchen from the living room, and the smell of cooking vegetables was coming from pots on the stove.

"That's a lovely quilt." Kay figured it was a good idea to keep up the small talk.

"Granny Mercer and her friends made it for Chris."

A box fan blew warm air through the house as June told them to have a seat while pointing to the couch.

"Had you heard that Mr. McKenzie is missing?" Kay asked. Jerome had quickly caught on that Kay was going to have more luck asking questions than he was, so he leaned back against the couch and took silent inventory of June and the house.

"We did."

"Your husband must be a good hunter." Kay nodded toward the pair of deer heads mounted on the wall. One was an eight point and the other a ten.

"I think hunting season is his favorite time of year," June said, and Kay thought she heard a little hesitation that suggested it wasn't *June's* favorite time of year.

"Men do love to get out in the woods," Kay said, nodding her head.

"Been worse lately than hunting season," June blurted with a trace of irritation in her voice. As soon as she said it, she looked at Jerome and Kay as though hoping they hadn't heard her.

"Really?" Kay said. "What's he doing in the woods this time of year?"

At first Kay didn't think June was going to answer, but with a sigh she spilled out her frustration.

"It's that crazy old man that got him going. Jerry's father owns almost two hundred acres of woods, and I think he's walked every foot of it twice in the last month. Takes his shovel out and just walks around looking for some fool treasure that ain't even out there. Like he can't just sit here with us, he's got to be hunting for that stupid gold." June's obvious anger made Christopher frown and pat at her face.

"So y'all met Professor Harrington?"

"Yeah, we met him," June said disdainfully.

"You know he died?"

June nodded. "Jerry said they were talking about it at the feed store."

"Would you mind telling us how you met?" Kay asked.

"It was Memorial Day weekend. We were cooking out and he walked up and introduced himself. Seemed like a nice old guy and... Well, we weren't sure he wasn't homeless, so we invited him to have a hamburger with us. That's when he got to talking about the gold. My husband's brother, Andy, was here, and the two of them were suckered into the whole story: the Spaniards, a hurricane, the gold. Andy's wife and I were like, 'This is crazy,' but guys are guys. And those two are worse than most. They've had at least a dozen get-rich-quick schemes since I started dating Jerry in high school."

"So your husband started looking for the gold?"

"First it was him *and* Andy, but Andy's wife shut that down pretty quick. They've got three kids and he works two jobs. She told him that dog don't hunt and if he wanted to still have a family, he had to spend some time with them."

She looked at Christopher and let him play with her finger. "I should have done the same thing, but it's harder living on the property."

"Did y'all see any more of the Professor?"

June rolled her eyes. "He was over here at least a dozen times. It wasn't all his fault either. Jerry would get some crazy thought about where the gold could be, or some clue he thought he saw, and go running around looking for the old guy."

"When was the last time that either of you saw him?"

"I don't know. You'd have to ask Jerry. He figured out how I felt about him hunting for the gold and stopped talking about it around me. I know he snuck over and saw the guy a few times and didn't tell me about it."

"Do you know Cody Morgan?" Kay decided to switch topics.

"Now he's a strange one. Jerry found him a couple times just… like, hanging out in our woods. Last fall, Jerry had to tell him to leave 'cause of hunting season. We've got family that hunts this land and… Now, *most* of them are really responsible, but I wouldn't trust no kid with buck fever some foggy morning, if you know what I mean."

"Was Cody also hunting for the gold?"

"I don't know what he's hunting. Jerry asked him a couple times why he was on our place, but the kid just gets weird. Never has a gun or anything so he's not, you know, really hunting." She shrugged and looked at Christoper, who was chewing on his own fingers.

"Did you ever see Cody and the Professor together?" Kay asked.

"No. I don't know for sure if they even knew each other. I just figured since both of them were creeping around in the woods, they'd've had to run into each other."

"How well do you all know Dwayne McKenzie?" Jerome

had tired of letting Kay ask all the questions.

"Me? Not that well. See, Jerry's grandfather got in a fight with Dwayne's father years ago, so the families kind of stick to their own."

"Didn't you say that Jerry went over to McKenzie's hunting property to see the professor?"

"He might have. It's not like there's any *real* fireworks between the families. At least not since the two old men died."

Now that June mentioned it, Kay remembered that her father had buried one or both men and that there had been a bit of a dust-up at the viewing or the funeral; she couldn't remember which.

"Where does Jerry work?" Jerome asked.

"He's an assistant manager at Creekside Feed. His daddy is part-owner." There was a hint of pride in her voice. "Andy works there too."

"Have you seen or heard anything odd or out of place in the last couple of weeks?"

"Around here?" June seemed to think about this for a few moments. "With little Chris here... I don't see or hear much going on outside."

They thanked her and got up to leave. June followed them to the door, the now-fussy toddler still in her arms.

"Did someone find the gold?" she asked.

"I don't know," Kay said honestly as she stepped outside.

"I hope they did," June said and shut the door.

Kay drove back toward the McKenzie property, but slowed down on the road before turning.

"Do you know who owns the house on the *other* side of McKenzie's property?" she asked Jerome.

"Keith Dandridge. He's a civil engineer with the county. Nice enough guy."

"You know him?"

"Met him a few times when he was working on a bridge or road in the county and I was directing traffic for them."

Kay passed the entrance to the McKenzie property and turned instead onto a tarmac drive that led up to a fine Victorian house with a pair of gables and gingerbread latticework. Camelia and azalea bushes were scattered around the yard, and daylilies lined flowerbeds holding four o'clocks and lantana.

"He's probably not home," Jerome said as they got out of the car and walked up to the house. He was proven right when their knocks on the door went unanswered.

"If you want to talk to him today, let's drive to the Fast Mart up the road and use the payphone to call Dandridge's office," Jerome suggested.

"We could just drive to the county road department," Kay pointed out.

"He's probably out at a project. His office will know."

At the convenience store, Jerome got out of the car and glared at the ne'er-do-wells hanging by the phones until they drifted off. Having scattered the crowd, he found the only phone in working condition and made a quick call.

"Dandridge isn't that far away," he said, getting back into the car. "They're surveying the bridge on Highway 190 at Otter Creek."

There were three county trucks parked along the shoulder of the road when they got there. Kay pulled up behind them and Jerome was out of the car by the time she'd turned the engine off. She followed him to a group of workmen standing next to a tripod. One of the men was pointing toward the bridge and talking animatedly. He looked puzzled and perhaps a little irritated when he saw Kay and Jerome walking toward them.

"Is there a problem?" he asked.

"We'd like to talk with Keith Dandridge," Jerome

explained.

Dandridge walked toward them with a thoughtful look on his face.

"I know you. You're a deputy. You've directed traffic at a couple of projects. What can I do for you?"

"We'd like to ask you a few questions about your neighbors," Jerome said.

Dandridge looked at Kay. "I don't think I've had the pleasure?"

"I'm Kay Lamberton," she said, stretching her hand out toward him.

Almost delicately, he took her proffered hand and shook it. "You own the funeral home, right?"

"I'm one of the owners." She smiled.

"Of course." He looked back and forth between Jerome and Kay. "I don't understand. You said you wanted to talk about my neighbors?"

"Dwayne McKenzie and Roger Harrington," Jerome said.

"Oh, I see." Dandridge didn't look surprised. He turned to the other men. "I'm going to be a few minutes. Take a half-hour break." Then he pointed to clearing near a spring-fed creek. "We can talk over there."

The air was cooler down by creek. Kay took stock of Keith Dandridge. He was an average-looking guy of average height and average weight. He bore the tan of a man who spent most of his days outside. His dark hair had a little grey around the temples and was cut short.

"Do you know that Dwayne McKenzie is missing?" Jerome asked.

"Of course. We've been friends since elementary school. If I didn't have to be on this project, I'd be out helping with the search now," he said regretfully.

"How well do you know him?"

"I've known him most of my life. We played football for

Melon County High School. I was just okay, but he was good. My place backs up to his hunting property. I guess that's why you're here."

"Exactly. When was the last time you saw Dwayne?"

"Gee, I'd have to say about a month ago... something like that. I think I ran into him at the bank."

"Did he seem all right? Did he mention anything that was bothering him?"

"No, we just said hi. Talked about the weather, the way you do."

"Had you met Professor Harrington?"

"Sure. He was a funny little guy."

"You heard that he died on McKenzie's property, right?"

Dandridge nodded. "I was sorry to hear that."

"What sort of relationship did you have with him?"

"I don't know if you'd call it a *relationship*. He came to my house... I guess it was in early spring. Told me that there could be Spanish gold buried on my property and offered to let me keep the gold, or as much as the state would let me keep, if I allowed him to search the property for clues."

"What did you tell him?" Jerome asked.

"At first, I said no, but he made it sound like the real deal. All that gold. Who's going to turn an offer like that down?" Dandridge laughed. "The county doesn't pay me that well."

"Did he find anything?"

"I'm still working for the county, aren't I?" He sighed. "Look, he spent a few days poking around and didn't find any clues. After that, he would come by sometimes and we'd sit around the firepit and exchange war stories. One thing we had in common was that we both had wives that ran off on us. A few drinks and we were cursing all the women of the world." Dandridge looked at Kay and tipped an imaginary hat. "No offense intended."

"None taken. Anyway, we're even. I've cursed all the men in the world after a few drinks," Kay said with an easy smile.

"Did Harrington ever mention any trouble he was having with other people?" Jerome asked.

"No. There were a few people who wouldn't let him search their place, but it wasn't a big deal."

"How big is your property?"

"Thirty acres. Nothing like Dwayne's hunting tract."

"That's your family home?"

"Yep. It's been in my family for eighty years. Dad turned the keys to the house over to me the day I married Kelly."

"Is that the wife who left you?"

Dandridge nodded sadly. "Ran off with a man from Alabama. She'd been drinking a lot and... I guess she just fell out of love with me." He looked down at the ground.

"When was the last time you saw the Professor?"

"Just over a week ago. He came by to talk about another clue he'd found. He thought I might could help him out."

"How so?"

Dandridge pointed toward the tripod up the hill. "Wanted me to do some survey work with him. He wanted to get better topographical maps of some of the property around us. One thing he was looking for was depressions in the ground that can't be explained naturally."

"What about them?" Jerome asked.

"Any time there's a human settlement and things like bodies or wooden structures are buried, when they rot away, the ground settles. He thought it was also possible that the Spaniards might have constructed a limestone room underground to store the treasure, and a depression in the ground might indicate the entrance to such a place."

"Did you help him out?"

"We never got that far. He came over and talked to me about it, then said he'd come back with maps so he could show me the area he wanted to survey."

"Not on your property?"

"I think he was talking about McKenzie's property or some of the other large tracts nearby.

"How long was this before he died?"

"A day, maybe two, I think."

"Were you concerned when he didn't come back right away with the maps?"

Dandridge shook his head. "The man was like a moth. If a light went on close to him, he'd go flying off to look at it. I just figured he'd gotten another hot lead. It wasn't like I could call him."

"Do you know Cody Morgan?"

"Sure, I've seen him around. I think he's an odd kid, but he's smarter than he looks and, as far as I know, he's never caused any trouble. Why do you ask?"

"He was hanging out with Professor Harrington on McKenzie's land. When you said he's a bit odd, what did you mean?" Jerome inquired.

"Oh, sometimes I would find him on my property or near it. Usually just sitting or standing and staring off into the woods. It was… unsettling."

"Did you ever talk to him about it?"

"I told him that I'd prefer he asked permission when he wanted to walk around my property."

"Was there anything concrete about his behavior, other than the trespassing and staring off into the woods, that bothered you?"

"Not really."

"Do you have any idea why he was on your property?"

"No. It started before the professor showed up, so it wasn't about the gold. I asked Cody and he just said he liked looking at the woods."

"Did you report him?"

"It wasn't like that. After he stopped coming on my property without permission, there wasn't anything to report."

"Did you ever talk to him about anything else?"

"I warned him about walking in some of these woods."

Jerome raised his eyebrows. "Warned him? About what?"

"Come on. Surely you know that there are some marijuana plots out there."

"We've found a few," Jerome admitted.

"You've found some of the bigger plots, but there are a lot of smaller ones. College-aged kids with a few dozen plants way back up in the woods. Some of those guys even lay out booby traps. That was one of the things that I warned Cody about. And, of course, I told him to cover himself from head to foot in orange during hunting season."

"What was his reaction to your warnings?"

"He said he'd seen some pot plants."

"Do you have any names or know exactly where these plots are?" Jerome asked.

Dandridge smiled and shook his head. "You aren't going to get me into that kind of trouble. *Live and let live* is my motto."

After a few more questions, they let him get back to work. When they returned to the car, Kay heard the loud squawk of the radio she'd been given. One of the volunteers, Megan Haynes, had tripped and broken her arm.

They were back at McKenzie's place in fifteen minutes. A frazzled Mrs. Cutter was trying to calm Megan when Kay hurried up to the tent.

"We had a snakebite out behind Mrs. McKenzie's house and now this."

"She'll be fine," Kay said calmly, examining Megan's arm. "But we need to get her to the hospital."

"I just want to call my boyfriend," Megan said nervously.

"We'll call from the hospital," Kay promised as she and Jerome helped her to the car.

CHAPTER THIRTEEN

Jerome went with them to the hospital in Gainesville. The ER was busy, though not as bad as it would have been if it was fall and the students were in town. Once they had Megan checked in, Kay left her in Jerome's care and went over to the bank of payphones to call the funeral home.

"Have you had anything to eat?" Ruby demanded once Kay explained why it would be a while before she got home.

"Just a bag of chips," Kay admitted, realizing that she really *was* hungry. But her stomach would have to wait if it wanted anything more than vending-machine food.

"Supper's in an hour." Ruby didn't sound happy with the way Kay was taking care of herself.

"Can you save me a little?"

Mollified by Kay's request, Ruby promised to make a plate for her.

As she walked back over to Jerome and Megan, Kay felt the sounds, smells and adrenaline rush of the hospital all calling to her. There was something about the way life and death could be decided in an instant that drew her back to nursing, despite the long hours filled with tedium and sore feet. She would need to decide soon if she was serious about going back to work and assisting Lee only as a silent partner.

Jerome interrupted her thoughts by pulling her into a corner where they could talk without being overheard.

"I want to talk to the Jerry Mercer."

"Who?" The events of the last hour had pushed much of the day's questioning to the back of Kay's mind.

"The treasure hunter. June's husband."

Kay nodded. "Someone that obsessed might do something crazy."

"Sounds like he may be at a crossroad, feeling the pressure of life with a young wife and new baby. I've seen it before. Anxiety and feelings of inadequacy can make a man act loony."

"We all come to those crossroads at different points in our lives. The first time you take on adult responsibilities, then when your life is half over and you realize you have more deficits than assets," Kay added.

"And when you get to the point where old age is looming and all you want is a bit of your youth back."

"You take one path and your life has dignity and hope, but if you take the other you risk falling into an abyss of shame and darkness." Kay almost giggled and realized that she was tired to the point of being silly.

"We're getting deep now." Jerome chuckled.

Kay took a deep breath and composed herself. "I think you're right about Jerry Mercer. His wife did look worried."

"She was pissed is what she was."

"It was more than that. I think she was really worried about him."

"And that's why I want to talk to him."

"Do it tomorrow. I'll go with you."

Kay looked up and saw a familiar, darkly handsome face approaching from the other side of the waiting room.

"Alan, I wondered if you were working this evening."

Kay was glad to see him, as much for his own self as for the fact that she wanted some relief from the boredom of waiting for Megan's name to be called. She noticed that he was carrying a grease-stained paper bag.

"I was just coming off duty. Ruby called and told me you were in the ER and informed me that a compassionate person would bring you some food," he said with a grin.

Kay introduced her patient. "This is Megan Haynes. Her arm is broken."

"I'm Dr. Eckhart." He kneeled down beside Megan and took her hand gently in his, feeling carefully from her hand up and down her forearm. "We need to get an X-ray to know exactly what's going on, but I can tell you the ulna is broken." He helped her to her feet while some of the other people waiting nearby watched with jealous eyes.

"Must be nice having a boyfriend in high places," Jerome joked as they walked toward the doors leading to the exam areas.

"I brought food for you too," Alan said good-naturedly.

"Nah, I'm catching a ride back to Lang with Henry Booker. He's here dropping off a Section 8 case."

Alan turned to Kay and Megan. "Y'all come back with me."

He led them to one of the break rooms used by the doctors and staff.

"Go ahead and eat a little. You're going to be here for a while," he told Megan. "I'll go arrange for you to get some X-rays taken."

"No good deed," Kay kidded Megan as she offered her one of the enormous biscuits Alan had picked up from

Skeeter's.

"I just wanted to help out," the girl said as she nibbled on the biscuit.

"Do you know Mr. McKenzie?"

"My brother works for him."

"Was your brother at the search?"

"He was leading the group that went out to search the hayfields. That's what Warren does. He takes care of the hayfields. Warren already thinks I'm clumsy so I'm glad he wasn't there to see this." She raised her hand slightly and winced in pain.

"Has your brother said what he thinks happened to Mr. McKenzie?"

"Robbers. He thinks maybe they were going to make him go the house and get the money he keeps in the safe, but he fought back so hard they had to kill him."

Kay thought of the Stern robbery that Mac and Jerome had told her about. "It's possible."

"Or maybe it was the gold they were after."

"What do you know about the gold?"

"Everybody's been talking about it. A lot of people didn't believe the gold was there until all of this happened."

"All of this?" Kay asked, confused.

"Mr. McKenzie being abducted and the old man being killed."

"So you heard about that too?" Kay was surprised at the efficiency of the local grapevine.

"I heard he was stabbed and hung up as a warning to anyone looking for the gold."

The grapevine may be fast, but it isn't always accurate, Kay thought. Playing along, she said, "Like someone is trying to scare people away?"

"My mother thinks it was the curse."

"Curse?" This was a new level of crazy that surprised

Kay.

"On the gold. The Aztecs or whoever's gold it was cursed it, which is why the Spanish ship was wrecked in the first place. Then all the Spaniards trying to transport the gold to St. Augustine died too." Megan made this sound like the gospel truth.

"I see what you mean," Kay said, though she really didn't.

"But I don't think it was a curse. Someone just doesn't want anyone else to beat them to the gold." Megan paused and frowned. "I know it all sounds like a *Scooby-Doo* mystery, but I can't think of any other reason all this stuff is happening."

The door opened and a nurse took Megan off to be X-rayed. A few minutes later, Alan came back.

"I've placed her in good hands. Did she get some food?"

"She would have gotten more if she hadn't been busy telling me about a curse." Kay smiled.

"I don't think you need a curse to explain a broken arm."

"She's not cursed. It's the gold." Kay went on to bring Alan up to speed on the search for gold and the disappearance of Dwayne McKenzie.

"I thought being an ER doctor would be exciting. Apparently, it's nothing compared to owning a funeral home." He picked up his own biscuit and started eating.

"I've been thinking about returning to nursing."

Alan looked up, clearly excited. "I think that would be great! Even if you didn't want to work here, you'd have no trouble getting on at Shands. Rumor has it that they're developing one of the best trauma centers in North Florida. With your military background, I'd think it would be a perfect match. Of course, if you *did* want to work here, well, that would be great."

"I don't know." Kay knew she was being indecisive and

she hated it. "It's frustrating. On the one hand I like… being at home with my brother. I missed a lot of family time when I went into the Army, and I find it… gratifying to help carry on Dad's legacy."

"Couldn't you continue to do the books and help out on the business end?"

"Sure. I could be a silent partner, keep the books and be there if he wants my advice." Kay wondered if she was trying to talk herself into it.

"And if you got a job here in Gainesville, you'd still be close enough to go over there any time you wanted."

"I know. I just want to take my time and try to make the right decision. I have a track record of jumping into situations without considering all the consequences."

"Like becoming a nurse, joining the military and then dropping everything to come down and rescue your brother's business?"

"To name a few." Kay gave him a wry smile.

"Those decisions all seemed to work out for you."

She waved her hand from side to side. "More or less."

"I think the only things keeping you at the funeral home are all the ad hoc investigations you get involved in."

Kay couldn't tell if there was criticism in his tone or not.

"When I see something that doesn't seem right, I have to look into it. I don't know how to turn off the part of me that cares."

"And that's what's going on now with the gold, isn't it?"

Before Kay could respond, a nurse came to tell them that Megan's boyfriend had arrived. Alan stood up and offered to take the man back to see her.

"If he's here, then I'm going to go ahead and leave," Kay said.

Alan stepped in close and took her hands in his.

"I love every opportunity I get to see you. I'll have to

find a way to thank Ruby for letting me know you were here."

"I was glad to see you too," Kay told him, and they shared a quick kiss.

"Next date?" he asked.

"I'll let you know."

She started to pull away, but he held onto her hands.

"This investigation or whatever you want to call it. Be careful."

Kay gave his hands a reassuring squeeze. "I promise."

The sun was low in the sky as Kay drove home, creating a soothing mix of pastel colors. She rolled the window down and let the warm summer breeze fill the car as the radio played "Jack & Diane" and "I Can't Go for That." As much as she tried to clear her mind of worry, it kept returning to the mysteries that surrounded the death of Professor Roger Harrington.

CHAPTER FOURTEEN

Lee had just finished cleaning up the embalming room when he heard Kay's car pull into the driveway. Lester had already left to join Ruby in watching *Happy Days* in the family room on the new twenty-five-inch color console TV they'd talked him into buying from Alison. Excited to tell Kay about his experience in St. Augustine, he stepped out the back door and waved to her.

"You look excited," she told him.

"You look tired."

"You took a trip to St. Augustine while I spent the day traipsing around in the woods, going door to door with Jerome and ending up with a trip to the ER."

"You have a point," Lee admitted, barely containing himself from jumping up and down.

"Let's at least go inside," Kay said.

As she crossed the drive, she stepped on a quarter-sized pebble on the concrete and stumbled. "Owww!"

"That's thanks to Yang. The goofy cat has started pulling

stones out of the flowerbed and batting them around."

"He needs to find a less painful game," Kay grumbled as she kicked the pebble back into the flowerbed.

"I know who killed Harrington!" Lee blurted once they were in the kitchen.

Kay looked at him to see if he was serious. "How?"

"Not who?" he teased.

Kay grabbed the plate of fried chicken and potato salad that Ruby had left for her in the refrigerator, then motioned for Lee to join her at the table. "Start at the beginning."

As she ate, Lee told her all about his meeting with Joyce Harrington, the strange way she had acted and how he'd snuck back to eavesdrop on her and her mysterious male visitor.

"Tell me exactly what they said."

"I did my best to memorize it," Lee said, scrunching up his face in thought and then repeating what he had heard. The expression on his face when he finished was that of a magician who'd just pulled a twenty-pound rabbit out of his top hat.

Kay leaned back in her chair. "They really said that if they got caught it would ruin them?"

Lee nodded.

"It certainly sounds incriminating," Kay agreed.

"So now what?" Lee asked. He'd been thinking about it all day but still hadn't decided on the best course of action.

"What would happen if we told this story to the sheriff's office?"

"They don't even want to believe he was killed."

"Maybe with a confession from the killers they will." Even as Kay said it, she wasn't sure if it was true. "And what about Dwayne McKenzie? Did they kill him too?"

"I don't know. They didn't say anything about him."

"Technically, they didn't even mention Harrington," Kay

pointed out.

"Which is one of the problems with going to the sheriff. It gives them an out."

"I can just see that oaf Wade Sutton saying that they could have been talking about anything."

"That would be more believable if I hadn't just been questioning her about her ex-husband," Lee said.

"I'd like to know about this guy she's with."

"Hugo Valero. She said that he's a muckety-muck when it comes to Spanish antiquities."

"Guess that explains how Joyce met him. I wonder if he was a friend of the Harringtons before he became better friends with Joyce." Kay looked thoughtful. "We might need Jerome's opinion on this."

"I don't want to let those two get away with murder."

"And did they have anything to do with McKenzie's disappearance? If they did, then he could still be alive. If we don't act soon, we could be inadvertently responsible for his death."

Kay got up and went over to the phone.

"What did you learn today?" Lee asked.

"Nothing that ties into what you heard. I'm calling Jerome."

The deputy picked up on the third ring. "I've got to be at work in an hour," he complained.

"Lee overheard Harrington's ex-wife and her current boyfriend basically admitting that they killed him."

Jerome took a moment to digest this. "Okay, I'll be there in twenty minutes."

Fifteen minutes later, dressed in his uniform, Jerome banged through the screen door and into the kitchen.

"What's all this about?" he asked Kay and Lee, who were eating homemade peach ice cream at the table while Kay told Lee about the interviews she and Jerome had conducted.

"Let's go to the office. Big ears." She jokingly pointed at Ruby, who was standing by the sink and popped her with a dishtowel.

"You know I'm just going to listen at the office door," she told them.

"What kind of ice cream is that?" Jerome asked.

"Peach. I made it myself this afternoon."

Kay and Lee were already heading for the office with bowls in hand.

"Make me a bowl?" he asked sweetly, and Ruby rewarded him with a big smile and a generous helping of three scoops.

Jerome joined the others in the office and sat down in a chair with his bowl, glancing at his watch. "I'm listening. You have half an hour."

Lee repeated what he'd told Kay.

"What can I do with that?" Jerome asked.

"That's what we wanted you to tell us," Kay said, frowning.

"We don't even have concrete proof that a crime has been committed, and this conversation you overheard means nothing. They could have been talking about anything."

"We have Roger Harrington's body in the cooler." Lee pointed in the general direction of the embalming room.

"And the coroner has left it a question mark. And your suspects didn't say they'd killed anyone."

"You don't think the conversation was suspicious?" Lee asked.

"I'm not saying that. But they aren't going to admit they said it, and all you can do is testify to what you heard which, without context, isn't proof of much. They could have been talking about their affair. A defense attorney would tear this confession up and shove it down the prosecutor's throat, which is why the sheriff won't go all-in on an investigation."

"All of that aside," Kay said, "what do you think it

means?"

"Sounds to me like they're guilty as sin… of something. Is it murder? I guess it's possible."

"So what now?" Lee asked.

"We keep doing what we're doing. Finding McKenzie would help. If he's dead, that will open up an investigation which could involve the death of Harrington. If that happens, then I can promise you even that idiot Wade Sutton will have to pay attention to what you overheard."

"Do you really think there's a connection between McKenzie's disappearance and Harrington's death?" Kay asked.

"If not, then it's a hell of a coincidence."

"I'm going back to the McKenzie place to help with the search tomorrow," Kay said.

"Someone should go with you. I would, but I have got to get some sleep. I don't have a day off until Friday."

"I'd go," Lee said, "but I've got to pick up a body from the airport in Gainesville and take it down to Ocala for the Armstrong Funeral Home. I promised them last week I'd do it."

"Maybe Lester can go," Kay suggested.

"Where is Lester? I don't believe he'd miss this." Jerome held up his empty bowl.

"After *Happy Days*, he went over to Alison's store to help unpack some TVs that came in today," Lee said.

"Don't worry. He's eaten two bowls already and will probably stop by on his way home for another," Kay said.

They followed Jerome back to the kitchen, where he put his bowl in the sink.

"When I get off in the morning, I'm going by the feed store and talk to Jerry Mercer," Jerome told them as he went out the door.

"I want to be there," Kay said.

"Meet me at the feed store on your way to McKenzie's place. I'll be there at eight." He gave a wave over his shoulder.

An hour later, Kay was in bed reading *Free Fall in Crimson*. Over the last four months, she had devoured almost all of John D. MacDonald's Travis McGee series. *Maybe that's why I'm seeing murders with every dead body*, she thought. There was a flash of lightning and a roll of thunder in the distance as she turned off the light.

On Wednesday morning, Kay came downstairs to the smell of bacon frying.

"I listened in enough to know you were heading out early this morning." Ruby smiled and handed her a plate with bacon, scrambled eggs and toast. "You need a good breakfast if you're going hiking in the woods."

"Thanks, Ruby. I'm actually glad we have some time to talk," Kay said, making her voice sound as ominous as possible. "Telling Jerome that I needed him yesterday morning and then calling Dr. Eckhart and telling him to bring me food at the hospital is not what you were hired for."

"Looking after this family is *exactly* what your daddy hired me for." Ruby wasn't going to show remorse for actions she deemed appropriate.

"I wasn't privy to Dad's negotiations with you, so let me make this clear. There are limits to how much I want to be watched over."

"You and Jerome made some progress looking into the death of the Professor, and last night at the hospital I'm sure that food sure tasted good." Ruby gave her a sly smile.

"Just because it all worked out for the best doesn't mean you were right to stick your nose into my business."

"We'll just have to disagree on that point," Ruby said, knowing that Kay wouldn't push the issue too far.

Kay wished she was angrier about it than she really was. With a sigh, she ate the bacon and used the toast and fork to finish the eggs.

"I suppose you think I need someone to go with me this morning." Kay took her plate to the sink and turned to get her keys from the hanger on the wall.

"Lester has already eaten and is waiting out by your car."

Kay whirled around and was about to tell Ruby she had gone too far this time when Ruby added, "Last night you *did* say you might see if Lester could go with you."

"I was leaving my options open," Kay said through clenched teeth.

"You can tell him to stay here," Ruby said innocently. They both knew that Lester would pout for a week if Kay told him to not come with her.

I will tell him to stay behind, Kay told herself as she turned and left without another word to Ruby.

Lester was watching Yang, one of Ruby's chubby tabbies, paw at the vent to the crawlspace under the house.

"He's been doing that for the last ten minutes," Lester told Kay.

"I wouldn't be at all surprised if there's a mouse under there. There's a rat in the kitchen," Kay said, looking over her shoulder to see Ruby glancing out the kitchen window.

"A rat?" Lester looked up at Kay.

She was about to tell him that she didn't want him to go with her to the McKenzie place when she got a look at his big, puppy-dog eyes. *Damn it, I just can't do it!* she thought.

"Come on. Let's go for a ride." She waved him toward her car.

Kay pulled up to the feed store where Jerome was already waiting. He was sitting on his motorcycle, smoking a cigarillo. Kay got out of the car after sternly telling Lester to wait for her.

"Smoking this early?" Kay shook her head as she walked over to Jerome.

"It's this or amphetamines at this point."

"Let's get this done so you can go home and get some sleep."

"Glad you remembered to roll the windows down." Jerome smiled and nodded toward Lester, who looked disappointed that Kay wouldn't let him get out of the car.

"Ruby doesn't think I should go anywhere by myself. He didn't want to stay in the car, but I explained to him that three people might be a bit overwhelming to Mr. Mercer."

"He's sure got that lost-puppy look down to an art." Jerome waved to Lester, who waved at them sadly through the open car window.

The feed store had started life as a warehouse along the railroad tracks, so it was built up four feet off the ground, making it easy for semis to unload their large pallets of feed and fertilizer. The shop also carried lumber and supplies for gardening and fencing.

At eight o'clock the store had already been open for an hour, and several farmers and builders were inside placing orders or searching various bins for equipment parts. Jerome, still in uniform, caused a few heads to turn as he walked up to the counter while Kay hung back.

"Is Jerry Mercer here?" Jerome asked.

The short, grey-haired man behind the counter stroked his beard and fiddled with his glasses, acting like he had to think about it for a moment before answering. "Yeeeep," he said, drawing out the word.

"I'd like to talk to him."

"He's out in the yard taking inventory." The man raised his arm slowly and pointed through one of the open bay doors. Fifty yards away, Jerome could see a man with a clipboard peering over stacks of lumber.

Jerome headed that way and Kay fell in line behind him. When they were ten feet away, Jerry Mercer turned and saw them. He looked to be a few years older than his wife, with brown hair that was longer than the current fashion. His eyes were green and clear, though they were rimmed by the dark circles of a man who hadn't been getting a lot of sleep.

"Can I help you?" He looked the odd pair up and down, as though trying to figure out what they would be interested in buying.

"Mr. Mercer, I'm Deputy Carter. I wanted to ask you a few questions about a neighbor of yours who's missing, Dwayne McKenzie."

Jerome had his full attention now.

"I heard about that, but I'm not sure how I can help you." He was tapping the clipboard against his thigh nervously.

"Your house isn't too far from McKenzie's hunting property."

"That's true," Jerry admitted. "Still, I haven't seen him." His eyes narrowed. "You're the ones who came by the house and talked to my wife."

Jerome nodded. "We did."

"She was kind of upset when I got home."

"I'm sorry to hear that," Jerome said in a tone that made it sound like he wasn't sorry at all. "She said that your family and McKenzie's didn't get along very well."

"I wouldn't say that. My grandfather had a beef with Dwayne's father, but the fight didn't trickle down to the rest of us. Heck, my brother Andy almost married one of Dwayne's nieces."

"Have you seen anything odd around your place in the last few weeks?"

"Like what?"

"Strangers, items that look out of place, your stuff disappearing, gates open or closed that shouldn't be."

"No, nothing like that."

"How well did you know Professor Roger Harrington?"

This question made Jerry visibly more nervous. The tapping of the clipboard increased, and his other hand began to open and close.

"I spent some time with him. He sure could talk." He tried to laugh, but nothing came out.

"What did you all talk about?" Jerome asked, causing Jerry to take a couple of gulps of air.

"I… just stuff."

"Like gold?"

"Yeah," Jerry admitted. "He couldn't stop talking about the gold he was looking for."

"Your wife tells us that you've been looking for the gold too."

Kay saw a flash of anger in Jerry's eyes. Kay guessed that June wasn't supposed to be telling people about his obsession with the treasure.

Jerome must have seen the anger too, because he added, "We didn't give your wife much choice. I wouldn't want to hear that you gave her a hard time for talking to us."

"No. Of course I wouldn't." Jerry looked frustrated at being questioned and at his apparent transparency. His eyes glanced past Jerome to the store, as though he were hoping someone would come and give him an excuse to escape the interview.

"The gold?" Jerome prompted.

"Yeah, I've looked around our place. Who wouldn't if a guy tells you there might be a fortune in gold buried in your back woods."

"How much time did you spend with Harrington?"

Jerry looked like he wanted to lie but thought better of it. "I guess a few days and a couple of afternoons. I can't really narrow it down too much. Sometimes he'd come over to our place and a few times I went and found him."

"And you all hunted for the gold?"

"Like I said, he could talk. Mostly he talked and I listened."

"Did he talk about anything other than the gold?" Kay asked, causing Jerry to focus his attention on her.

"He talked about his ex-wife a bunch." He paused as though he wasn't sure he should say the next part, but he finally added, "I thought he was obsessed with her."

"What exactly did he say about her?"

"I couldn't possibly remember all of it. There was a lot about how badly she treated him. He had a whole list of grievances, and he also talked about all the complaints she had about him. I was interested in his stories about the gold and was bored with all the talk of his ex. He definitely hadn't moved on."

"Did he mention any recent arguments he'd had with her?" Kay asked.

"No. It sounded like she'd cut him off. You know, wouldn't answer or return his calls. He made it sound like he left long messages on her answering machine."

"Did he ever mention any other man in her life?"

"Oh yeah. Went on and on about him. Some guy with a weird name. Spanish, I think. Again, I wasn't interested in the Professor's personal life."

"Try and think of something specific he said about the man," Jerome urged.

"Weasel. He liked to call him a weasel. There were also a bunch of Spanish words he used. When I asked him what they meant, he just said they were curse words. Actually, he said that if I understood them my hair would catch on fire, they were so vulgar."

"Did he mention the last time he had talked to them or saw them?"

"Not that I can remember."

"Tell me what you know about Cody Morgan," Jerome said, changing tack.

"The kid's a bit creepy. His grandfather is okay. I used to do some work for him when I was younger. That's what a kid like Cody should be doing, mowing grass or doing chores to earn extra money, not sneaking around on other people's property."

"He works at the Fast Mart," Kay pointed out, surprised that she found herself defending Cody.

"Yeah, he put in an application here too. I dropped that one right in the round filing cabinet. Last thing we need is some guy staring off into the woods all the time or giving the women the heebie jeebies."

"Did he come onto your property?" Jerome asked.

"Yes, you can ask June. He freaked her out."

"What did you do about it?"

"What do you think I did? I told him to get off my property."

"Did you argue with him?"

"What's this about? You think he killed Harrington?"

"We want to understand everyone who is in the area and what their relationships are. When I ask a question, there isn't always a specific purpose behind it."

"A fishing expedition," Jerry said.

"There's nothing wrong with throwing a line in and seeing what bites." Jerome's tone was stone-cold serious.

"So did you argue with Cody Morgan?" Kay wasn't going to let him avoid the question.

"No. That's part of what's creepy about him. You tell him to get off your property and he just turns and leaves."

Jerry shook his head, then tapped the side of it. "He's just off, if you know what I mean."

"Do you think he killed Professor Harrington?" Kay asked.

"Was Harrington murdered?"

"We're looking into the possibility," Jerome answered diplomatically.

"We. Is that the sheriff's office or you and the owner of the funeral home?" He pointed at Kay.

Kay admitted to herself that Jerry was smarter than she'd originally thought.

"Officially, Harrington's death is not currently being investigated as a homicide." Jerome stepped lightly through the minefield. "However, there *is* an official investigation into the disappearance of Mr. McKenzie."

Kay was sure that Jerome was hoping Jerry Mercer wouldn't ask if Jerome was part of that investigation. He didn't.

"Our store's been helping with the search. My dad sent over some supplies for the mounted posse and 4-H horses they've been using to comb through the property. That's a lot of land to search. McKenzie must own five thousand acres in the county."

"What do you think happened to Dwayne McKenzie?" Jerome asked.

"At first I figured he ran off with some woman."

"Why would you think that?"

Jerry looked down at the ground, considering his next words.

"The man is arrogant. Just the type of guy that thinks he can have anything he wants. Even other peoples' women."

"Have you heard about him moving in on another man's girlfriend or wife?"

"No," Jerry admitted. "I just know the type."

"So if he didn't run off with a woman, what do you think happened to him?" Jerome continued to push.

"I go back to him being arrogant. He probably pissed someone off on a deal."

"Do you know anyone who was angry with him?"

Jerry was quiet and looked down at the ground for a minute.

"We're talking to everyone. If there's something we need to know, it'll be better if it comes from you." Jerome's tone had changed from aggressive to gently urging.

"He screwed me over. A couple of years ago, I'd just started taking over some of my dad's responsibilities here at the store. One was working with our suppliers. Dwayne knew I didn't know the specifics of all the deals we had, and he came to me one day with a contract to provide the store with hay for the next two years. Since hay prices can fluctuate depending on the cost of fuel and fertilizer, we do a percentage deal. I didn't know that we'd been getting twenty five percent of the price. He handed me the contract he'd made up saying we got fifteen percent and acted like it was the same as the last contract. Not knowing any better, I signed it."

"Guess that didn't make your dad too happy."

"Made me look like a fool to everyone. When I confronted Dwayne, he said I should take it as a lesson in doing business. Know what you're doing before you sign a contract. Didn't make it one bit better that he was right."

"I'd have kicked his ass," Jerome said, nodding.

"I…" Jerry looked at Jerome and chose his words carefully. "…did two things. First, I learned my lesson, and now I read anything I sign backwards and forwards. Second, once that contract ran out, I never did business with McKenzie again. I've driven a hundred miles to buy hay rather than buy it from him."

"Have you seen McKenzie in the last two weeks?" Jerome held up his hand to stop him from speaking right away. "Think carefully about your answer."

"I saw him at the Fast Mart last Monday. We didn't say anything to each other. He was at the counter paying for gas when I came in." Jerry shook his head. "That's all. It'd been a month at least before that."

"You went over to McKenzie's hunting cabin to see Harrington."

"I knew I was taking a risk."

"What would have happened if McKenzie had been there when you came to see Harrington?"

"I would have left."

"And if he showed up when you were already there?"

"I was careful not to go over there if there was a chance of that happening."

Jerome decided he'd gotten all the information he could out of Jerry Mercer. He shared a glance with Kay, who'd come to the same conclusion. They thanked Jerry for talking to them, and Jerome told him they'd be in touch.

CHAPTER FIFTEEN

"So what's your opinion of Jerry?" Kay asked when they were out of earshot.

"There's a lot of anger there," Jerome said.

"Probably built on the foundation of a sense of inadequacy. A man trying to walk in his father's footsteps and never quite living up to his own expectations, let alone his father's."

"You could be right. Not sure what that has to do with Harrington or McKenzie." Jerome stopped at his motorcycle.

"I don't either."

"Keep an eye out for trouble today. Even though it pains me to say it, if you need me, call," Jerome told her.

"We'll be fine. Won't we, Lester?" Kay asked the sad face in her car window.

"Can we go now?" Lester said petulantly.

Kay rolled her eyes and got into the car while Jerome put his helmet on and spun out of the parking lot.

There were less people at the McKenzie place than the day before, but the yard was still filled with cars.

"Where are we going to go look?" Lester asked excitedly as they got out of the car.

"Who's answering the phone at the funeral home?" Kay had just realized that everyone except Ruby would be gone.

"Lee doesn't have to leave until noon, and I'm supposed to check in every hour or so after that to see if Ruby has taken any calls."

Kay nodded. "Let's go sign in."

Once their names were on the list, Kay pointed out Beth McKenzie to Lester.

"She doesn't look too well," Lester observed.

Kay had to admit that there was a marked different in Beth's appearance. The last time Kay had seen her, her hair had been brushed and her make-up in place. Now her make-up looked like it had been put on in the dark and her clothes were wrinkled, with sweat stains under her arms. What hadn't changed were her piercing, determined eyes.

Beth moved through the groups of volunteers, earnestly talking to all of them. Her desperation and drive were palpable. Then Kay noticed her attention shift to the row of parked cars. Following Beth's gaze, Kay wasn't happy to see Wade Sutton strutting toward them.

Sutton locked eyes on Beth and went straight to her. Kay thought about moving closer to Beth so she could hear what they talked about, but she needn't have worried.

"Where are the deputies?" Beth asked when Sutton was still fifteen feet away. Her voice was loud and accusatory.

Sutton didn't answer until he was standing right in front of her.

"Now, Mrs. McKenzie, I told you we aren't going to commit a bunch of resources to a search until we know for sure that foul play is involved." He looked down at her condescendingly as he spoke.

"And I told *you* that Dwayne wouldn't just run off." Beth was vibrating with anger.

Kay thought Beth looked like a very pissed off rattlesnake. Anyone with a lick of sense would have taken her tone, posture and flinty eyes as a warning, but not Wade Sutton. He looked right and left, checking to make sure he was the center of attention.

"Now you never know. Your husband might have found a cute little filly to run off with," Sutton said with a smile that lasted less than a millisecond. That's how long it took for Beth's hand to fly up and slap him across the face.

The smack resonated across the yard. Everyone was staring, some of them with open mouths. Kay was sure that everyone who had heard Sutton's comment was resisting the urge to clap. She knew she was.

Sutton's face had turned a menacing shade of red. Kay decided she didn't want to give this encounter a chance to escalate any further, so she quickly walked across the space that separated her from the two combatants. Sutton caught the movement out of the corner of his eye and turned to see what new threat was advancing on him. When he saw that it was Kay, he refocused his fury on her.

"You! What have you been telling her?" he said in a preposterous attempt to divert blame to Kay.

"Sutton, I'd suggest you watch what you say to Mrs. McKenzie," Kay warned him.

"If someone has killed McKenzie, then the first suspect will be the wife." As the words came out of his mouth, Sutton's eyes looked startled at the audacity and bad taste of his own accusation.

"You will rot in hell," Beth McKenzie prophesized, and the only thing that stopped her from launching herself at him was Reverand Sam Beck from the Methodist church, who hurried over to calm things down, positioning himself between Sutton and Beth.

"I'd suggest you go," Kay told Sutton.

She thought he was going to argue with her until he looked around and noticed that the audience was staring angrily at him. With a sneer, he wheeled about and stomped back to his unmarked car without another word.

Kay turned back to see Beth wiping away tears of frustration while Reverand Beck awkwardly patted her shoulder.

"We need to get the groups out there looking," Beth said to everyone and no one.

Kay turned to see Lester watching from a distance. She walked back over to him.

"You were a big help," she said.

"I don't like Wade Sutton," Lester replied. "And I don't want to end up in jail."

"What have you done that could land you in jail?" she said, then added, "Besides smoking pot."

"I don't smoke that much. Now my roommate—" He smiled when he realized that Kay was only kidding him. "No, I meant I might hit him."

"Come on." She half pulled him over to a spot where they could watch everyone while waiting to be given an assignment. "Watch the crowd for anyone who looks suspicious."

"You think the killer could be here?"

"It wouldn't be the first time a bad guy inserted themselves in an investigation."

Within half an hour, they were assigned to go out to one of McKenzie's hay fields. They were told that it had been searched once by horseback, and now they wanted people on foot to walk the ground looking for clues. Kay had to admit that the searchers were being thorough.

Kay and Lester had walked most of the field when Lester stopped, bent down and held something up in his hand.

"Look what I found." Lester walked over to Kay, carrying an arrowhead with a broken tip.

"You're supposed to be looking for clues to McKenzie's whereabouts, not Indian artifacts."

"Do you have to carry that everywhere?" Lester slipped the arrowhead into his pocket and pointed to the canvas bag on Kay's shoulder.

"I made the mistake of being useful yesterday," she joked.

As if on cue, the radio inside the bag came to life with a series of squawks and voices saying that they needed to find Beth McKenzie.

"I think the game's afoot." Kay turned up the volume on the radio.

"I can't understand half of what they're saying," Lester complained.

Kay shushed him. "We need to head back to the car."

"What's going on?" Lester shouted from behind her.

Other volunteers searching the field turned to look at them as they passed. Kay slowed and let Lester catch up.

"They've found something."

"McKenzie?"

"I don't think so. Maybe his body."

"Where?"

"Not close by. I heard them say that a car was waiting for Mrs. McKenzie."

"Maybe they found his truck?"

"Yeah," Kay agreed.

They drove back to the McKenzie house and Kay went to the tent that was still manned by Mrs. Cutter. She looked both nervous and excited.

"I want to turn the radio back in. We've got to leave."

Kay held out the canvas bag, hoping to get the older lady talking. From her expression, it was clear she'd heard some news.

"Sorry you have to go, but I understand. Everyone appreciated you taking Megan up to the hospital yesterday."

"I heard some chatter over the radio. Have they found something?" Kay asked.

Mrs. Cutter looked conflicted. "I shouldn't say a word, 'cause I don't really know what they've found. But someone came to pick up Beth."

"I hope Mr. McKenzie is found safe."

"I know. It's so sad, and that ogre Wade Sutton had to go and make things worse this morning. The nerve of that boy. You know, I taught him in my sixth-grade reading class and he was dense as a brick even back then. I can tell you, he is lucky there's family to support him 'cause he wouldn't be able to get a job as a ditch-digger without them." Mrs. Cutter was on a tear. She'd clearly been appalled by Sutton's behavior.

"I've had my own run-ins with Wade Sutton, and I can tell you that he hasn't gotten any smarter." Kay paused for a second, then asked, "You didn't hear where they were taking Mrs. McKenzie?"

"Just that it's somewhere east of here. Everyone was in such a hurry."

"Who came for her?"

"Not Sutton, I can tell you that. It was some other young man from the sheriff's office."

Kay thanked Mrs. Cutter and headed over to her car with Lester in tow.

"What now?" Lester sounded confused.

Kay went to start the car, then realized that Lester had a point.

"I don't know." She leaned back in the seat and tried to

decide what to do. "Let's go over to Jerome's house."

"I thought he needed sleep."

"Sleep's overrated." Kay felt a little bad about disturbing Jerome, but she wanted to know what was going on.

Jerome lived in the house that had belonged to his grandmother. It was made of cinderblock and painted dark green with yellow shutters, his grandmother's favorite colors. The house was located in the historically black section of Lang, where most of the residents were solidly middle-class craftsmen, teachers and businessmen.

Kay felt a touch of guilt as she knocked lightly on the door. She was surprised to hear a soft, female voice from inside asking her to wait a minute.

Jerome's mother opened the door. She was petite with grey hair and a smiling face. Kay had met her a few times and had never seen any expression on her face other than that smile.

"Honey, you timed that just right. He tried to call you and was getting ready to come over looking for you." She turned her head back toward the interior of the house and shouted, "Jerome! Miss Lamberton is here." She turned back to Kay. "Would you like some cinnamon cake? I just brought one over for Jerome."

"That sounds great!" said Lester, who had been half hiding behind Kay. He barged his way through the door with a quick, "Hi, Mrs. Carter," thrown over his shoulder.

"Lester, I wouldn't have bothered to ask if I'd seen you back there." Mrs. Carter laughed.

"I left a message at the funeral home," Jerome said as he came down the hallway.

"They found something, didn't they?" Kay asked.

"McKenzie's truck. At least they're pretty sure it's his truck. It's in the St. John's River."

"Have they brought it up yet?"

"No. They're waiting for Townsend to get there. Mrs. McKenzie is on her way too."

"Townsend?" Bill Townsend was a competent investigator with the sheriff's department who had been stuck working non-violent crimes for years while Sutton had been given the best cases.

"Seems Sutton said the wrong thing to Mrs. McKenzie and she called in some favors. Had him removed from the investigation." Jerome's voice was filled with glee.

"She slapped him," Kay reported.

"I wish I'd seen that. I went ahead and told Townsend what we've been up to and he wants us over there too."

"Then let's go!" Kay turned and jogged back to her car.

"What about the cinnamon cake?" Lester asked from the kitchen.

"You can stay here and have some, then go back to the funeral home when you're done," Jerome told him, then generously offered, "You can take my motorcycle. But be aware—I know that it only has one scratch on the rear fender."

The truck had been found about fifty miles away from Lang. Kay tried to rein in her thoughts as she took directions from Jerome, who was reading the road map.

"The truck being found in the St. John's River supports Lee's theory that the ex-wife and her lover are behind Harrington's murder and McKenzie's disappearance," Kay said.

"It *is* on the way to St. Augustine. But you're putting the cart before the horse. We don't know what they'll find when they pull the truck up out of the water," Jerome told her, then gestured for her to take the next left.

As they turned down the short road that ended at the

river, there was no question they were in the right place. A dozen cars and trucks lined the road, and workmen and first responders stood about talking. Kay found a place to park behind a crime-scene van from the Florida Department of Law Enforcement. Jerome admired it as he got out of the car.

"That's the kind of thing we need."

"You all collect evidence," Kay said.

"Yeah, but most of the time it's just the deputy or investigator taking pictures and recovering prints. Did you know that, due to the cost of film, we get written up if we take more pictures than our supervisor thinks is necessary?"

They walked toward the bank of the river where a tow truck sat with its winch facing the slow-moving water.

"There's Townsend." Jerome pointed to an unassuming man who looked more like an accountant than an investigator. He stood with a group of first responders and county workers, watching a man on a jon boat about twenty feet from shore. Beth McKenzie stood a few feet away, looking nervously at the water.

The man on the boat held the hook and cable from the tow truck. As the driver let out the cable, the man pulled the hook toward a diver in the water. Ten minutes later, after the hook and cable had been secured and checked, the diver made a circular motion with his hand and the slack in the cable was taken up by the winch.

As the winch began to turn, Kay could see a disturbance in the water, and she thought about turning away. She wasn't sure she wanted to see McKenzie's bloated corpse. But one look over at Beth, who was keeping her eyes focused on the water, steeled Kay's resolve.

Slowly, the blue-and-white truck surfaced as the tow truck pulled it into shallower water. When the water was still halfway up the doors, Townsend told them to stop. Without regard for his clothes, he waded out into the river and peered through the windows, careful not to put his hands on the truck.

Kay saw him shake his head and wave to the tow truck driver to start the winch again. Once the truck was on shore, everyone moved forward, their curiosity irresistibly drawing them closer.

"We need some nets and buckets," Townsend told them as he looked at the truck. It was leaking water, but the water was still all the way up to the partially open windows of the cab. "We can't do anything until we've drained the water, and I want to make damn sure we don't lose any clues that might be floating around in there."

There was a discussion between the county workers and the crime-scene team from FDLE. Townsend left them and walked over to Jerome and Kay.

"I want you to tell me everything you know about the McKenzie disappearance and the death of this character, Harrington. All I got from Sutton was a one-page report. I've seen more thorough reports on a lost wallet."

"Are they going to let you keep the case?" Jerome asked.

"They only gave it to me because Sutton screwed himself with Mrs. McKenzie. She even brought out her lawyer, Charles Dean. Said if the sheriff didn't take Sutton off the case and start treating it like a serious crime, she was going to sue the department and the sheriff and Sutton individually."

"Bet that went over well." Kay grinned.

"They told her they had qualified immunity, at which point she said her lawyer would dig until he found something the sheriff didn't have immunity for."

"There's more than one skeleton in the sheriff's closet," Jerome said knowingly.

"Next thing I knew, Sutton was giving me his third-grade-equivalent report and stomping off like the petulant child he is. Of course, they're happy to send me over here to do the hands-on policework, but I've already been told that the sheriff will be handling the case directly, which is a joke, and that I'm just to be his front man. Honestly, I'm ready to find another job."

"Hang in there. We're only a year from the election," Jerome encouraged him.

Townsend gave him a suspicious look.

"I've heard a rumor that someone in the department might challenge the sheriff. Are you going to go up against him?"

"Not me. Let's just say I might know of someone with a lot better chance who *is* thinking about it."

"I don't care if he's the janitor. He's got my vote," Townsend said. "I hate to see victims like Mrs. McKenzie have to fight assholes like Sutton just to get justice for their family."

"I witnessed the confrontation between Mrs. McKenzie and Sutton. It was a thing of beauty," Kay admitted.

"She's a tough woman." Townsend turned to look at Beth. "She's going to tear our county apart to find her husband. I'm not sure my wife would even notice I was gone until the delinquent payment notices started arriving."

"What do you think happened to him?" Kay asked.

"It's early days. I'm hoping this truck can give us some clues. The fact that it's over here tells me he probably didn't have an accident. No one can suggest a good reason why he would have been over here near the St. John's." He paused and looked at Jerome and Kay. "Now tell me what you know about his disappearance."

Kay and Jerome went back and forth, occasionally stepping on each other's words as they told Townsend about the people they'd talked to.

"There's one more thing you need to know. My brother

overheard what he considers a confession to Harrington's murder," Kay said. "But it would be best if you got it directly from him."

"I'll talk to him later. Go ahead and give me the CliffsNotes version."

Kay went into as much detail as she could remember of what Lee had told her about his meeting with Joyce Harrington and his subsequent eavesdropping that had led to the overheard confession.

"I'd say that's very interesting. Especially considering where McKenzie's truck ended up. But right now, it's all academic. We've got to see what spills out of the truck and go from there."

"What do you want us to do?" Jerome asked.

"Stay around. I'll know more when we open the doors."

Kay and Jerome watched as the crime-scene techs siphoned most of the water out the windows into buckets. Several samples of the water were taken so they could be analyzed for blood or other substances. Then they opened the passenger door and the remaining water gushed into a net set up to catch any debris from inside the truck. This included pens, notepads, receipts, fast food wrappers and a work glove. The other glove was later found under the seat.

There were no body parts, and no wallet or jewelry that should have been with McKenzie if he'd gone into the water with the truck. The keys were still in the ignition, and a Colt Python in an engraved leather holster was still under the seat where Beth said McKenzie always kept it.

"Professor Harrington's journal wasn't in the truck," Kay pointed out.

"We know that Dwayne drove off in this truck Sunday morning, and that he had the journal with him at the time. The odds that whatever happened to him revolve around the journal have just gone up a notch, since he either still has it with him or someone else removed it from the truck." Townsend spoke like a professor explaining a problem to his class.

"How are you going to proceed from here?" Kay asked.

"First, I'm going to tell you all to back off." He held up his hand to ward off Kay's objections. "It's for a couple of reasons. Miss Lamberton, you and your brother are putting yourselves at risk. There is a real possibility that a very bad person is lurking around these cases. If you make them nervous, you could find yourselves in the crosshairs." He turned and looked at Jerome. "I know you can take care of yourself. What you're at risk of is losing your job."

"We were trying to help." Kay knew that the excuse sounded lame. "No one would have even looked into Harrington's death if it hadn't been for us."

"Now that the head of Mensa is off the case, you can feel confident that I will look into all aspects of McKenzie's disappearance and revisit the death of Professor Harrington. I'm going to start by having some of the water from the cab of the truck analyzed for blood." He paused for a second and looked at the two of them, as if considering his next words. "I might want one or both of you to come out to McKenzie's hunting property and walk me through it."

"Lee saw the body when it was hanging from the deer stand," Kay told him. "But I *do* want to go out there with you too. I just think Lee might be able to answer some of your questions better than me."

"What the heck, we'll make a party of it." There was only a touch of sarcasm in Townsend's voice.

"Where do you think McKenzie is?" Kay found that she liked Townsend and respected his opinion.

"I don't have any idea. The options are suicide, accident, murder or abduction. Of course, there's always the chance that he just walked away, but from what I know of the man and what others have told me, I don't think he ran out on his wife and business. What your brother overheard tips the scale toward murder or abduction. One job that has to be done is searching this river. Whoever drove the truck into the river might have dumped the body here too."

"How did the truck get in the river?"

"My guess, based on the evidence so far, is that the suspect—and that could still be McKenzie himself—drove it at about ten miles an hour into the water, then swam away from it."

"The doors were closed," Jerome observed.

"They could have closed from the backwash as the vehicle moved forward into the river. I'd say the driver jumped once most of the inertia was expended, just as it hit the water and the wheels lost traction. I know a guy at the university who might be able to analyze it and give us a better idea of what happened."

"If someone killed McKenzie and drove his car into the river, they would need a way to get home. They could have called a friend or arranged to be picked up ahead of time," Kay suggested.

"Maybe they live around here. We'll check with Mrs. McKenzie and see if anyone connected to her husband lives near here."

"If it was Joyce Harrington and her boyfriend, it would have been easy enough for one of them to drive a separate car," Kay said.

"Good point. Their alibi will be at the top of the list. They have a motive for killing Harrington. If they did, and if McKenzie figured it out, then that could give them a motive for getting rid of him too." Townsend looked at Kay. "That visit your brother made to Joyce could put him in their crosshairs."

"I'll talk to him when I get home." Kay hadn't thought

that far ahead, and it chilled her to think that Joyce and Hugo could target Lee. "When are you going to go after them?"

"It's too early. I want to know more about this," he waved toward the waterlogged truck, "and more about Harrington's death before I bring them in."

"But if they're going around killing people…" Kay felt her blood rising.

"He's right. If he pulls them in too soon, they'll get a lawyer and clam up," Jerome assured her.

Kay took a couple of deep breaths in an attempt to calm down and process everything rationally.

"Okay, but don't wait so long that someone else dies."

"You don't have to guilt me into doing my job," Townsend said through gritted teeth. "I'm not like some of the other people working for this department."

"I understand." Kay still wasn't happy.

"The law is not a perfect instrument, but it's the only one I have. When it works, it moves slowly, but with precision."

CHAPTER SIXTEEN

Kay and Jerome didn't talk much on the way back to the funeral home, both lost in thought about everything they'd recently learned.

"Are Joyce and this Hugo guy the killers?" Kay asked when they were fifteen minutes from Lang.

"Townsend is right. We can't focus on particular suspects until the evidence is clear," Jerome reminded her.

"Isn't a confession clear enough?" Kay knew he was right, but she was worried about the possible threat Joyce and her boyfriend might pose to Lee.

As if reading her thoughts, Jerome said, "Lee could be misremembering what he heard. And even if his memory of the conversation is perfect, it's still open to interpretation."

"Do you think Lee could be in danger?"

"I've never met Joyce or her lover." Jerome shrugged. "There's a part of me that wishes Townsend hadn't been assigned to the McKenzie case."

"Why? He's better than that moron Sutton."

"I don't feel right interfering in Townsend's case. If Sutton was still in charge of it, then I'd find a way to meet our two prime suspects and get an idea of how dangerous they are."

"I see your point. It's a little different going behind Townsend's back," Kay agreed.

They pulled into the back drive of the funeral home and noticed that Bertha was backed up to the entrance to the embalming room. Jerome went straight to the kitchen while Kay went upstairs to change out of her sweaty clothes.

"Who'd you pick up?" Jerome asked Lester, who was eating chocolate chip cookies fresh out of the oven while Ruby washed the mixing bowls at the sink.

"Some guy that was shipped down here. He's already embalmed and we're going to have a viewing for him tomorrow and the funeral on Saturday."

"This isn't the body that Lee was supposed to take to Ocala?" Jerome found it novel that they had so much business that he couldn't keep track of the bodies.

"No, different one." Lester spoke through a mouthful of crumbs, reminding Jerome of Cookie Monster.

"Try the chocolate chip," Ruby said over her shoulder, and Jerome was happy to oblige.

Lee came into the kitchen and Jerome started to ask, "Where did—"

"He was living with some relatives in Tennessee. His wife is buried here, and he's still got a few friends in the area. I got the funeral announcement to the paper just in time, so we might have a few people show up. I don't expect a crowd."

"Who did you pick up?" Kay asked as she joined everyone in the kitchen.

Lee repeated what he'd just told Jerome.

"Have a cookie," Ruby told all of them.

"This just came up?" Kay asked.

Lee shrugged. "I might have forgotten to mention it with all the excitement. It's not a big deal. No embalming, a small viewing and even smaller funeral. No graveside service."

"What about Harrington?"

"He's fine in the cooler for now." Lee sighed. "I got a call from his sister. They want him cremated. Actually, that's all they can afford. I told them we'd give him a small memorial service for any of his friends at the university that want to pay their respects."

"Didn't we talk about giving our services away?" Kay asked, scowling at him.

"His sister was so grateful she was crying. Besides, it's not like she lives around here and is going to tell everyone that we gave her a free memorial service. And since she wants to be here for it but can't come down here right away, it gives us more time with our investigation. That's why I don't mind keeping Harrington on ice for a while."

Kay appeared mollified by his explanation, so Lee helped himself to a couple of cookies before asking, "What about McKenzie? Was he in the river?"

"They haven't found him yet," Kay said.

She and Jerome went on to fill them all in on the afternoon's events, making Lester and Ruby swear to keep the information to themselves.

"That's on the way to St. Augustine," Lee couldn't help pointing out.

"Yes. But remember that if Joyce and Hugo killed McKenzie, then they might decide to eliminate you," Kay admonished him.

"They don't know I overheard them."

"But Joyce thinks you suspect them of the murder of Harrington."

"They can't go around killing everyone who suspects

them," Lee said nonchalantly, eating his second cookie.

"But they were free and clear until we started making a big deal about the way Harrington died."

"And now more people suspect them, and they can't kill all of us. You said Bill Townsend is on the McKenzie case now and is looking into Harrington's death. Joyce and Hugo have more to worry about than me."

"Still, you need to keep a sharp look out for anything strange," Jerome warned him.

There was a flash of lightning followed by a crack of thunder that shook the room and caused everyone to jump.

"Okay, I get it." Lee put his hand on his chest and laughed weakly.

"That was close." Kay looked out the window and saw that the western sky was a dark and ominous purple.

"I think I'll bring Yin and Yang in."

Ruby walked away from the sink, drying her hands on a dishtowel, and called to the cats from the back door. They both came running and flopped down on the kitchen floor. Lee and Kay had told her that she was welcome to bring the cats into her apartment above the carport, but that they'd prefer she not let them into the funeral home itself. Of course, she hadn't listened to them, no matter how many times they asked. All they had managed to do was get her to promise to only let the cats in if the weather was bad and there wasn't a funeral service.

They all watched the storm build until it settled into a steady drum of rain. Jerome finally decided he'd have to get wet and headed off on his motorcycle to get ready for work. Kay wandered upstairs to her book, leaving Lee and Lester to plan out the details for their latest client, Arthur Malone.

"I want you to handle the viewing and funeral," Lee told Lester.

He had decided that the small service would be a good

chance to see how well Lester could do on his own. The more independent Lester could be, the more flexible the funeral home could be. If Lester could conduct a viewing and funeral on his own, then that would allow them to have multiple events at the same time. Maybe someday they could even open another funeral home. Lee knew his father had always struggled with the idea of expanding. He had been a hands-on mortician and had found it difficult to delegate. Lee had some of those same tendencies, but the couple of years that he'd struggled to keep the business afloat had, oddly, instilled in him a desire to grow the business.

"I can do this," Lester said, sounding like he was trying to convince himself.

"It'll be simple," Lee promised him. "I doubt we'll have more than twenty-five people tomorrow. His daughter and her family are going to come into town for it, but he hasn't lived here for almost twenty years. How many friends are going to remember him?"

"And you expect even less for the funeral?"

"I just hope there are enough people to fill a couple of pews in the Old Westside Church."

The church had just been the Westside Church when it had been built in the 1850s. It had been lovingly kept up for more than a hundred years, even after a new brick sanctuary was built on adjoining property. The congregation still held services in the old church a few times a year.

"Did they get the air conditioner fixed?" Lester asked, and Lee smiled.

"Now you're thinking like a funeral director. They've got a temporary unit that does a decent job cooling the building down. But you'll need to turn it off during the service or no one will be able to hear Reverand John."

"I got this." Lester's hands tapped nervously on his thighs.

"I'm not just giving you responsibility for the service. I expect you to do all the paperwork too. You've done all of this before." Lee had sent Lester to get documents signed and to collect receipts many times.

"Yeah, but you always told me what to do. Now I have to think of it myself." Lester chewed his lip.

"Exactly." Lee smiled. "I'll be in the office if you need me."

The next morning, the Florida landscape was a steam bath, with the bright morning sun turning the puddles from the night before into one-hundred-percent humidity.

Lester was already fussing around the office and the viewing room, planning for the evening's event.

"I think I've got everything they paid for," Lester told Lee, who was heading to the kitchen.

"I'm sure it's fine. The family is lucky that we don't have anyone else's viewing tonight or they'd be in the parlor."

They had been rushing around for the last month, often with two or three funerals or viewings a week, and now it was like the faucet had been turned off. Lee's father had always told him to enjoy the quiet times. *Death may take a vacation, but the grim reaper always returns with a vengeance*, he'd said with a sad smile.

"I'm sorry about the picture," Ruby said as Lee entered the kitchen.

"What picture?" Lee took the plate of eggs and toast that she handed him.

"Yin broke a picture frame in the office and was dragging that around." She pointed to a photo on the kitchen table.

Lee set his plate down and picked up the photo. The image was one that he knew by heart, a photo of his mother and father in Key West on their honeymoon. They were posed in front of Hemingway's house, with a gleam in both their eyes that spoke of love and happiness. Yin had chewed and scratched the image of Lee's mother completely off the picture.

"Don't worry. I've got a copy up in my room." His room used to be his parents' room, and when he'd moved into it, he'd left a dozen of their pictures hanging on the wall.

"Yin is very sensitive. I think the lightning hitting so close upset him."

"It's not a big deal."

"I love that picture." Kay had come in and was looking over Lee's shoulder. "What happened to Mom?"

After Ruby explained the situation, Lee smoothed Kay's ruffled feathers by reminding her about the second photo in his bedroom and offering to move it to the office.

"Lester didn't eat much this morning." Ruby sounded hurt. "You might be pushing him too hard."

"This is just a small viewing and funeral. I'm glad he's taking it so seriously," Lee said as he put a light dusting of salt and pepper on his eggs.

"Before I even finished breakfast, he was asking me questions about what he could and couldn't do that wouldn't bust the family's budget," Kay said, sitting down at the table and picking up the *Gainesville Sun*. "Here's an article about them finding McKenzie's truck. Hey, you can see Jerome and me in this picture." She laid the paper open and tapped the black-and-white image of the tow truck pulling McKenzie's vehicle out of the river.

"You're famous," Lee joked.

"I don't know if I wish they'd found his body in the truck or not," she mused.

"All depends on whether he's dead or not," Ruby said in her typically odd manner.

"Without the body, Mrs. McKenzie's hopes stay alive,"

Kay said.

"Which isn't necessarily good for us. We bury people for a living. Our whole *raison d'être* is to give the loved ones an opportunity to say goodbye and begin the process of moving through their grief," Lee said.

"That sounds like Dad." Kay looked again at the image of her father.

"Dad believed in the mission." Lee stopped eating for a minute and looked at Kay. "I know it sounds corny, but I believe we really help people."

Kay looked into her brother's eyes and saw the sincerity. *The question is,* she thought, *am I also committed to this crusade of helping people to express their grief, or do I want to go back to being a nurse and trying to prevent the grief from ever happening?*

The rest of the day passed quickly as Kay and Lee assisted Lester with preparations for the viewing. Jerome stopped by when he got off work.

"I just met with Townsend," he told Kay.

"Has he learned anything?" Kay leaned her elbows on her desk, anxious to hear any news.

"They haven't found McKenzie's body in the river or anywhere in the area around the spot where the truck was found."

"No witnesses?"

"A couple of earwitnesses. Seems like the truck went into the river around two in the morning on Monday. One couple woke up when they heard a car engine and an odd splashing sound. They told Townsend that if they hadn't been half asleep, they might have gone outside to take a look. In hindsight, they said it sounded like a car driving into the river." Jerome sighed. "I can't say I blame them. There's a lot of fishermen in the area and kids come down to the river to party sometimes, so hearing noises isn't anything new. Who wants to get out of bed at two in the morning to get involved in someone else's business?"

"Still, you just wish they could have looked out a window."

"If they did hear the truck going into the river, it gives us a solid mark on the timeline that we can check against any suspect's alibi."

"I wish Townsend would go ahead and interview Joyce and Hugo."

"This is exactly why he's waiting. Yesterday he didn't know that two o'clock on Monday morning was important. Today he does," Jerome told her.

"I know." She shook her head in frustration. "I thought I would be glad to have Sutton off the case. Now I see you were right. It forces us to sit on our hands and let a real investigator do his work."

"The word on Henry running for sheriff is getting around. Townsend told me that he's already heard the sheriff and others are putting together a list of traitors. My name will be front and center on that list." It was obvious that the situation was bothering Jerome more than he wanted to let on.

"I'm sure everything will work out okay." Kay tried her best to sound reassuring.

"Y'all better have a full-time position opening up around here. I've got a feeling I'm going to need it."

Lee stuck his head in. "I heard that. I'm sure we'll figure something out."

"What about tonight?" Jerome asked.

"I'll let you and Lester handle the viewing and I'll stay out of the way. That way, Lester won't have me looking over his shoulder. Oh, and Kay said she'd help out in the viewing room."

It was always a good idea to have someone close by the coffin in case one of the older mourners needed a handkerchief or started to get wobbly.

"I'll be back for dinner," Jerome said and headed for the door.

CHAPTER SEVENTEEN

Anytime there was an evening viewing, dinner was served early. By five o'clock, everyone was sitting around the table enjoying the chicken and yellow rice that Ruby had made. According to her, it was a recipe she'd picked up during her time in Havana before the revolution.

By six, Lester had everything in order for the viewing. He and Lee had been unimpressed with the job the embalmers had done on the deceased, but there wasn't anything they could do about it except touch up the cosmetics a bit.

"Thank you for doing this," Arthur Malone's daughter told Lee when she arrived. "Dad wanted to be buried next to Momma."

"We're glad to be able to help your family at a time like this. Let me introduce you to Lester Andrews. He'll be in charge of the viewing tonight."

Lee faded into the background and watched as Lester talked with the deceased's family. Lester managed a comfortable, down-home rapport with them that impressed him.

"How's it feel to be the one in charge?" Lee asked once the relatives had gone to sit with the body.

Lester looked as nervous as a new father with triplets. "I'm glad this is a small one."

"It's all yours. I'm going over to the store and spend time with Alison."

Upstairs, Kay looked at herself in the full-length mirror in her room.

"Am I a nurse or a funeral director?" she asked the mirror. Her reflection gave her a small smirk. She smoothed her dress down and squared her shoulders before heading downstairs.

She was surprised to see that a dozen people were standing in the viewing room. A glance at her watch told her it was five minutes before the official start of the viewing. With Lee's assurances that it would be a small affair, she hadn't expected anyone but the family to be there yet.

There were several folks talking to Jerome at the front door. Kay went into the viewing room where Lester was directing people to the guestbook and handing out the printed commemorative obituary. He caught her eye and came over to her.

"Maybe this is just the after-work rush." There was a glean of sweat on his forehead.

Kay discreetly sniffed the air but didn't smell the distinctive odor of pot. Lee had taken the time to sit with Lester and discuss how his smoking habit wouldn't lend itself to the professional impression necessary for a mortician. Lester had been much better since the conversation, but Kay had wondered if the stress of his first real funeral would cause him to backslide.

"Mr. Malone was apparently more popular than Lee thought," Kay said softly, so as not to be overheard by the mourners.

"I don't think I had them print up enough obituaries," Lester said worriedly.

"It'll be fine."

They could hear more people arriving at the front door.

"Would you mind standing by the casket?" Lee asked.

"Of course."

As Kay took her place at the foot of the casket so she could better direct the mourners, she noticed that the people in the room looked familiar. Lang was a small town and she had at least a passing familiarity with almost everyone, but she'd seen some of these folks very recently.

"Keith Dandridge. We met the other day," she said as she noticed the man standing out of the way of the other mourners. And that's when she realized that a lot of people in the room had been helping with the search for McKenzie.

"I remember," Dandridge said, shaking her hand. "It was awful to hear that they found Dwayne's truck in the river."

Kay nodded, looking past him to see who else was there.

"I just hope he's okay. We've been friends most of our lives."

"I think everyone hopes that nothing bad has happened to him." Kay saw Jerry Mercer and another man standing in the hallway. They were dressed in new-looking jeans, white shirts and ties. Both of them looked uncomfortable.

"Guess they've searched about every foot of his property. But now with the truck found in the river… it makes you wonder," Dandridge said.

"I think everyone is puzzled," Kay agreed.

Jerry Mercer poked his head into the viewing room and his eyes met hers. He quickly looked away.

"What does the investigator think happened to him?"

Dandridge didn't seem to care that her attention was focused everywhere but on him.

"I don't think he's formed an opinion."

An older man wearing a worn black suit with a narrow tie entered the room holding his hat up in front of him with both hands. Kay recognized Bert Morgan, Cody's grandfather. The old man made his way straight to Kay.

"I knew Art Malone for years," Morgan told her.

Looking irritated, Dandridge edged away from them and drifted toward the center of the room, which now felt rather cramped.

"I'm sure he'd be glad you came," Kay told the old man.

"Doubt it. We didn't see eye to eye on much."

Kay didn't know what to say. After a couple of awkward moments, she asked, "If you weren't good friends, why are you here?"

"I saw in the paper that you were there when they pulled Mr. McKenzie's truck from the St. John's River." He paused, looking down at his hat, and lowered his voice. "I'm worried about Cody."

"Would you like to go somewhere and talk about it?" Kay asked, equally quietly.

"What?"

Kay realized that the old man's hearing wasn't going to allow them to have a whispered conversation.

"I'll be right back," she said loudly enough for him to hear her, and he nodded.

Kay found Lester in the hallway, looking shellshocked.

"Where'd all these people come from?" he asked, his voice cracking.

"They're here because they saw the article about McKenzie's truck being found and, thanks to that photograph, they know I was there."

"So what?"

"Mostly, they're just rubbernecking, but there are some suspects here." She reached out and took his arm. "Look, the grandfather of one of the suspects wants to talk to me. I'm going to take him into the office."

"But..." Lester looked at the crowd filling the entry hall and viewing room.

"I won't be long. Most of them aren't interested in the deceased anyway."

Before Lester could respond, Kay went back to retrieve Bert Morgan and led him to the office. She settled him into a chair across from her desk, thinking that he looked older and less sure of himself than when she'd met him at his house.

"Why are you worried about Cody?" she asked gently.

Morgan looked down and his hands nervously kneaded his hat.

"I... You won't turn him in to the police, will you?"

Kay thought about this. She didn't want to lie to the old man, but she also didn't want to tell him that if Cody had killed someone, then she wanted him in jail. If she said that, she knew he'd just get up and leave.

"I won't do anything that I don't think is for Cody's own good." This was the truth. "I'll also promise that if he's done anything short of murder, I won't turn him in."

"What about the deputy? The one who came to my house with you. I saw him when I came in."

"Like me, Jerome wants to catch the person who killed Roger Harrington. He's not interested in trespassing or anything else that Cody might have done."

"I don't think he's hurt anyone, but he might know who did." Morgan looked up and into her eyes. "My daughter is already mostly lost to me. I can't lose Cody."

Kay pulled a chair next to Morgan's.

"I'll do everything I can to help you and Cody," she assured him, then pressed on. "Why do you think he knows the person who killed Harrington?"

"I heard him talkin' to himself the other night, in his bedroom. He was sayin' things like, 'I know you couldn't have done this. You wouldn't hurt anyone.' Stuff like that. It was kind of like he was tryin' to convince himself that someone he knew didn't do something bad."

"Did he mention Harrington or McKenzie?"

"No, nobody by name. Just seemed upset and talkin' about somebody hurtin' someone else."

"I know your daughter has had some problems. Could it have anything to do with her?"

"I thought about that. Thing is, he hasn't seen her for months that I know of."

"Is it possible that he could have seen her without you knowing about it?"

"I don't think so. He hates her. Says he does."

"Who are his friends?"

"Maybe some of the folks at the Fast Mart."

"Does he hang around with anyone when he's not working?"

"Harrington was the only person I've heard him talk about since he moved in with me. He dropped out of school a year ago. Kids were awful to him. Now he's either workin' at the store or wanderin' around in the woods."

"What's he do in the woods?" Kay wondered if Cody could be involved with a pot-growing operation.

"Just watches." Morgan looked down at his hands again. "I know how that sounds. But he really *is* just lookin' at the woods. He knows a bunch about the animals. One day I went for a walk with him, and he was pointin' out all the different tracks and tellin' me how big the animal was. I know he's got a… He calls it a field notebook that he writes in."

"Has he been acting different this past week?"

"Guess he's been quieter. That's not sayin' much. Even on a good day, Cody's not much of a talker. That's one thing we have in common." He smiled sadly.

"Do you think he would let us look in his room?"

"If he won't, I'll let you look. It's my house." He sounded scared. "I don't want him goin' down the same path as his mother."

"I think we should ask him first. Going into his room and looking around without his permission could destroy the trust he has in you. No matter what's happened, I want to help you and your grandson."

He stood up without warning.

"I better go pay my respects to Art and head on back home." Morgan went to the door without another look at Kay.

When Kay came out of the office, she saw Jerome with four people hanging around him. She was sure they were asking him about McKenzie and the truck. *Maybe he'll get a tip from someone who doesn't want to go through formal channels*, she thought.

In the viewing room, Lester was moving around, trying to answer questions and encouraging people to go up to the casket if they wanted. He looked worn out.

"Lee's at Alison's store. I can call him if you want some help," Kay offered.

Lester looked undecided for a moment, then said, "I've got this."

"Good for you." She smiled. "What do you want me to do?"

Lee was helping Alison rearrange the stereos along the north wall of her shop.

"It's quiet in here tonight," he observed.

"Looks like everyone's at the funeral home." Alison was looking out through the plate glass window at the front of the store.

Lee joined her and looked down the street toward the funeral home.

"Wow! I guess Arthur Malone was more popular and better remembered than I thought."

"If you need to go help Lester, you can. I can finish this."

"I told them where I was going to be. They can call if it gets out of hand."

"I could tell that Lester was both proud and nervous about being in charge tonight," Alison said.

"If we're going to continue growing, he's going to need to step up."

"What about Kay?"

"What about her?"

"Is she going back to nursing?"

"Never occurred to me that she'd want to." Lee looked surprised at the question.

"She gave up her job to come down here and help you. I don't think she planned on it being a permanent thing." Alison went back to the stereos.

"We're making good money now. I don't know." He handed her the wires to a set of large speakers.

"I'm just saying that when I came to dinner last week, she was talking a lot about nursing and Dr. Eckhart. Sounded to me like she missed her old life." Alison took the wires and twisted them before inserting the ends into a turntable cassette combo.

"I didn't get that."

"I'd chalk that up to you being a guy."

"Maybe it's about Eckhart."

"Ummmm, didn't seem like that to me. I'd say it's the other way around."

"You mean she likes him because she wants to go back to nursing? That doesn't make sense to me."

"Again, you're a guy."

"And you're a girl." Lee leaned over and kissed her as he handed her another set of wires.

"And because I'm a girl, I pick up on vibes you don't. Believe me, Kay wants to go back to her career."

"How would that work? She's the business person in the family." Lee frowned.

"You might want to talk to her about it," Alison warned.

They shifted two console TVs to make room for a shipment of VCRs that had been delivered earlier.

"Lester is pestering me to buy one of these. I just spent a fortune on the new TV," Lee said, studying one of the VCRs.

"I gave you a great deal on that TV," she reminded him.

"I'm just saying that Lester thinks I can just throw money around for his entertainment."

"Wait another year. The prices are going to come down, and by that time maybe we'll know whether VHS or Betamax is going to win out."

"I don't understand why they have to have two different systems."

"Don't ask me. Just hand me another box."

When they had the shelves stocked, Alison turned to Lee and took his hand.

"I saw the picture of Kay and Jerome in the paper. What's going on with Dwayne McKenzie?"

Lee gave her a quick summary of everything that had happened so far.

"You think you know who Harrington's killers are?" she asked when he'd finished.

"I wish I'd been wearing a tape recorder like they use on *Hill Street Blues* or *Magnum P.I.*"

"If I'd known you were going on a spy mission, I could have rigged something up," Alison told him with a grin. She looked toward the door that opened into the workshop as if she meant to get started on it.

"Is it legal?" Lee asked.

"I don't know." She scrunched up her face. "Probably not."

"Townsend told Kay that I might be in danger if Joyce and her boyfriend think I know something."

"And you walked over here by yourself?"

"It was daylight."

"It will be dark when you walk back."

Alison sounded upset and Lee was surprised at her reaction.

"I don't think they'll try anything," he assured her. "Like I told you, I snuck back and listened at the door. They don't even know I was listening."

"Maybe. And maybe they're going to try and tie up loose ends now that the truck has been found."

Lee could hear the fear in her voice and pulled her into a hug. He remembered that she owned this shop because her father had been murdered, which would leave scars on anyone's psyche.

When she finally pulled out of the hug, Alison looked thoughtful. "What do the cats think?"

Lee had no idea what she was talking about. "Huh?"

"Ruby's tabby cats. What have they been doing?"

"You aren't serious?"

"Every time y'all have gotten involved with a murder case, those cats have done weird things that have predicted who the killer is."

Lee thought Alison was exaggerating the cats' contributions, but he humored her. "Yin and Yang are always acting crazy. Yin broke one of our picture frames and was carrying the photo around today, and Yang's been tearing up the latticework around the crawlspace under the house."

"See! What was the picture of?"

"It was of my parents, and they certainly didn't kill anyone from beyond the grave," Lee said with a note of sadness in his voice.

"No... Hey, I'm sorry. I just..."

"I know what you were saying. Ruby's always trying to convince us those cats have some otherworldly power."

"Ruby is... interesting."

"And if she were any more interesting, and didn't cook as well as she does, I'd be reconsidering her employment."

"You don't mean that."

"No, not really," Lee said grudgingly. "She's kind of become part of the family. Mind you, the crazy part of the family."

"Everyone needs a loony aunt. But keep an eye on Yin and Yang anyway."

"Believe me, I keep my eye on them. If I didn't, I'd step on one of them or trip over them."

An hour later, with the store in good order, Lee told her he was going home.

"Walk with you?" she said.

"It's only a block." He smiled.

"A lot can happen in a block."

"But you'll have to walk back alone."

"Okay, I'll drive you."

"That's..." Lee was going to say that it was silly but he understood her fears. "Okay, that way I can be sure you're safe too."

Alison parked her car in the back of the funeral home. The building was dark except for a light in the kitchen, Ruby's apartment above the carport and Kay's room upstairs.

"A movie tomorrow night?" Lee asked after several goodnight kisses.

"Yes! *The Thing!*" she said excitedly. "I loved the original. Dad and I used to watch it together on the late-night spook show."

"I'll pick you up at seven." Lee opened the door and stepped out into the warm, moist summer air.

"See ya!" Alison waved as she backed out and drove away.

Lee took a minute to smell the jasmine in the air and look up at the half-moon in the sky before walking toward the house. He decided to enter through the embalming room so he could check to see if Lester had cleaned up before he left.

Lee tried the door and was glad to see that it was locked. Funeral homes could attract weirdos, so he always made sure the house was secure before going to bed. Especially the door to the embalming room. He took out his keys and was holding them up close to his face, trying to find the right one, when the world went dark.

"Hey!" he yelled as he felt a hood pulled over his head and noticed a strong smell. A second later, he was dealt a paralyzing blow to his stomach and fell to his knees. The pain and the odor left him dazed as he tried to stand, then blackness overwhelmed him.

CHAPTER EIGHTEEN

Ruby was mixing pancakes by the time Kay came downstairs the next morning. When she entered the kitchen, she saw Lester reading the comics with a piece of toast in one hand and a glass of milk in the other.

"Does your contract include breakfast?" she teased him.

"It does when I'm cooking." Ruby smiled at Lester, who nodded his head.

"I deserve breakfast after last night." Kay heard a note of pride in his voice.

"I guess you do," Kay told him and sat down in her usual seat at the table, where Ruby had already placed a plate. "Lee up yet?"

"He hasn't been down."

"I didn't hear him in the bathroom." Kay was a bit surprised.

"Maybe he and Alison had a late night," Lester said with a wink.

"He has been known to stay over at her house," Ruby

said. Kay knew the slight tone of disapproval in her voice had nothing to do with morals. Ruby just didn't think it was right for anyone to miss one of her breakfasts by choice.

They spent the rest of their time at the breakfast table talking about the Malone funeral that was scheduled for eleven o'clock. By the time they were finished, Lester was looking about indecisively.

"You think Lee's upstairs or at Alison's house?" he asked. "After last night, I've got a few questions about the funeral today."

"You can go up and check," Kay told him.

Lester left the kitchen, thumped up the stairs and returned a few minutes later.

"He's not up there."

Ruby and Kay looked at each other.

"I started breakfast about seven and haven't seen him."

"I guess he stayed over at Alison's house. Good for him." Kay looked thoughtful. After a few uncomfortable minutes, she finally said to Lester, "I think you should call Alison."

"Why me?"

"Nobody wants their big sister checking up on them. You can just tell him, quite honestly, that you have a few questions about the funeral."

Lester approached the phone on the wall like it was a cobra.

"I don't want him to be mad at me," he said, slowly reaching for the phone.

"He won't be," Ruby said, nodding in encouragement to Lester.

She and Kay watched as Lester dialed the phone.

"Is Lee there?" he asked when Alison answered.

"I dropped him off last night," she said firmly.

"He's not here."

"I'm coming over there," Alison said and hung up before

Lester could say anything more. He looked at the phone and put the receiver back on the hook.

"He's got to be someplace." Kay's mind was racing. She knew she should try to remain calm and rational, but she was losing the battle with a sense of panic.

"We need to search the house." Ruby was already moving toward the kitchen door. "I'll take the ground floor. Lester, you take the outside; Kay, check upstairs." Before the others could say anything, Ruby was in the hallway and heading for the viewing room.

Kay headed upstairs and, without a word, Lester slammed through the screen door.

"Nothing," Kay reported to Ruby when they met at the door to the embalming room five minutes later.

"Ground floor is clear." Ruby's voice was almost military in its brusqueness.

Before they could say anything else, they heard Lester yelling from outside. Ruby and Kay fought to get through the kitchen door together, but Kay squeaked through first. Lester was standing outside the embalming room door, pointing down at a set of keys on the ground.

"Those are Lee's," he said in a small voice.

"Don't touch them," Kay instructed. "I'm going to call Jerome."

"Now you aren't even letting me get to bed before you wake me up," Jerome grumbled over the phone.

"Something bad has happened to Lee." Kay's words were sharp and urgent. She went on to explain how they had found his keys.

"I'm on my way," Jerome said. "And I'll bring Townsend."

Half an hour later, Jerome, Townsend, Kay, Lester, Alison and Ruby were standing in a half circle, staring at the keys.

"How sure are you that he's not somewhere else?" Townsend asked.

"My brother has a very narrow circle that he moves in." Kay was tapping her foot nervously. "His life is this funeral home and spending time with Alison. And all of our vehicles are here."

"I haven't seen him since I dropped him off last night." Alison's anxiety was palpable.

"Hard to tell if his bed has been slept in. He's not exactly a make-the-bed-in-the-morning type of person," Ruby said with a frown.

"I can back up what Kay said. Lee doesn't do much besides hang out with Alison or attend to funeral business," Jerome said.

"That's too bad." Townsend's face had a grim expression as he bent down closer to the keys. "Is anything missing?"

Kay, Lester and Ruby looked at each other.

"I didn't notice anything." Kay didn't sound certain of her answer.

"I'll go look around the embalming room and the storage closet." Lester started toward the embalming room door.

"Don't touch that!" Jerome reached out and grabbed his arm.

"Fingerprints. Got it." Lester nodded.

"Don't touch anything you don't have to, and,when you do need to touch something, use a clean cloth and do it carefully," Townsend instructed them.

"I'll go take another turn around the house and see if I can tell if anything is missing," Kay said.

"No." Townsend looked at her with regret in his eyes. "I don't want you to look without an escort."

"What?" Kay said, not understanding.

"Someone needs to be with you. You're the next of kin?" he asked.

"We don't have any other family."

"So you would inherit the house and the business?" Townsend kept his voice slow and soft.

"What are you getting at?" Kay's anger was rising. "I already own half the business and the house."

"Still, there is value in Mr. Lamberton's half. Therefore, you have a motive for disappearing your brother. I know it seems absurd to you, but you have to consider how it would look to outsiders."

"He's right." Jerome looked at Kay. "This could eventually involve other investigators… even lawyers."

"The actions we take now are going to affect the whole investigation moving forward," Townsend said.

"But…" Kay tried to make a pertinent argument, but she didn't have one.

"I'll go with you." Townsend waved her toward the kitchen door. "We need to make sure he didn't pack a suitcase or take any clothes. Maybe he ran off. Stranger things have happened. Go watch the other man," he told Jerome, nodding at Lester.

Ruby put her hand on Alison's shoulder as the younger woman fought back tears.

"You need to find Joyce Harrington and her boyfriend," Kay said as Townsend followed her through the kitchen.

"You think the same person is responsible for Mr. Lamberton's and Mr. McKenzie's disappearance?" Townsend asked.

"We've been nosing around both cases. I'd be surprised if there isn't a connection," Kay told him.

"I'm not going to give you a hard time about it because I figure you're already doing it to yourself. But as civilians, you need to keep away from criminal cases."

"Sutton wasn't doing anything, and the sheriff had already declared that Harrington's death wasn't a crime,"

Kay said stubbornly.

"Sutton's a buffoon and the sheriff's only concern is politics."

"Jerome says Henry is going to—"

Townsend put his palm up toward Kay. "Just stop. I don't want to get involved in office politics. I need to have this job when next November rolls around."

"What good is having a job if you can't do it properly?"

"I have a family, thank you very much. Drop it."

"Sorry. I just want to find my brother."

"I wish one of the cars was missing. It's a lot easier to find a car than a person."

"We've got to do more than just look through the house." Kay felt despair creeping into her soul as she wandered from room to room, looking for any clues as to what happened to Lee.

"I'll put out a BOLO for him," Townsend told her.

"What about Joyce Harrington and Hugo?"

"I can have someone go by and talk to them. See if they have an alibi," he promised.

"Alison dropped Lee off around ten-thirty. So we can figure whatever happened to him happened between ten-thirty and eleven." Kay continued to look around as she talked.

"It's two hours from St. Augustine, so four hours round trip. If they can prove they were in St. Augustine any time between eight-thirty and one o'clock, they'll have a solid alibi." Townsend watched as Kay went around the office, checking to see if the checkbook, business credit card and other valuables were still present.

"I'd like to get a look at their vehicles too," he said. "If they won't give us permission to search them, we'll need probable cause for a warrant."

"You can use our phone. I'm not worried about the long-distance charges," Kay told him.

He looked at her for a moment before nodding his head.

"The sooner we check them out, the better. I've got a friend who's a deputy with the St. John's County Sheriff's Office." Townsend took out an address book from his breast pocket.

It took him a few minutes to get connected to his friend. After a few words of greeting, he explained what was going on and the background on the McKenzie case, as well as what they knew about Joyce and Hugo.

"Are they going to check on them?" Kay asked when he hung up.

"He's going to get an investigator to go to their residences and the college. He'll call if they find them, and we'll go from there."

They looked at each other with grim expressions. Neither of them liked the way this was going. They walked glumly back to the kitchen, where they found Jerome, Lester and Ruby talking with Alison.

"I knew something bad had happened when Lester told me he wasn't here." Alison was having difficulty fighting back tears.

"Maybe there's an innocent explanation," Kay said without conviction.

"You say you dropped him off last night?" Townsend asked Alison.

"We'd been at my store moving some displays around and unpacking new equipment."

"You own the electronics store down the street. It's barely a block away. Why did you drive him home?"

"Lee told me he'd overheard those people confessing to murder or whatever and that Kay was worried, so I got worried too. I should have made sure he got inside the funeral home. I just never thought." She wiped at the tears that finally escaped her eyes.

"You can't dwell on all the *what if*'s," Ruby assured her.

"When you dropped him off, did you see anyone else around?" Townsend asked.

"No."

"Don't answer so fast. Think about it. Maybe someone you weren't surprised to see."

"At ten-thirty, anyone out and about around here is unusual," Alison said. She frowned and looked thoughtful for a minute, then shook her head. "No, I definitely didn't see anyone."

"What about cars?"

"There might have been a couple of cars driving around. There usually are when I leave the shop. The gas station was still open, but I don't remember whether there was anyone at the pumps." The gas station was half a block up on the other side of her store.

"Miss Lamberton, Jerome, let's walk out back." Townsend turned and headed for the back door.

"If your brother was attacked, then whoever did it didn't park in your driveway. Probably didn't park on the street." Townsend was standing in front of the embalming room door, where the keys still lay on the ground. He looked at Jerome. "Go call the office and speak with Ed. Have him come out, collect the keys and dust this door and any other surface out here that he thinks might take a fingerprint."

Jerome nodded and headed back to the house.

"There's an alley that runs behind the house. That gate leads to it," Kay said, pointing at the aged wooden gate.

Townsend nodded and walked to the gate. With a pen from his pocket, he lifted the latch and nudged the gate open with his shoulder. "Don't touch anything."

On the other side of the gate were four banged-up metal trashcans off to one side.

"The alley is used by the garbage trucks, as well as a couple of the neighbors who use it to get to their garages," Kay said.

"Three years ago, I nabbed a mugger in this alley. He ran back here to go through the purse he'd stolen from a woman at the gas station." Townsend seemed to be talking to himself as much as to Kay.

He looked at the alley, which was really just a dirt path wide enough for a vehicle to get through. There were seven houses that had access to the alley and three of them had garages that looked like they were used regularly.

"Even with the recent rain, this ground back here doesn't hold tire tracks, but there's some litter that could be from someone sitting in their cars," Townsend observed.

"I don't know if kids still park back here, but I know that when I was younger, I parked back here with a few boyfriends." Kay felt herself blush as she thought of how that sounded. She cleared her throat. "We just kissed, you know."

"I parked in a few out-of-the-way spots myself." Townsend gave her a kindly smile. "I'll have Ed or one of his men come back here and check out the trash to see if any of it looks like it's been left here recently. I'll need to talk to your neighbors. See if any of them saw a strange car or person back here last night or in the last couple of days."

Kay was impressed with Townsend's professional bearing. As terrified as she was for Lee's safety, she felt better with Bill Townsend working with them.

CHAPTER NINETEEN

Lee's head was pounding as he tried to remember what had happened to him. As he became more aware, he realized he was blindfolded and his hands and feet were tied. His mouth was dry and there was a sickly-sweet aftertaste that made him gag. He realized that he was on a mattress, one that smelled old and musty.

"Hey!" he shouted.

There was the sound of a door opening and heavy footsteps crossing a wooden floor.

"You're awake," said a voice he recognized as Hugo Valero's.

"You better untie me!" Lee was beginning to understand what had happened to him and who had done it. He thrashed around on the mattress.

"Make all the noise you want. No one will hear you. I promise we'll let you go after we get some answers and some assurances from you." Hugo's voice was calm and without inflection.

"At least take the blindfold off."

"I don't think so." Hugo's voice was smug.

"Why have you done this?"

"We needed to talk."

"You could have just called me on the phone." Lee couldn't keep the exasperation out of his voice.

"You need to give us the right answers..." Hugo's voice trailed off with an implied threat.

"What do you want?" Lee didn't know how to play this. He could be coy and see how long it took Hugo to get down to the nitty gritty, but he didn't think that would help him. Hugo was going to do what he was going to do, and Lee thought the sooner everyone's cards were on the table, the better.

"Why did you come to see Joyce and ask her all those questions?"

"I told her. We needed background on Roger Harrington. I don't like to bury people I don't know."

"That is an absurd answer. Try again," Hugo said.

Lee sighed.

"I thought Harrington's death was... odd. So I decided to ask around and see what I could learn about him."

"That sounds closer to the truth."

Lee heard some other, lighter footsteps approaching the room.

"He's awake." Joyce sounded surprised and relieved.

"I told you he would be fine."

"Mrs. Harrington, I'm not fine. I need to go home."

"Don't call her Mrs. Harrington," Hugo said, clearly irritated.

"We need you to understand..." Joyce sounded like she was seeking Lee's forgiveness.

"I could understand all of this better if you'd untie me," he told her.

"Hugo, we—"

"No! We can't trust him."

"I thought that's what we were trying to find out? If we can trust him."

"First we have to find out what he knows," Hugo said, and Lee felt someone kick the mattress. "When you were eavesdropping, what did you hear?"

"I didn't eavesdrop."

Hugo kicked the mattress again with real force this time. Lee was rocked as the mattress moved and he decided it must be sitting directly on the floor.

"Don't lie!" Hugo thundered.

"Hugo, please," Joyce pleaded.

"Go. Let me deal with him."

"I think this was a mistake." Her voice wavered.

"Go!" Hugo's command was gruff.

Lee heard Joyce retreat from the room seconds before the door slammed shut.

"Did you kill Harrington?" Lee asked.

"Why would I kill him?"

"For the gold," Lee said.

"That's right, for the gold." Hugo sounded amused, which Lee thought was odd.

"What about Dwayne McKenzie?"

"I don't even know him," Hugo scoffed.

"You didn't kill or abduct him?" Lee was puzzled. Since he assumed they were going to kill him, why wouldn't Hugo admit what they had done?

"Why? Why would I kill a man I don't even know? You ask stupid questions. Now you will answer my questions. What do you know about us and Harrington's gold?"

"What everyone else knows. Harrington told everyone he was looking for Spanish gold," Lee explained.

"Harrington was a loud-mouthed fool. He didn't deserve

a woman like Joyce."

"Is that why you killed him?"

Hugo kicked the mattress again. "Are you wrong in the head? I told you we didn't kill him. It was probably his big mouth that got him killed."

Lee didn't know whether to believe him or not.

"If you didn't kill Harrington or McKenzie, then why did you kidnap me?"

"Because I need to know what you know, stupid." Another kick to the mattress.

"I don't know anything. That's why I was talking to Joyce."

"Liar." Hugo stomped out of the room and slammed the door.

Lee could hear him talking to someone in the other room. He assumed it was Joyce, but the second voice was too soft to hear through the door.

"He is lying!" Hugo's voice boomed.

There was an indistinct mumble.

"No! He will destroy us!"

More mumbling from the second voice.

"I don't know. Maybe I can pay him to keep quiet. If he'll admit what he knows… Possibly."

Joyce said something else.

"If I have to. No one is going to ruin my career."

"You can't hurt him!" Lee heard Joyce this time as she raised her voice.

"Don't tell me what to do. I'll remind you that this is all your fault. You insisted we do something to get rid of your ex-husband. It was all your idea. Now here we are. Don't tell me what I can and can't do to save myself."

Lee heard more stomping feet and another door slam.

Kay was in the office, her hands trembling as she set the phone receiver down for the twentieth time. She'd called everyone she could think of who might have some political or law enforcement connection. The first call had been to Chester Madison, who had shown his political muscle in the past when they'd needed it. He'd promised her that he'd talk to people in Tallahassee and try to get FDLE involved in Lee's missing person case. He had assured her that she'd have all the help she needed to find her brother.

She'd also called old friends of her father. Even though many of them were retired, they still knew people and liked to show that they could make the cogs move when they wanted to. She was reaching for the phone to make another call when it rang under her hand.

"The St. John's County guys can't find Joyce Harrington or that guy Hugo," Jerome reported. He'd been sticking close to Townsend and updating her whenever he had a chance.

"It has to be them!" Kay gritted her teeth in anger and frustration.

"Townsend is checking property records to see if they own any other homes or buildings."

"Has he sent out information to the airport and bus terminals?"

"I made sure our people in communications did that. I also called all the law enforcement agencies within a hundred miles of St. Augustine, as well as the highway patrol to make sure they all distributed the BOLOs for Lee and Joyce."

"We've got to find Lee."

"I wish I could get permission to go over to St. Augustine and talk to their neighbors and friends," Jerome said in a way that made it clear he wouldn't be offended if Kay found some strings to pull to make it happen.

"I'll see what I can do."

"St. Augustine's police and the St. John's sheriff's deputies are good, but they don't have that fire in the belly that we do," Jerome said.

Kay called Chester Madison again, who promised to lean on Sheriff Pratt to get permission for Jerome to travel to St. John's County.

Kay was of two minds. She wanted to go with Jerome to search for Joyce and Hugo, but she knew that someone needed to be at the funeral home. Lester had gone to oversee the funeral of Arthur Malone, which she expected to be mercifully small since all the gawkers in the county had got their fill last night at the viewing.

"Do you need anything?" Ruby stuck her head through the office door.

Kay looked up at her.

"Do you think you could manage things here if I went with Jerome to St. Augustine?"

Ruby smiled. "Don't you worry about a thing. I know you'll go crazy sitting around here. Why do you think Yang keeps going into the crawlspace under the house?"

Kay was used to Ruby's abrupt shifts in conversation. "I wouldn't know. We'll see about replacing some of the broken latticework."

"Yang is a fair mouser. If he's going under there, it's probably to hunt."

Kay doubted that the fat tabby cat ever bothered to hunt anything, but she nodded.

Jerome called again an hour later.

"Townsend said that Sheriff Pratt told him to let me go to St. Augustine to act as a liaison with local law enforcement. I guess you had something to do with that."

"I told Madison you wanted to go."

"I figured as much since I don't think the sheriff even knows what a liaison is."

"I want to go with you."

"I'm not surprised. Give me half an hour."

Lee rubbed his face on the mattress and managed to push the blindfold up onto his forehead. The light filtering into the room through the lowered blinds was dim and dusty. When he looked around, he saw an old nightstand and an open closet door. Like he thought, the mattress sat directly on the floor. While it was dirty, he was relieved to see that there weren't any suspicious stains or rips in the material.

The sound of feet approaching caused him to panic. He tried to put the blindfold back on, but with his hands tied behind his back there was nothing to do but hope that whoever came through the door wouldn't be too angry that he'd taken it off.

The doorknob turned and Joyce entered the room. She glanced around as though she expected to find someone else in the room with them.

"You shouldn't have taken the blindfold off," she scolded him. "Hugo is mad enough as it is."

"I'm thirsty and wouldn't mind some food," Lee said, remembering something he'd read about hostages and how they should strive to humanize themselves in the eyes of their captors.

"First, get that blindfold back in place." She came over and pulled it back down across his eyes. "I'll be right back."

Lee listened to her leave and wondered what his best plan of action would be. Could he get the ropes off his wrists? He moved his hands around, testing the bonds. There was wiggle room, but not enough. He remembered a movie he'd watched about Harry Houdini. He had been able to dislocate his thumbs in order to get out of handcuffs and chains, but that wasn't in Lee's skillset. *Maybe there's a knife or something sharp in the nightstand I can use to cut the ropes*, he thought. He'd have to wait for Joyce to come back with the water before he tried to get to the nightstand.

"I'm not going to untie your hands," Joyce said when she came back into the room. "You'll just have to do the best you can while I hold the glass."

Lee heard her get down on the floor next to the mattress, then she put a glass to his lips.

"I'm going to tilt it back," she warned him.

Lee hadn't known how thirsty he was until the cool water entered his mouth and he started to swallow.

"Careful," she said when he moved away, choking.

Lee drank the whole glass. "Thanks," he told her.

"I brought you some crackers if you want them."

"Please." He felt gratitude as she put a cracker up to his lips. He remembered how the article on hostages had also talked about Stockholm syndrome. Was his gratitude for the basics of life the start of him becoming emotionally as well as physically dependent upon her? *It's too soon*, he told himself. *I can still feel resentment toward them for kidnapping me.*

"I'm sorry about all this," Joyce said.

"What happened to your ex-husband?"

"I don't know. Until you showed up at my office, I thought it was an accident."

"And you and Hugo didn't do anything to Dwayne McKenzie?"

"I'd never heard of the man until he called me to tell me that Roger was dead."

"Could Hugo be behind all of this without you knowing about it?"

"No. We've been together most of time, and besides, all he cares about now is his reputation."

"If you haven't done anything wrong then you can just let me go." Lee didn't know whether he believed her or not, but he was willing to pretend that he did in order to gain her trust.

"I can't. Hugo… He's out of his mind now. You don't know what his career means to him."

"What's his career have to do with this?" Lee was confused. If they hadn't murdered Harrington or abducted McKenzie, then what was Hugo worried about?

"It's all my fault. Hugo is such a proud man. He was an orphan in Spain. His father fought against Franco during the civil war, and in the 1950s he was reported to the BPS, Franco's secret police. Hugo's father died in prison. His mother was disgraced and died a few years later working as a prostitute."

"I can't imagine…" Lee sympathized in spite of himself.

"A benefactor of the orphanage took note of Hugo's intelligence and his interest in Spanish history and adopted Hugo. His new status allowed Hugo to go to the best schools in Madrid. By the time Hugo was twenty-three, he had earned two doctorates. Now he's recognized as one of the world's foremost experts on historical Spanish documents."

"I still don't see how—"

"It's all my fault," Joyce said again, breaking down in sobs. "I've killed Roger and destroyed Hugo."

Lee had spent most of his life seeing people cry at funerals, but it was disconcerting to hear a woman cry while he was blindfolded and tied up.

"Explain what happened. Maybe I can help," he said in his best sympathetic and encouraging tone of voice.

They heard the sound of footsteps on bare wooden flooring coming toward the room.

"Joyce?" Hugo stepped into the room. "Get out of here!"

Lee heard her get up and mentally kicked himself for not pushing the conversation along faster.

"I just brought him some water and crackers," Joyce explained.

"You've been crying. What have you two been talking about?"

"Roger, that's all. I told him we didn't kill him."

"I've already told him that." His anger was rising again.

"I don't know why you're so mad at me," Lee said and immediately regretted it.

Hugo went berserk, kicking the mattress, stomping his feet and screaming at him.

"You had to stick your nose in where it didn't belong! If you had let Roger's death go without meddling, none of this would be happening! You are destroying me!"

Lee heard fear as well as anger in Hugo's voice, and he thought about what Joyce had told him about Hugo's childhood. Lee didn't know why, but he knew that Hugo was terrified of falling back into the poverty and scorn of those early years before a patron had pulled him out of the orphanage.

"I'll do anything I can to help," Lee pleaded as Hugo spent his rage on the mattress and the floor.

"What can you do?!" Hugo yelled.

"Give me a chance. Explain to me what's going on," Lee pleaded.

"There's nothing you can do. It's probably already too late!" Hugo raged, but his footsteps retreated and the door slammed behind him.

Lee wasn't sure if Joyce had gone with Hugo or not.

"Joyce?" he whispered, but there was no answer. With a sigh, he rolled over on his back and cursed under his breath.

CHAPTER TWENTY

Kay and Jerome met Scott Burket, the St. John's County Sheriff's Office investigator, at Hugo Valero's house.

"Nice place." Kay frowned as she looked at the two-story, Spanish mission-style home. It was similar to others in the neighborhood that dated back to the 1920s. Several of the homes had men in the yards trimming hedges and mowing lawns who clearly weren't the owners of the homes.

"This is one of the safest neighborhoods in the county. Mostly older people who don't cause trouble and who keep a sharp eye out for suspicious activity," Burket said.

Burket was in his forties with close-cropped grey hair and green eyes that were constantly moving. Kay could recognize a man who'd spent time in a war zone.

"Appreciate you meeting us." Jerome looked past him to the house. "Whose car is that?" he asked, pointing to a silver Honda Civic parked in front of the garage.

"It's registered to Joyce Harrington. Don't bother looking in the garage. There aren't any other cars here.

We've knocked on the doors. No answer. The college hasn't seen either one of them since yesterday."

"Does Joyce have her own house?"

"The college has a post office box listed for her. Everyone I asked assured me she was living here with Hugo Valero."

"Family?" Jerome asked.

"Neither one has any family in the area. I got the names of some friends and have worked through about half the list without any luck. No one has admitted to seeing them since yesterday morning, and they don't know where they could be. Though several went into detail about how Hugo travels a lot, mostly to Spain and Central America."

"Flights?"

"I've got someone checking the airports from here to Atlanta and Miami."

Kay was impressed. She'd imagined St. John's County getting the request and doing little more than coming over here and knocking on Hugo's door.

"What about his car?" Jerome asked.

Burket looked down at his feet for a moment, then back up at the other deputy. "What do you think? You haven't given us enough cause to issue a BOLO for the man's car."

"Couldn't you call it a welfare check?"

"I *could*. That might get past the watch commander, but I hate to do that if these people are involved in a kidnapping. I put the word out that it's a welfare check and uniform pulls them over not knowing they could be dangerous..." He shook his head.

"Yeah, I get it," Jerome said.

"How sure are you that these people *are* involved in your brother's disappearance?" Burket asked Kay.

"I think it's likely, but... I don't know," she admitted.

"If I could call our investigator working the case, he

might have something for us. Townsend was going to talk to the neighbors who could have witnessed something," Jerome said.

"We can go to my office and you can call from there," Burket told them.

"Let's take a look around the place first," Jerome said.

"You're getting into tricky territory with admissible evidence," Burket reminded him.

"Finding Lee is our top priority," Kay said in a voice that didn't allow for argument.

"Of course. I'll stay here," Burket said, pulling a cigar from his coat pocket.

Jerome and Kay walked up the drive. Kay peered into the Honda's windows where she saw an atlas sitting on the seat.

"Damn it. That atlas might tell us where they went."

"It could have a mark where the truck was dumped in the river, or your address written in it. Doesn't do us much good now 'cause even I draw the line at breaking a window," Jerome told her.

"Is that a hint that I should do it?" Kay asked seriously.

"No, it is not!" Jerome looked back at Burket, who was smoking his cigar and looking down the street. "Not yet. If we haven't found anything by this afternoon, we can talk about it."

They continued walking around the house. There was a fence surrounding the back yard, but the gate was unlocked. Behind the house was a nicely landscaped half acre with a koi pond large enough to submerge a station wagon.

"Hugo does all right for himself," Jerome said.

There were curtains over the French doors that opened onto the back patio, so they couldn't see inside the house.

"They could just be hiding in there." Frustrated, Kay stood back and looked at the house.

"Doesn't feel that way."

"I'm the woman. I'm the one that's supposed to have intuition."

"I don't think I'd trust your judgment right now." Jerome looked at Kay and frowned. "I won't tell you that I know how you're feeling, because I don't. What I *will* tell you is that I would do anything right now if I thought it would bring Lee home safe."

"I know you would." She reached out and touched his arm. "And you aren't wrong. I'm on the very edge of a steep cliff right now."

"Come on. Let's go call Townsend and Lester and see what's been going on."

They followed Burket to his office, which was next to the county jail.

"Sheriff O'Loughlin is working on getting us a new jail and some decent offices, but this is what we have to offer right now," Burket told them as they walked from their cars to the old railroad depot where his office was located.

"You can use my desk." He pointed to an eight-by-eight room crammed with the desk and a couple of chairs. "You'll need to put your calls down in the log next to the phone."

"I've got two cars and a van seen near the alley," Townsend told Jerome once he got him on the phone. "Also have a couple of people seen lurking about, but one of them I'm pretty sure is Stinky."

Jerome knew all about Stinky. He was a panhandler whose personal hygiene was an assault to all the senses. When Stinky needed to be picked up by law enforcement, they always sent the youngest rookie out in the oldest patrol car.

"The other one was a guy in overalls near a suspicious van."

"You got all this from the neighbors?"

"They're older and very talkative. I think the best bet is a light-colored, newer Cadillac that was seen parked in the alley. The man who saw it said that if it had been a beater instead of a nice car, he would have called us."

"Did he see anyone near the car?"

"No. He was taking out the garbage and it was late."

"Anything else?"

"No. I called the guy at the funeral home…"

"Lester?"

"That's him. He gave us the names of some people who know Lee. I was calling and setting up meetings with them when you called."

After Jerome hung up with Townsend, Kay called Lester.

"I've been trying to get Yang out from under the house," he told her. "I think Ruby is just trying to keep me busy." Lester sounded like a guitar string about to snap.

"Where's Ruby?"

"She's talking to Alison." He lowered his voice. "Alison looks scared."

"We all are," Kay told him. She reported what they'd found at Hugo's house.

"A guy that rich might have a second house," Lester suggested.

"Sometimes you can be pretty smart. We'll check the property records while we're over here."

After they were done making calls, Jerome told Burket about the three vehicles.

"A Cadillac?" Burket snapped his fingers and pulled out a folded piece of teletype paper from his pocket. "I pulled Hugo's DMV records. Bingo!" He tapped the paper and handed it over to Jerome. Hugo was the owner of a beige 1979 Cadillac Fleetwood.

"If you have an eyewitness that saw a car matching this description near the scene, that's enough for me to put out a BOLO for the car and Hugo Valero as a material witness in a missing person case."

Burket spent the next thirty minutes sending out the BOLO over the teletype and contacting local dispatch units.

"Can you tell us where the property appraiser's office is? We'd like to check and see if Hugo or Joyce have any other properties in the county," Kay said.

"I can do better than that. I have a friend who works in the office. I can give him a call and have them check it out." Burket picked up the phone as he spoke.

Again, Kay was impressed by Burket's willingness to follow through on their suggestions.

"He said it would take an hour before he'd have a chance to check the records," he said as he hung up with his friend.

"We'll check back with you," Jerome told him.

Kay and Jerome decided to drive by Hugo's house again before grabbing something to eat as they waited for Burket to hear back from the property appraiser's office. Nothing had changed at Hugo's house, and they resisted the urge to break into the house or Joyce's car.

"I can't stand this." Kay dropped her half-eaten hamburger onto the plate and shoved it to the middle of the table. "We've got to do something to find Lee."

"Waiting is a lot of what cops do," Jerome told her. Then he put down his own hamburger and said more kindly, "It won't help Lee for us to go dashing around looking in places he isn't, or getting ourselves in trouble breaking the law."

Kay frowned but nodded. "When you're done, let's go to the college and try to find some people who know Hugo and Joyce."

"Honestly, I'm not that hungry." Jerome looked down at what was left of his hamburger. "Going over there'll kill some time before we call Burket back."

They found a parking space near the building that housed Hugo's and Joyce's offices.

"Where do we start?" Kay asked once they were inside.

"Sometimes it's best not to have a plan. We'll just talk to whoever we see." Jerome shrugged.

They found Joyce's office first.

"Let's split up. I'll go this way; you go that way." Kay pointed left and then right.

"When you get to the end of the hall, we'll meet back here," Jerome said.

Kay nodded and headed for the first door on the left. She had to knock on three different doors before she finally received an answer.

"Yesss, come in!" sang a lyrical male voice from the other side of the door bearing a name plate that read: *Professor Jonathan Glover.*

Behind the desk sat a small man in a tweed suit and a bowtie, who smiled brightly at Kay. Without going into detail, she simply told him that she was trying to contact Professors Valero and Harrington.

"Ahhhhh, yes, the lovebirds," Glover said with a twinkle in his eye.

"Have you seen them today?"

"Who are you, sweetie?" he asked, pinning her down with his eyes and waving her toward a chair. Clearly, his somewhat silly affectations hid a perceptive personality.

"I'm sorry. I'm Kay Lamberton." She perched on the edge of the chair in front of his desk.

"And why are you looking for Hugo and Joyce?" Glover raised his eyebrows and smiled.

"Actually, I need to touch base with my brother. I think he's with them," she said, coming up with an explanation on the fly.

"Ahhhhhh, I see. Funny, they seem to be missing at the moment. Normally one or the other of them is striding up and down the halls making some sort of commotion. But the last day or two, it's been very quiet. I guess that just goes to answer your question. No, I haven't seen them today or yesterday." He held up his hands and shrugged.

"You called them lovebirds?"

Glover laughed and wagged his finger at her.

"Young lady, you aren't going to get away with that. I'm a devoted fan of Raymond Chandler, Perry Mason and John D. MacDonald. I know when someone is mining for information. So what's your game?" he asked in a comical gangster voice.

"Okay, you got me." Kay raised her hands in surrender. "Have you heard that Joyce's ex-husband is dead?"

"Yes. A very sad thing." All of his jovialness vanished. "I knew Roger and liked him. What does his accident have to do with you asking me about Hugo and Joyce?"

"My brother and I run the funeral home down in Lang. We have Harrington's body and, well, we thought there was something odd about his death."

"But you have no legal authority?"

"We are working with the sheriff's office," Kay said, stretching the truth only a little bit.

"I see." Glover scrunched up his face as he thought. "Can you prove any of this?"

"A deputy is here with me. I can get him if you'd like." Kay liked this doughty professor. There was an air of integrity about him, and she wanted to hear what he had to say about Hugo and Joyce.

Glover stared at her for a moment before shaking his head. "Go ahead and ask your questions."

"You said you liked Roger. What do you think about Joyce and Hugo?"

"Individually, Joyce is a dedicated instructor who maybe didn't have enough excitement in her life. Hugo has an enormous ego, but he also has the knowledge and brains to back it up. There is no problem with each of them by themselves. The trouble came when they got together."

"When did they get together? Before or after the Harringtons' marriage ended?"

"As soon as they saw each other, they were together. I was with Hugo in Gainesville the night he met her. We were at the university for a Spanish Historical Society meeting. Of course, Roger and Joyce were there too. I'd known them both for a number of years, while Hugo had just started here at the college six months earlier. The Harringtons knew Hugo's reputation with old Spanish documents, and both were excited to meet him."

"You said that Hugo and Joyce were attracted to each other immediately. Did Roger notice?" Kay asked.

"Roger was a very self-involved man. Not an egotist; his focus wasn't on himself. Instead, it was on whatever excited him at the moment. It could be some obscure book, an unknown Spanish philosopher or a new library he'd discovered. Whatever he was interested in was *all* he was interested in. So, no, he did not notice the frightening chemistry between Joyce and Hugo." Glover shook his head sadly.

"Frightening?"

"It was like watching someone mix two nondescript chemicals together to watch them boil and smoke. There was too much need in both of them. Joyce needed the excitement that Hugo could bring, and Hugo desired the love and adoration that Joyce could provide him."

"When did Roger realize what was going on?"

"That's an interesting question." Glover frowned. "I think he learned of the affair shortly before he became obsessed with the lost Spanish treasure."

"How angry was he?"

"That's what I mean about it being an interesting

question. For maybe a week or two, his emotions seemed to be building into a real anger, but then things changed. He discovered a written account of a Spanish shipwreck and the crew's effort to transport the gold to St. Augustine. It was typical Roger. Once he was on the track of the gold, everything else became secondary. Even the affair between Joyce and Hugo."

"You're telling me that he cared more about an old legend than he did the disintegration of his marriage?" Kay asked skeptically.

"If you think about it, it makes sense. Roger had two choices: he could throw himself into this new project, or he could face the humiliation that Joyce and Hugo were doling out. Once his eyes were opened to the affair, even Roger could see that there was little chance of getting Joyce to give up her relationship with Hugo."

"An ostrich with its head in the sand." Kay understood the reaction.

"More like the ostrich had its head in the library, but yes, that's the idea. And even better, his little gold hunt gave him a reason to get out of Gainesville."

Kay had seen enough nasty breakups over the years to understand why someone would want to go into hiding rather than face their partner.

"So where are Hugo and Joyce now?" Kay asked, leaning forward.

"Like I said, I haven't seen them for a couple of days. I would assume they're at Hugo's house."

"Who would know where they are?"

"It's the end of summer session, so they're under no obligation to tell anyone where they went." Glover shrugged.

"Don't they have any friends?"

"Hugo doesn't have friends. He puts people into three categories: those who worship him, those he thinks might be useful and those he considers enemies."

"What about Joyce?"

"Joyce cares only about Hugo. Oh, she has acquaintances, but so many people find Hugo off-putting that she hasn't had many opportunities to make real friends here in St. Augustine."

They both jumped at a sudden knock at the door.

"Probably a student," Glover said softly to Kay, then he called out in a loud, cheery voice, "Come in!"

Jerome popped his head into the door.

"Nope, not a student of mine. Perhaps a friend of yours?" Glover said knowingly.

"Professor Glover, this is Deputy Jerome Carter."

"Professor, nice to meet you," Jerome said, then he looked at Kay. "I didn't have any luck."

"That's okay. The professor here has been a font of information."

"Before we continue," Glover said, looking up at Jerome, "she said that you are a deputy…?"

Jerome smiled and pulled out his wallet, flashing his star and badge. "Pretty much anything Miss Lamberton tells you can be considered gospel," he said.

"I'm still trying to wrap my mind around the idea that Roger's death was anything but an accident or natural causes." Glover shook his head.

"There are just some questions about it," Jerome said carefully.

"Hugo and Joyce aren't at his house," Kay said to get back on topic. "There must be somebody else at the college that they socialized with."

"As I told you, Hugo isn't well… Wait, there *is* one couple that they hang out with occasionally." Glover looked thoughtful. "Nelson and Lila Cardenas. She's a Spanish historian who works with the city on Old St. Augustine and an adjunct professor with the college. Nelson is a lawyer who's worked with the college on some legal issues."

"And Hugo and Joyce have spent time with them?" Kay asked.

"Yes, I think they meet Hugo's high standards. I know they've dined together on occasion and maybe even played cards."

"Do you have their number?" Jerome asked.

"Lila should be in our faculty register." Glover reached down and opened the bottom drawer of his desk as he spoke. He took out an official-looking binder with the college insignia on it and began to flip through it. "Yes, here it is!"

Jerome stepped up to the desk and pulled out his pocket notebook to write the number down.

"May I use your phone?"

Glover nodded and Jerome picked up the receiver and dialed. After a minute, he replaced the receiver.

"No answer and no answering machine." He looked apologetically at Glover. "One more call?"

Glover nodded and Jerome dialed a number from his notebook.

"Scott, have you heard anything from your friend at the property appraiser's office?" Jerome asked.

Kay saw him frown, then he told Burket what they had learned from Professor Glover.

"That would be great." Jerome hung up the phone. "Scott says he knows the Cardenases and he's gonna try and track them down."

They thanked the professor and headed back to the car.

"Let's go back to Scott's office," Jerome suggested. "With luck, maybe he'll know something by the time we get there."

CHAPTER TWENTY-ONE

Lee woke to the sound of the door opening. It took him a moment to remember where he was and why he couldn't see anything. He struggled with the ties that bound his hands as footsteps crossed the room.

"Quiet," Joyce told him. "Hugo is taking a nap."

He stopped struggling. A part of him wanted to trust Joyce, but he couldn't help but jump as her hands touched him.

"You've got to get out of here," she whispered as she pulled off his blindfold. "I'm going to cut you loose."

Light burned his eyes. Before his eyes could adjust, Joyce was tugging at his arms and cutting off the bindings.

"Thank you," he whispered, remembering her admonishment to be quiet.

"I'm scared that Hugo's going to hurt you. You need to leave now."

"Yes, of course." Lee shuffled around so she could reach his feet and cut the cords that bound them together.

He started to get off the mattress, but Joyce placed her hand on his shoulder to stop him. "Wait. Let me make sure he is still asleep." She quietly hurried from the room.

Lee's heart was beating fast as he waited for her to come back. All he wanted to do was get up and run from the room. It took all of his willpower to sit still.

When the door opened again, Joyce waved him over. As he stood up stiffly, she put her finger to her lips in a shushing gesture. As quietly as he could, he walked over to the door, then followed her out of the room and down the hallway to a sunroom at the back of the house. The jalousie windows looked out over the St. John's River. The sun was falling low in the sky as Joyce carefully opened the back door.

Once outside, Joyce grabbed Lee's arm and began tugging him down toward the river. "There's an old canoe on the dock."

The back yard sloped down to a rustic-looking dock. Lee could see the upturned canoe resting against a wooden box.

"Can't I take a car, or go down the road to one of the neighbors?" Lee wasn't so sure about the canoe.

"If he wakes up and finds you're gone, the first thing he's going to do is head down the road looking for you. The easiest way to get to the neighbors is by the river."

"How close are the neighbors?" Lee asked, still not comfortable with the idea of the canoe.

"Couple hundred yards upriver or a little farther downriver. The quickest way is to go downriver. You may have to try a few places before you find anyone. Most of the houses along here are weekend homes."

They were only fifty yards from the dock now.

"Will you be okay?" Lee asked.

"Don't worry about me. Just get away. I'll be fine."

They reached the dock and Joyce looked back nervously

toward the house. Together, they eased the canoe down to the water with a small splash.

"Where's the paddle?" Lee asked frantically.

"Oh, over here." Joyce moved to the other side of the dock where a paddle hung on hooks and handed it to him.

After getting down into the canoe, Lee looked up at Joyce while he held onto the dock. "Before I go, you've got to tell me why Hugo is so upset. The truth this time. Did he kill Roger? And where is McKenzie?"

Joyce rubbed her hands on her jeans and glanced back at the house nervously.

"No, we didn't kill anyone!" She shook her head vigorously. "Okay, I'll tell, I'll tell you! It was all my fault. I wanted to distract Roger. When he found out about Hugo and me, he was going crazy. So I came up with this idea."

Joyce paused and Lee wasn't sure if she'd say anything more.

"If you didn't kill Roger, then someone else did. You've got to tell me what's going on," Lee urged.

Reluctantly, she said, "I talked Hugo into making a fake document describing the Spanish shipwreck and the crew's attempt to hide the gold. Ironically, Hugo is probably the only person in the world who could have done a good enough job to fool Roger. After I suggested it, Hugo took the idea and ran with it. He already had some old paper he could use, and an ink mixture that would produce an excellent fake. After a week or two, he managed to come up with an incredible forgery."

"You mean the whole story about the gold was a lie?" Lee asked incredulously.

"Exactly! And if it gets out that Hugo faked a Spanish document, his reputation will be ruined. He won't be able to get an academic job anywhere. Everything he's worked for his whole life will be gone. And it's all my fault." Joyce looked like she was about to cry. "And… maybe what I did *did* cause someone to kill Roger." Tears were rolling down her cheeks as she reached out and shoved the canoe away from the dock.

"Good luck," Lee told her as he steadied himself in the rocking canoe and began to paddle away. He was annoyed at himself for feeling sorry for her, but he didn't look back.

Unbidden, he suddenly thought of a time when he'd visited a campground in Georgia with his mother. He'd been only seven or eight at the time, but she'd taught him how to paddle a canoe in a straight line and how to guide it with a twist of the paddle. He whispered a quiet thanks to his mother as the memory flooded back.

Lee took the easiest course and headed downriver. After only a few minutes, he spotted a couple of houses along the bank of the river. Seeing the houses energized him, and he dug in hard with the paddle. On the second heavy stroke, the paddle broke in half. Without a second thought, Lee grabbed what was left and paddled quickly toward the nearest house.

He pulled himself out of the canoe and scurried up the bank, but no one answered his frantic knocking. He stumbled back down the bank and around a picket fence that ran down to the water, then started back up toward the next house. He'd barely made it halfway before an old man in a fishing vest came out of the back door.

"I'm sorry, but this isn't public access," the man told him.

Lee tried to explain the situation, but the words came out sounding like crazy gibberish even to him. He'd started to explain about his kidnapping, but then he wondered: *Do Hugo and Joyce really deserve to be arrested for kidnapping and have their lives ruined over something that stupid?*

"Never mind. Can I use your phone?" Lee asked the man. Regardless of whether he decided to report Joyce and Hugo, it was clear that Hugo was in a very volatile mood and

Lee needed to get out of the area as quickly as possible.

The man squinted at him as though trying to assess Lee's level of craziness. Lee knew that his rumpled appearance and sense of urgency weren't helping.

Finally, the man said, "I've got one in my garage. I guess you can use that one."

"I'm Lee Lamberton, by the way." Lee stuck his hand out, trying to put the man at ease.

"You can call me Marvin." He ignored Lee's hand. "Go in that back door."

The man pointed up the slope to the detached garage, then waited for Lee to go first as though he didn't like the idea of Lee being behind him.

Inside the garage, there was a rotary dial phone on the wall. Confronted by the phone, Lee realized he'd didn't know who to call. He'd decided not to call the police, but if he called the funeral home it would be more than an hour before anyone could pick him up, and Marvin didn't look like he wanted to play host to Lee for that long. Maybe a taxi? Lee felt his pockets and realized he didn't have his wallet. He looked at Marvin frowning in the doorway and felt sure the man wouldn't loan him the money for a taxi ride. With a sigh, he decided that calling the funeral home was his best choice.

"Collect call," he told the operator, then he heard Lester answer the phone.

"Collect call from Lee Lamberton," the operator informed him.

"He's not here," Lester said, obviously mishearing her.

Before Lester could hang up, Lee shouted over the operator for Lester to accept the charges.

"Where are you?" Lester asked excitedly.

"Will you accept the charges?" the operator insisted.

"Yeah, sure!"

Once the operator had disconnected, Lester asked, "Where are you? Everyone's been looking for you all day."

"Where's Kay?"

"She's over in St. Augustine looking for you."

"Really? I'm somewhere on the St. John's River. I need someone to pick me up quick," Lee said and glanced over at Marvin, who wasn't looking any less suspicious.

"What happened to you?"

"I don't want to go into that right now. Can you get ahold of Kay?"

"Maybe. She's with Jerome."

Lee tried to think of the best way to handle the situation. "Hold on." He looked over at Marvin. "He's going to have to call me back."

Marvin didn't look happy, but he gave a short nod.

"You've got to get ahold of Kay and Jerome, then call me back." Lee read off the number on the phone.

Lee waited nervously for almost half an hour before the phone rang. It was Kay, and he quickly told her the address that Marvin had given him.

Kay silently gave thanks to God and her lucky stars as she and Jerome drove to pick up Lee. Lester had called the sheriff's office and spoken with Townsend. In turn, he'd been able to contact Scott Burket while Kay and Jerome were still at his office. Now they were driving twenty miles over the speed limit to the address Lee had given them.

"I don't understand why Lee was so cryptic about what happened to him," Jerome said.

"I don't care about any of that. I'm just glad he's okay."

"Just seems odd." Jerome pursed his lips and added, "Still, you're right. It's good to know he's okay."

"I don't think it's a coincidence that we found out that

Hugo and Joyce have friends with a house on the St. John's River and then, almost immediately, we find out that Lee is on that same river," Kay said.

"I think we should have let Burket come along," Jerome said.

"Lee said he was fine and that he didn't want law enforcement involved."

"And I'm saying that sounds odd." Jerome tapped the steering wheel emphatically as he spoke.

Lee had found a place beside Marvin's garage where he could watch the road without being seen. As soon as Jerome pulled into the driveway, Lee hurried out to the car. Kay started to get out, but Lee waved her back in. As he climbed into the back seat, Jerome and Kay started asking him questions simultaneously.

"I'll tell you everything. Just drive."

"You're acting like you just robbed a bank," Kay said as Jerome pulled out of the driveway.

Lee saw Marvin peering out of the windows as they drove off. "That's probably what he thinks," he said ruefully.

"Now tell us what happened," Kay said, turning around in her seat.

With a sigh, Lee dove into the story of his last eighteen hours.

Kay shook her head in disbelief. "We knew you'd been grabbed, and it seemed pretty obvious it must've been Hugo and Joyce. But I still can't believe they did it."

"They need to be arrested," Jerome said, looking at Lee through the rearview mirror.

"Especially since they probably killed Roger and did something with McKenzie," Kay said.

"That's kind of the rest of the story. I don't think they killed anyone," Lee said.

"If they kidnapped you—" Kay started.

"It's what Joyce told me when I was leaving. See, there isn't any gold. They made it up to distract Roger from their affair." Lee explained why Hugo was so desperate that he'd decided to kidnap Lee.

"No gold." Kay was stunned.

"That changes things." Jerome shook his head as he drove.

"It strikes Joyce and Hugo off the suspect list, for one thing," Lee said.

"And it means no one killed Roger because he found the gold," Kay added.

"What about that guy, Jerry Mercer? According to his wife, he's pretty invested in the search for the gold. He could have found out that there wasn't any gold and blamed Harrington for stringing him along," Jerome suggested.

"Maybe, but then what happened to McKenzie?" Kay asked.

"There's that strange kid too," Lee said as he watched the pine trees go by outside.

"Cody, our country boy Peeping Tom. He's certainly not at the bottom of the list. In fact, he's at the top of my list to interview again." Jerome sounded determined.

"He's a little odd," Kay agreed, "but what's his motive?"

"We could've been looking at this all wrong. Maybe the gold angle was just a red herring," Jerome said. "Maybe Roger Harrington caught Cody Morgan peeking in windows and threatened to go to the police."

"Then McKenzie found out that he killed Roger, so Cody had to get rid of him too," Lee added.

"I'm not sure about the kid," Kay said doubtfully. "Maybe you dismissed Hugo and Joyce too quickly. What if Roger found out that he'd been tricked, so Hugo had to kill him to keep him quiet?"

"Joyce wasn't lying," Lee said emphatically.

"It could be that Joyce doesn't know the truth," Kay pointed out.

"I guess…" Lee didn't sound convinced.

"My problem with Cody as the killer is his age," Kay said.

"You want me to list all the horrible crimes that kids nineteen years old and younger have committed?" Jerome asked.

"No, I get it. And he *is* hiding something," Kay agreed.

"A teenage boy wandering around in the woods spying on people isn't that surprising. The question is: Why is he spying on people? How dark are his motives?" Jerome asked.

"Still, if it's not Hugo, then I think my money would be on Jerry Mercer. Like you said, he could have learned that there wasn't any gold and killed Roger out of frustration. He might have even been angry enough to torture him," Kay said. "Let's talk to both Cody and Mercer tomorrow."

Jerome nodded.

When they finally pulled into the driveway of the funeral home, Ruby met them at the car and took charge of Lee.

"I know you must be starving." Ruby dragged him into the kitchen and soon had him sitting at the table with a mountain of food in front of him.

But before he had a chance to start on the food, Alison ran in.

"I closed up the shop as soon as I heard they'd found you." She sat down close to him and put her hand on his arm with a smile. "You don't know how glad I am that you're okay."

Lee leaned toward her, and they shared a gentle kiss.

"That reminds me. Your boyfriend left a message," Ruby told Kay.

"Alan isn't exactly my…" Kay stopped and rolled her eyes. There wasn't any point in arguing with Ruby. "Where's the message?"

"He said he had some news and wanted you to give him a call as soon as you could."

Lester came in and sat down on the other side of Lee, looking enviously at his plate of food. "Glad you're back, boss! Hey, I got Yang out from under the house."

Ruby smiled and patted him on the back. "Yang and I appreciate you crawling under there and getting him out. You've already had dinner, but how about I get you another bowl of blackberry cobbler? With ice cream?"

"Yes ma'am!" Lester's face brightened.

Kay decided to call Alan from the office where there would be fewer ears to hear the conversation.

"One of our senior ER nurses announced she's retiring," Alan blurted as soon as he recognized her voice. "I've already talked to a hospital administrator who's very impressed with your experience in Vietnam."

"What does it pay?" Kay was surprised to hear herself ask.

"I talked them into giving you credit for your time in the military, so you wouldn't be starting at the bottom of the pay scale." He went on to give her the numbers and a list of benefits.

Kay was even more surprised to hear herself tell him that she was interested in the position.

"Great! I'll get an application. Can we get together tomorrow?"

Kay thought about Cody Morgan and Jerry Mercer. "I might be tied up most of tomorrow. I'll call you."

CHAPTER TWENTY-TWO

On Saturday morning, the sky was overcast as a tropical depression pushed clouds in from the Gulf Coast.

"You could wait till tomorrow, then I could go with you," Lee said.

Lee was following Kay around as she gathered her things so she'd be ready when Jerome picked her up.

"I'm sorry. I don't know why, but I feel like we're close to figuring this out," Kay said as she looked through her denim purse, checking it for her keys and wallet.

"If you've got this figured out, you're smarter than me." Lee frowned.

"Little brother, I've always been smarter than you." She gave him a light punch in the arm and a smile to let him know she was kidding. "It's probably wishful thinking. Look, I just want to follow through with this."

"And I don't? Remember that I'm the one who was kidnapped!"

"Then come with us."

"I've got work to do, including fixing the latticework so that stupid cat will stop going under the house. And there's some funeral business that Lester isn't up to yet," Lee said in a low voice. He didn't want to hurt Lester's feelings, but Lester didn't quite know all the ins and outs of selling funerals and handling families.

They heard the roar of a motorcycle outside. A moment later, Jerome slammed through the screen door. "We better take your car. Looks like it's going to rain later," he said when he saw Kay, then he motioned to Lee. "You should come with us."

"We just had that discussion. He's staying here." Kay brushed past Lee and Jerome.

Jerome shrugged and followed her out the door.

The wind was brisk and damp as they got into the car.

"Where to first?" Kay asked.

"I talked to Townsend this morning. He's got a traffic homicide he's dealing with right now, but he suggested that we talk with Mrs. Mercer again before we talk to her husband. I went by the feed store on the way here. He's at work, so we should be able to talk to her alone."

"Sounds good." Kay backed out of the driveway and headed out of town toward the Mercer place.

As she pulled into the yard and turned off the engine, Kay saw June Mercer pull back the curtain at the front window. By the time Kay and Jerome were out of the car, June had opened the door and stepped outside.

"I'm not talking to y'all again without a lawyer."

"We just have a few questions," Jerome said, still walking toward her.

"Jerry told me you didn't have any right to ask me questions without my lawyer." June glared at them.

"Call your lawyer. We'll wait." Jerome called her bluff, stopping in the yard and looking at her with his hands spread.

June glared at them as though hoping she could wish them away.

"We might actually be able to help you," Kay said. This caused both Jerome and June to look at her.

"How are you going to help me?" June demanded.

"What's the biggest problem you're having right now in your marriage?" Kay asked.

June tilted her head as though giving the question serious consideration.

"My husband is never home. What can you do about that?" Her voice was still defiant.

"You might be surprised," Kay told her. "But we're going to have to make a deal."

"I'm listening.

"Can we go inside?" Kay asked. A clap of thunder underscored her question.

Reluctantly, June opened the door and went inside, leaving it open for them to follow.

"Baby's asleep, so keep your voices down," June told them as she dropped onto the couch. She waved them over to a couple of chairs.

"Your husband still looking for the gold?" Kay asked.

June narrowed her eyes and stared past them as though remembering a particularly painful experience.

"You know what that idiot did? He paid that old lawnmower guy a hundred bucks to dig holes on the old man's property. Jerry even has to fill the holes back in. That hundred dollars was the money for our power bill," she hissed.

"Is he at work this morning?" Jerome asked, even though he knew the answer. He just wanted to hear what June would say.

"Who knows anymore. Yesterday I found out he's been

skipping work some days to go gold-hunting." Her frustration was boiling over.

"We're going to solve that problem for you," Kay said and gave her a little smile.

June leaned forward and looked interested.

"The only way you can keep him and his brother from hunting for that gold is to lock them up in jail. Is that what you have in mind?" This time she was the one to smile.

"You want him to go to jail?" Kay asked.

"At least I'd know where he was," June shot back.

"I think we can do better than take him to the county bed-and-breakfast," Jerome said.

"I'm listening." June leaned back.

"You need to answer a few questions first. To begin with, we need to get a timeline of your husband's movements over the past week," Jerome said.

June answered his questions as well as she was able. When she was done, Jerome had filled three pages of his notepad.

"So how are you going to get them to stop hunting for this stupid gold?" June demanded.

"I'll tell you, but you have to promise not to say anything to your husband until we've had a chance to talk to him," Jerome said.

"Like he and I ever talk anymore." She rolled her eyes.

"There's no gold. It was all a trick," Kay told her.

"I never thought there was any gold," June said, though her eyes were wide at the revelation. "You say it was a trick?"

"You don't need all the details, but yeah, it was a trick. I think I can convince your husband he's been wasting his time," Kay assured her.

June burst out laughing. It took almost five minutes and the baby waking up before she got control of herself.

"You better go talk to him fast because I won't be able to

contain myself when I see him." She gave another laugh as she bounced the baby on her hip and watched them head out to the car.

"How do you want to handle this?" Kay asked Jerome as they drove toward the feed store.

"Listen to you! You're going all super cop," Jerome said with a grin. "I think we should hit him with the news that he's been made a fool of as soon as we can. Shake him up and see what falls out."

"What if he won't talk to us?"

"He wants that gold so bad he can taste it. If he thinks we know anything about his precious treasure, he's gonna listen to us."

They found Jerry Mercer loading deer corn into the back of an old Chevy pickup truck.

"I don't have time for you today," he growled at them.

The man in overalls whose truck Jerry was loading watched the three of them curiously.

"Finish with that corn and then we'll talk," Jerome said.

The man with the pickup looked disappointed as Jerry finished putting the last two bags of corn into the bed of the truck and handed him his receipt. For a minute, Kay thought the driver was just going to stay there to find out what was going on, but he finally got into his truck and drove away.

Jerry turned his back on Jerome and Kay and headed toward the loading dock.

"You can walk away, but if you do, you won't find out what we know about the gold," Jerome said to Jerry's back.

Jerry took one more step before coming to a stop. Kay could almost see the wheels whirling in his head. Then, as if a giant hand were turning him against his will, Jerry turned back to them.

"I don't believe you."

"We haven't told you anything yet." Jerome laughed.

"I don't think you know anything about the gold," Jerry scoffed.

"We know a damn sight more about it than you do."

Jerry came stomping back over to them.

"I'm listening," he said through clenched teeth.

"It was all a joke played on Roger Harrington. It's a long story, but the gist of it is that his ex-wife made up the story of the gold to screw with him."

Jerry was clearly shocked.

"No! No, that guy Harrington was a professor. He knew what he was doing. He had, like, some real old document. You can't fake that. Not with a guy like Harrington." Jerry's face was turning red. As much as he denied the truth, a part of him must've realized that they weren't lying to him.

"You see, his ex-wife found a guy who knew more about those real old documents than Harrington did. They just made themselves a fake and Harrington bought it lock, stock and barrel." Kay couldn't help digging the knife in a little deeper.

Like a dropped bottle of nitroglycerin, Jerry exploded. Childishly, he stomped around and threw pieces of lumber, PVC piping and anything else he could get his hands on. Jerome and Kay stood out of the way and watched the tantrum.

"You're lying!" Jerry pounded an eight-foot two-by-four on the ground. "I know you're lying! I can prove it!" he screamed. "His journal shows—"

Jerry froze when he realized what he'd said.

Kay looked at Jerome, who was suddenly tense. Before either of them could react, Jerry took off running with Jerome a second behind him.

Jerry's advantage was that he knew the feed store's lot much better than Jerome. For a couple of minutes, they ran around stacks of concrete blocks, wood, packs of shingles and other supplies. Jerry finally made a mistake when he went around a stack of lumber and Jerome just stopped and grabbed one of the boards, swinging it into Jerry's chest. Like a cartoon character, Jerry's hair flew up as he fell backwards and landed with a thud on the concrete. By this point, they had attracted half a dozen spectators and more than one of them laughed.

Before Jerome could grab Jerry, they heard a shout from the loading dock and a man carrying a baseball bat jumped down and ran toward Jerome.

Calmly, Jerome pulled his .38 Colt from the concealed holster on his side and pointed the revolver at Andy Mercer's chest.

"Drop the baseball bat!" Jerome kept the gun pointed at Andy's chest as he stepped back so he could see Jerry, who was still lying on the ground, semi-conscious.

Andy stopped and let the bat drop to the ground. "What did you do to my brother?" he demanded.

"I'll check on him." Kay started toward Jerry and added for everyone's benefit, "I'm a nurse."

No one moved except Kay. She knelt down beside the prone Jerry, who was now spewing an epic string of curse words. It was unclear whether they were meant for himself or Jerome.

"He probably has a concussion, but other than that he'll be fine," Kay said after a cursory examination.

Jerome, keeping a wary eye on Andy, slipped his gun back into its holster and pulled a pair of handcuffs from his back pocket as he approached Jerry.

"I didn't do anything," Jerry moaned as he rubbed his head.

"Where's the journal?" Jerome asked as he took one of Jerry's hands and pulled it behind his back.

Jerry tried to avoid answering the question by pretending

he hadn't heard it, but he put up no resistance as Jerome brought his other hand back and handcuffed him.

"Tell me where the journal is and I'll make the charge petty theft," Jerome offered.

"Look, I admit I took it out of McKenzie's truck, but I didn't do anything to him. I swear I don't know where he is." Jerry shook his head.

"You still haven't answered my question. Where is the journal?"

"I've got it stashed here." Jerome pulled him to his feet and Jerry staggered a little. "My head's killing me."

"Show me," Jerome ordered him while keeping a strong hand on Jerry's arm and one eye on Andy, who was still watching them. "If you want to be a part of this, I can get another pair of handcuffs. Otherwise, I suggest you keep your distance."

Jerry started for the loading dock on unsteady legs. "It's in the bathroom," he mumbled.

The journal was hidden in the space between the drop-down ceiling and the roof. Jerome uncuffed Jerry and let him climb up on the toilet to retrieve the spiral-bound notebook. He climbed back down and handed it to Jerome.

Jerome flipped through it quickly, then handed it to Kay.

"As best I can tell, it's all here," Kay said after thumbing through the pages.

"Read his notes. The gold is real," Jerry insisted as Jerome pushed him out of the bathroom door.

"Don't say a word. I've called our lawyer!" Andy Mercer yelled as Jerome steered his brother toward Kay's car.

After checking the back seat to make sure there wasn't anything that could be used as a weapon, Jerome shoved Jerry into the car.

"First time it's been used to transport a prisoner," Kay joked as she got behind the wheel.

"You'll have to drop us off at the sheriff's office. I gotta get up with Townsend and see what we're going to do with our prisoner," Jerome said.

"You'll let me go when my lawyer gets done with you," Jerry said.

"Where was McKenzie's truck when you stole the journal out of it?" Jerome asked him.

"I don't have to tell you anything."

"You're already talking. It's your choice whether you say things that will help you or not," Jerome informed him.

"Man, you did a number on my head."

"We'll get someone to look at your injuries. Now pay attention to what I'm going to tell you. Once we get to the office, everything becomes official. Right now, I still have plenty of leeway to help you, but once we walk through those doors, it'll be out of my hands."

"My head is pounding. I can't think."

"Anything you say to me now is off the record," Jerome lied.

"What can you do for me?" Jerry asked, and Jerome knew he had him where he wanted him.

"I don't have to charge you with anything. Just tell us what we want to know. You can start off with where you found the truck."

"It was on McKenzie's property. I was just scouting around. You know, looking around for the gold. Then when I saw the truck, I hid."

"Were you afraid McKenzie would kick you off his land?"

"That was part of it, but it's not like the old days when my grandfather hated his father. He would have just wanted to know what I was doing, no big deal. The real reason I hid was 'cause I wanted to see if McKenzie was hunting for the gold too."

"What did you do when you saw him?" Jerome was hoping Jerry would admit to seeing McKenzie, which would lead to a whole other line of questioning.

Kay listened as they talked. When it looked like Jerome was getting somewhere, she purposely turned the wrong way so they could stretch the time they had with Mercer.

"I never saw him. After about ten minutes, I crept up to the truck and looked inside. I found the journal tucked behind the seat."

"What did you do then?"

"What do you think I did? I ran like hell!"

"With the journal?"

"Yeah," he said quietly.

"Do you really want us to believe you never saw McKenzie?" Jerome badgered him.

"I didn't. I swear. Hey! Are you guys looking for the gold too? I bet you aren't really taking me to jail," Jerry said, agitated.

"Oh, you're going to jail." Jerome chuckled. "Like I told you, the only question is what you're going to jail for."

"You aren't even going the right direction!"

"Sorry. I thought this was a shortcut," Kay said unconvincingly.

At that point, Jerry clammed up and didn't say another word the rest of the way to the sheriff's office.

"I'm going to take him inside. There's no point in you waiting. It could take hours," Jerome told Kay as he pulled Jerry out of the back seat.

"What do you think?" Kay indicated Jerry with a nod of her head.

"I think the idiot is probably telling the truth. He only has eyes for the gold." He turned to Jerry and said sternly, "The *nonexistent* gold."

Jerry just glared at him.

"What about talking to Cody?" Kay asked.

"Don't go talking to him by yourself," Jerome warned.

Kay promised she wouldn't. As she pulled out of the parking lot, she decided she'd convince Lee to go with her to talk to Cody Morgan.

CHAPTER TWENTY-THREE

Kay found Lee in the casket room with Lester. They were unpacking a new delivery and rearranging the room to highlight it.

"I didn't expect you back so soon," Lee said as he shifted one of the biers.

Kay told them what had happened.

"So Jerry Mercer killed Harrington and did something with McKenzie?" Lester asked.

"I'm not so sure. He had the journal, but I think I believe his explanation about how he got it."

"Pretty suspicious that he had it." Lee frowned.

"We'll see what Jerome finds out when they question him. I'd still like to talk to Cody Morgan."

"Y'all didn't get that far?" Lee asked.

"We dealt with Mercer first, which ended with his arrest. And Jerome didn't want me to go talk to Cody by myself…"

Lee looked around at the casket room.

"Give me half an hour and I'll go with you."

The clouds were keeping the summer temperatures bearable as they left the funeral home, and so far, it still wasn't raining.

"Where do you want to check first?" Lee asked as Kay drove.

"We'll go by the Fast Mart. If we don't find him there, we'll go to his grandfather's house."

A quick stop at the store proved that Cody wasn't there.

"What's his grandfather like?" Lee asked as Kay drove away from the Fast Mart.

"All country, no-nonsense, seems to care a lot about his grandson."

When they arrived at the farmhouse, they saw Cody pushing a green lawnmower around the front yard. He looked up when he noticed the car approaching. For a second, Kay thought he was going to run. Instead, he reached down and choked off the lawnmower while he kept an eye on them.

"Hi Cody." Kay did her best to sound cheerful and casual.

"Who's that? Is he a deputy?" Cody pointed at Lee.

"That's my brother, Lee."

"Hi." Lee stepped forward with his hand out.

Cody took his hand hesitantly. "What do y'all want?"

"Some things have happened, and we wanted to talk about them." Kay didn't want it to sound like they were there to treat him like a suspect. Though she was beginning to wonder...

"I don't know anything I didn't tell you before." Cody clearly wasn't fooled by her euphemistic approach.

"Jerry Mercer has been arrested," Kay told him, hoping the news would cause him to let his guard down.

"Arrested? He killed the Professor?" Cody didn't sound too surprised.

"You think he killed him?" Lee asked.

"I don't know," Cody mumbled.

"What do you know about Mercer?" Kay asked.

"Nothing really." He scraped the ground with his foot, then looked up at the dark clouds. "Look, I gotta finish the lawn before the storm comes."

"The last time I was here, it sounded like the Professor was your friend. My brother and I just want to find out what happened to him. Isn't that worth a little bit of your time?"

Cody looked back at the house. Kay followed his gaze and half expected to see his grandfather looking out the window at them, but there was no one there.

"If we're going to talk, I gotta put the lawnmower up in case it rains." Before Lee or Kay could say anything, Cody started pushing the lawnmower toward a shed at the back of the house.

"What do you think?" Kay asked when Cody was out of earshot.

"He's definitely a little strange," Lee said, then added, "and big enough to hang Harrington up by his foot."

When Cody came back, he looked more sure of himself. With his back straight and taking long strides across the lawn, Kay noticed just how powerful Cody was.

"I guess I've got something to tell you." Cody's face was solemn as he spoke. "I saw that guy Jerry Mercer around McKenzie's truck the other day."

"Was this before or after McKenzie disappeared?" Kay asked.

"I don't know. It was before I heard about it. I guess it was Sunday morning."

"Where was this?" Lee asked.

"It was on the other side of McKenzie's property, not far from the cabin where the Professor was staying. It was near a spot I call the Canebreak Trail because of all the rattlesnakes I've seen there."

"That's comforting," Kay said with a little shiver. "What exactly did you see?"

"The guy was carrying one of them Army shovels, the kind that fold up, and just walking along, looking at stuff. When he saw Mr. McKenzie's truck, he got all funny and cautious. You know, he was looking over his shoulder, and I thought for a minute he saw me, but I guess he didn't. It was weird 'cause he, like, hid for a few minutes, watching the truck while I watched him."

"What were you doing there?" Lee asked.

"Just walking in the woods," Cody said unconvincingly.

"What were you really doing there?" Kay asked as gently as she could.

"Looking for deer tracks." Cody's voice made it sound more like a question than an answer.

"No, you weren't," Kay told him.

"I always look for deer tracks," Cody said, trying to bluff his way through.

"But there's something else you were looking for. Was it the gold?" Lee asked.

Cody just stood there, looking at the ground. The wind had picked up and ruffled his hair.

"Does this have something to do with a girl?" Lee asked, knowing what it was like to be a teenage boy.

Cody laughed. It was deep and honest as he shook his head.

"Then what?" Kay pressed him.

"You won't believe me."

"The only way to find out is to tell us what you were hunting in the woods," Lee said firmly.

"Bigfoot." Cody's voice was so soft and low that they could barely hear him.

"What?" Lee was confused.

"I don't understand." Kay shook her head as if to clear her ears.

Cody started walking away from them like a scared and embarrassed child. Kay and Lee had to jog to catch up.

"Wait!" Kay was almost alongside Cody, but he kept his head down and continued walking toward the woods.

"We aren't making fun of you," Lee told him. "That was just a surprise, that's all."

Cody glanced back at Lee.

"He's right. We want to hear about… it," Kay assured him.

Cody stopped abruptly and Lee almost collided with him.

"You'll make fun of me." Cody was breathing heavily, not from exertion but from the fear of exposing his secret.

"We won't. I promise." Lee held up his hand as if taking a pledge.

"Promise," Kay seconded.

"I saw him once when I was fifteen." Cody looked at them with a defiant expression.

"Saw who?" Lee still wasn't sure what Cody was talking about.

"Bigfoot. I had just moved here and was…" He pointed away from the road into the dense woods behind the house, "…about five hundred feet back there. It was almost dark, and he came out from behind a bunch of wax myrtles that were covered in grapevines."

"How far away was he?" Lee felt himself drawn in despite his skepticism.

Kay was experiencing a form of déjà vu as she remembered her conversation with Ruby about the ape-men in Vietnam.

"Fifty-four feet. I went back and measured it. There were tracks, but not any that were good enough to cast. Not that I knew how to cast tracks back then."

Cody was looking off into the distance and his eye seemed to glow with the memory. Kay and Lee could tell that he absolutely believed what he was saying.

"You're telling us that you spend all your free time walking around in the woods looking for Bigfoot?" Kay was trying to wrap her head around this.

"Yeah." He reached into his pocket and pulled out a Kodak Instamatic camera. "I want to get a picture of him so I can prove to everyone he's real."

Lee and Kay were stunned by this revelation and just stood there staring at him.

"Oh, I'm saving up for a better camera. I almost had the money a couple of months ago, except that Grandad had to go to the doctor and needed the money for medicine."

"Why is it so important to you to prove Bigfoot exists?" Kay asked, puzzled by his motivation.

"Right after I saw him, I told some of the kids at school. We'd seen that movie, *The Legend of Boggy Creek*, so I thought they would believe me. Instead, they made fun of me. Started calling me Bigfoot."

Lee and Kay could hear the humiliation in Cody's voice.

"That must've been awful," Kay sympathized.

"Every time they called me Bigfoot, I promised myself I'd prove to them that I'd really seen what I'd seen." His eyes were narrowed and his teeth clenched in determination.

"So for the last four years, you've been walking around in these woods trying to get a picture of Bigfoot," Lee said with more than a little admiration.

"I can see why you and Professor Harrington got along," Kay said.

"He didn't laugh at me. In fact, a few times he pointed out broken saplings and trampled-down areas that I hadn't seen."

"And did you help him look for the gold?" Kay asked.

"Sure. I pointed out the rock quarry and some other landmarks he was looking for."

Kay wanted to chastise him for not telling them earlier why he'd been out in the woods, but she understood why he'd be hesitant to tell anyone he didn't know about his mission in life.

"Can you show us where McKenzie's truck was when you saw Mercer looking in it?" she asked.

"We can walk there from here. I know a trail."

"That's gotta be at least a mile or more," Lee protested.

"Going the back way, it's barely a mile."

Lee frowned and looked up at the sky. "It's gonna rain."

"The weather guy on Channel 20 said it's not going to rain until this evening," Kay scoffed.

"That guy's wrong more times than he's right," Lee argued.

"Come on, you won't melt." Kay sounded like the big sister she was.

"Fine! I give up. Lead on."

Cody smiled at the siblings arguing about the weather, then led them into the woods.

The path was four feet wide and looked like someone had mowed it in the last month. There were game trails crossing the path as it wound through both pine and oak woods.

"How did Harrington search for the gold?" Kay asked Cody.

"What do you mean?"

"Did he ever use a metal detector or dig holes?"

"He dug a lot of holes, but he was really good at filling them in. He had a friend that was an archaeologist, and he showed the Professor how to take a... core sample to see if the ground had been dug up in the past. You know, the soils would be all mixed up if it had. It was pretty interesting."

"Do you know where he was looking right before he died?" Lee asked.

"I know right about then he'd been looking around the old limestone quarry."

"How far is that?"

"Not too far. The old quarry road runs along the edge of Mr. McKenzie's property."

"We should check that out," Kay said.

"Let's see if we survive this hike." Lee was panting more than the other two. *I better start getting more exercise*, he thought.

"You'll want to check yourselves for ticks too," Cody said over his shoulder.

"Great," Lee mumbled.

Lee was thrilled when they turned a bend in the trail and saw McKenzie's cabin across the clearing.

"Where was McKenzie's truck?" Kay was feeling energized by the brisk walk.

"This trail goes on past the cabin and the truck was parked where it reenters the woods."

"So not much farther?" Lee was trying to console himself with the knowledge that Cody's legs were longer than his and that's why he was having a hard time keeping up. He just had to ignore the fact that Kay wasn't having any problems.

As they passed the cabin, they took a minute to look around. The area around it had been trampled down by all the searchers and their vehicles, but the cabin was locked up tight and nothing looked damaged or disturbed.

"The truck was about here." Cody pointed to a spot near the trail about five hundred feet on the other side of the cabin.

"Why would McKenzie park over here?" Kay asked.

"They've got a couple of food plots between here and Mr. Dandridge's property," Cody told them. "From here, you've got to walk or ride a horse."

"So what brought him out here that morning and where did he go?" Kay wondered.

"Did he drive his truck away from here or did someone else?" Lee mused.

"We know where his truck ended up," Kay pointed out. "If we've eliminated Hugo and Joyce, anyone else who drove his truck the fifty miles to the St. John's River would need a way to get back. Did they have help?"

"If it was Jerry and his brother, one of them could have driven McKenzie's truck to the river while the other brother followed in another vehicle," Lee suggested.

"That's what I was thinking. Anyone acting alone would have had to ride a bus or get a taxi back if they didn't involve a friend or family member."

"When you saw Jerry Mercer here by the truck, where were you?" Lee asked Cody.

"I was over there." He pointed to a copse of trees and palmetto bushes about a hundred feet away. "I've got some netting I've fixed up as a blind. You know, to see if... you-know-who comes around the cabin."

"You were watching for Bigfoot when you saw Mercer go up to the truck. Where did he come from?" Kay asked.

"Looked like he walked in along the path from the main road. After he rummaged through the truck, he ran off back toward the road with the journal."

"Did you see anyone else?"

"No."

"When did you get here?"

"I guess around eight."

"And the truck was already here?"

"Mr. McKenzie comes out early sometimes to spot deer and work on the food plots."

"When did you leave?"

"Not too long after I saw Mr. Mercer run off. He kind of

spooked me because he was acting so weird."

"Still, if McKenzie went farther out on the trail, and Mercer came from and returned to the road, would they have even met?" Kay posed the question as much to herself as to Lee and Cody.

"Maybe Mercer did something to McKenzie and then came back for the journal," Lee suggested.

"You wouldn't have thought he was that worried he'd be caught at the truck. Besides, why not drive the truck off then?"

"I can't believe I'm going to say this, but let's walk out this trail and see if we can find any clues as to what McKenzie was doing that morning." Lee was too curious to let it go.

Kay and Cody were more than game, so they all started down the trail.

"A bunch of people have been over this trail since Sunday morning," Kay observed. "The day we were here with the search effort, there were dozens of people."

"Which means we're probably wasting our time. But we might as well check it out." Lee puffed as he tried to keep up with Cody and Kay.

After they came to the clearing where McKenzie had planted a food plot, they stopped and looked around.

"Looks the way it always does," Cody told them.

"Who's putting out the corn?" Lee asked, looking at the corn under a drop feeder made out of a fifty-gallon drum with a couple of car batteries hooked up to it.

"Mr. McKenzie lets about a dozen people come out here and hunt. They all pitch in to fill the feeders and plant the food plots. It might be Mr. Dandridge. His place is just a quarter mile that way," Cody said.

"You said the old quarry road is out here?" Lee asked.

Cody nodded and pointed down the trail. "It's between

here and Mr. Dandridge's property." Without waiting, he started down the trail again.

"I know I've been whining the whole time, but seriously, the weather is looking dodgy," Lee said to Kay. Even as he spoke, there was a strong gust of wind.

"This could be from the tropical depression." Kay looked up at the dark clouds moving across the sky. "We'll turn back after we get to the quarry road."

Lee nodded, knowing that they probably wouldn't stop until they were walking in the pouring rain.

CHAPTER TWENTY-FOUR

The old quarry road was better defined than the trails. When the quarry had been in use, the quarrymen had taken limestone from the pit and paved the road with it, creating a hardpacked surface that defied the second-growth woods.

"The quarry is down there a couple hundred yards." Cody pointed to the right down the road. "And Mr. Dandridge's property starts over there." He pointed back fifty feet along the trail they'd come from to an aging heart-of-pine fence post with a faded "No Trespassing" sign tacked to it.

"How far is Dandridge's house from here?" Kay asked.

"Not far. Just through those trees is a clearing, and from there you can see the house. I guess it's another hundred yards or so," Cody said.

"Let's go look at the quarry and then head back," Lee said as he tried not to think about how far they were from the car.

As they walked along the old quarry road, the sides were

lined with large chunks of limestone. Some were the size of a Volkswagen Beetle.

"Do you know how long they used the quarry?" Kay asked.

"No. It's never been open since I've lived with my grandfather."

"I think Dad did a funeral for some guy who was killed here. But that was back when I was maybe twelve years old." Lee didn't add that he remembered it because he'd overheard his father talking about the body being crushed by a piece of limestone that had weighed a couple of tons.

The quarry covered almost ten acres. Standing on the edge, they looked over the twenty-foot drop to the floor of the pit. Scattered around the bottom was a variety of trash, including plenty of tin cans and bottles that had clearly been used for target practice.

"Lots of people must come here to shoot," Kay observed.

"I know guys who come here to sight in their rifles for hunting season," Cody said.

"Would that include you?" Lee asked.

"I've done it a couple of times. Last year, I got Granddad a new scope for his rifle and came out here to sight it in."

"At least there's not a bunch of water in the bottom of it. Otherwise, I'd want to know if McKenzie's body was down there," Kay said.

"When we get a ton of rain, there will be four or five feet of water in the middle. But most of the time it's dry," Cody told them.

"Do you want to go down in the quarry?" Lee asked, hoping the answer was no.

Kay sighed. "I don't see the point. The searchers were here and there's so much trash down there, it would be hard to figure out if any of it has anything to do with Harrington's death or McKenzie's disappearance."

They turned and headed back the way they'd come. It was starting to sprinkle as they reached the intersection of the trail and the old quarry road.

"Could McKenzie have walked to Dandridge's house?" Lee asked.

"They're good friends," Cody said.

"When we talked to him, Dandridge said he hadn't seen McKenzie in a month," Kay said.

"Could he have done anything to McKenzie?" Lee asked.

"Cody's right, by all accounts they've been friends for years."

"I've seen them together a lot. They always acted close," Cody said.

"Gold has broken up many friendships, but since there isn't any gold then I guess that doesn't apply," Lee said.

"There isn't any gold?" Cody seemed surprised.

Lee explained about the fake manuscript.

"I feel bad for the Professor," Cody said sadly.

The rain had picked up and the wind whipped through the trees as they stood at the crossroads.

"The weather isn't getting better," Lee shouted over the wind and rain. "Why don't we go up to Keith Dandridge's house? Maybe we can even get a ride back to our car."

"That actually sounds like a good idea," Kay agreed.

"Okay." Cody started down the trail through the spitting rain. He stopped at the "No Trespassing" sign. "This is Mr. Dandridge's land."

They ignored the signs and headed down the trail onto his land. There were a few limestone rocks beside the trail.

"Those things must weigh a ton," Lee observed when they passed the second rock.

"Yeah. Once in a while, Mr. Dandridge hauls one up from the quarry or moves one around with his tractor,"

Cody said.

"A lot of work to mark a path," Lee said.

"He *is* an engineer," Kay pointed out.

"The Professor was interested in the rocks and wanted to know if any of them had been here before Mr. Dandridge was here," Cody said.

"No doubt thinking they might be landmarks to the treasure. I think there were some drawings of rocks in his journal." Kay's hair was hanging down in front of her face, and she could feel her wet shirt sticking to her back.

"It's raining harder. Let's hurry." Lee squinted as the rain blurred his vision.

Cody nodded and went off down the trail at a brisk pace that had Kay and Lee hurrying to keep up. With the rain in their eyes, they could barely see the Victorian house until they were at the foot of the steps leading up to the wrap-around porch. The windows of the house were putting out a glow of light that promised warmth and the chance to dry off.

Soaked to the skin, Lee knocked on the imposing oak door.

"I can't say I was expecting company." Keith Dandridge smiled as he opened the door wide for the trio of travelers.

"Sorry to stop without calling first. We were on this side of Dwayne McKenzie's property when it started pouring," Kay explained.

"Now I know Cody, and you're Kay. I met you the other day at a worksite and at Malone's funeral. This must be your brother. I've seen him at several funerals."

Lee stepped forward and extended his hand. "I'm Lee Lamberton. Oh, sorry," he said as water poured down his sleeve.

"Don't worry about it." Dandridge took Lee's hand and shook it. "Come on into the kitchen while I get dry towels for all of you."

Fifteen minutes later, they were dried off and sitting around the kitchen table, with drinks and an open package of Oreo cookies between them.

"Sorry I'm not a better host. Since my wife left me I've devolved into my old bachelor ways."

"You never need to apologize to me for milk and Oreos." Lee smiled and took another cookie from the pack.

"Has there been any word about Dwayne?" Dandridge asked.

"No, not since his truck was found in the St. John's River," Kay told him.

"I can't imagine what could have happened to him. I try to hold out hope that he'll come back, but it doesn't look good." Dandridge appeared deeply concerned for his friend.

"We were trying to retrace his last steps when we got caught in the rain," Lee said.

"Were you? You've got a great guide there." Dandridge nodded toward Cody, who looked slightly uncomfortable sitting with them. "I think he knows more about the woods around here than just about anyone else."

"I guess," Cody mumbled, embarrassed.

"Sunday morning when he went missing, McKenzie's truck was seen parked near the trail that leads to your house. Did you see him on Sunday?" Kay asked.

A strange look flashed across Dandridge's face. Kay thought it might have been anger, but he quickly got it under control.

"No. If I'd seen him around that morning, I certainly would have told someone once I heard that he was missing. Don't you think I would have told you and that deputy?" There was an edge to Dandridge's tone.

"Of course." Kay figured she'd also be a little irritated if a friend of hers went missing and someone thought she had failed to report an important clue. "But maybe you saw or heard something that didn't seem directly related to McKenzie's disappearance. Like someone else walking around near your property. Or a strange car."

"You have a point." Dandridge appeared to relax. "Let me think…" After a minute or two, he shook his head. "I can't remember anything unusual happening that Sunday."

"I know y'all were good friends. If he was this close to your house, would he normally come by?" Kay asked.

"It depended on what we were both doing. You said that we *were* good friends. I'm still holding out hope that we'll be good friends again when he comes back." Dandridge's words sounded sincere and heartfelt.

"You know, we think that his disappearance is related to Professor Harrington's death. Which brings up one new fact you probably haven't heard. There is no gold," Lee said.

"I never thought there was." Dandridge rolled his eyes. "The only thing that made me wonder was the Professor's fervor. He wouldn't let anything stop him from looking."

Lee told him about the fake documents that had led to Harrington's obsession.

"The old guy seemed a bit crazy, but he also seemed very intelligent."

"It was a very good fake," Lee assured him.

"I guess it would have had to be. All of this seems like a tragic comedy of errors." Dandridge shook his head.

"Is it possible that Dwayne McKenzie had something to do with Harrington's death and took off?" Kay didn't believe it, but she wanted to see what Dandridge would say.

"No. Not Dwayne. If he did, he would be a standup guy and admit it." He paused and looked thoughtful. "Now if it turns out that, heaven forbid, Dwayne committed suicide, then I could see that. Maybe there was an… accident where Harrington died, and Dwayne felt responsible. That would fit his moral code."

"Was Dwayne interested in the gold?" Kay couldn't help remembering how he had wanted to look through the journal and insisted on taking it with him.

"I think he was curious like everyone else. Beyond that, I couldn't say."

Lee felt a rumbling in his gut. He didn't know if it was the milk and cookies or the hike, but he suddenly needed the bathroom. He hated to use a stranger's bathroom. *But sometimes you don't have a choice*, he thought and stood up.

"Can I borrow your restroom?" he asked, rubbing his grumbling stomach with one hand.

"Just down the hall to the right," Dandridge said graciously.

On his way down the hall, Lee looked around for a book or magazine, something he could read to take his mind off of using someone else's facilities. Just as he reached the bathroom, he saw a hall table with several magazines. His need urgent now, he randomly grabbed a Florida auto swap magazine.

As he let his system work through all the queasiness, he flipped through the magazine. There were several cars marked with ballpoint pen, including a Chevy Nova, a couple of Ford Fairmonts and a Dodge Aspen. He idly wondered about the cars that were marked. They seemed like odd choices for Dandridge to be interested in. *Maybe he has a son or daughter who needs a car*, he thought.

He went back and looked at each of the cars again. Something about the ads bothered him. He compared them again and realized what it was. All four cars were listed in St. Augustine. He flipped back to the cover of the magazine and saw that it was the August edition.

What does this have to do with anything? Lee asked himself as he finished up and washed his hands. He left the bathroom, putting the magazine back where he'd found it.

Still a little confused by his reaction to the car ads, he walked back to the kitchen where Kay was talking with Dandridge. On the other side of the table, Cody looked bored and stared out the window at the rain, which was still coming down steadily. Everyone politely acknowledged Lee's return to his seat.

"It does seem ominous that his truck was found in the St. John's River," Dandridge said.

"And whoever drove it over there either had to get back, is still in the area or is long gone," Kay said. "What do you think of Jerry and Andy Mercer?"

"I'm not going to point fingers." Dandridge looked down at the table. "But I will say that they blur the line between country and redneck. I also know that Jerry Mercer has been obsessed with Harrington's gold."

Kay went on to tell him about Mercer's arrest while Dandridge nodded sagely.

"That is all very suspicious," he said.

"What makes the Mercers such good suspects is that the two of them could have easily transported McKenzie's truck to the St. John's River."

"One drives McKenzie's truck, and the other drives a second vehicle. Makes sense," Dandridge agreed.

Lee had been sitting there, still thinking about the cars in the auto trader, when he realized what Kay and Dandridge were talking about. He sat bolt upright in his chair, his brain on fire.

Could I be right? he asked himself. *How do I check it?* He looked at Dandridge and tried not to stare. *Why would he do it? What if he did do it and finds out I suspect him? How do I make sure he doesn't get rid of the evidence?*

Lee knew he had to call Jerome.

"I should probably check on Lester," Lee said. Kay gave

him an odd look. "We've got that… call coming in about the funeral." It sounded like a weak excuse, even to him. "May I use your phone?"

Everyone at the table was looking at him now, even Cody.

"Of course. It's right over there." Dandridge pointed to a small desk in the corner of the kitchen.

"Actually, I wanted to go over a few of the funeral arrangements which are… private."

Dandridge smiled obligingly. "I have a phone in my office you can use." He stood up and gave Lee a smile. "I'll show you where it is."

Lee followed Dandridge to his office. There were blueprints and survey maps scattered on the desk and tables in the room.

"I'm sorry it's a bit messy. The phone is right over there." Dandridge pointed to a phone on the desk. "I'll leave you alone."

As soon as Dandridge was out of the room, Lee rushed over to the phone and picked it up. Then he realized he didn't know what number to call. He needed Jerome, but he was probably still tied up at the sheriff's office with Mercer. Sighing, he dialed the operator and asked her to connect him to the sheriff's office's main line.

It was a nerve-racking ten minutes before Jerome came on the line.

"What's wrong?" Jerome knew that Lee would not be calling him at work if it wasn't important.

"It's a long story. We're at Keith Dandridge's house and I think he's involved in McKenzie's disappearance," Lee said in a harsh whisper.

"What are you talking about?"

"I found a car magazine where he'd circled several vehicles for sale. They were different makes and models, but all of them were near St. Augustine. Don't you get it?" Lee hissed.

"No," Jerome said bluntly. "What does that have to do with McKenzie?"

"That's how he got back from dumping the truck. All the ads specified cash. He dumps the truck and then walks to a guy selling a car nearby. He buys the car for cash and drives it back. If he gets rid of the car without ever filing the title, then there's no paper trail." Lee rattled this off quickly, trying to convince Jerome. "Please come over here. I've got to get back before Dandridge gets suspicious."

"I must be crazy because that kind of makes sense. But why would he kill McKenzie? They're good friends."

"I don't know, but McKenzie's truck was seen near the path to Dandridge's house on the morning he disappeared."

"Okay, we can't fly off the handle. Townsend is tied up, but I can get off and come over there. Give me forty-five minutes. Not that I know what I'm going to do when I get there." Jerome hung up.

Lee set the receiver down and never heard the click as another phone in the house was hung up. When he got back to the kitchen, only Kay and Cody were at the table.

"Where's Dandridge?" Lee asked with a sinking feeling.

"He never came back from showing you where the phone was," Kay said.

Lee felt like someone had poured ice water down his back. He wanted to tell Kay about his suspicions but was afraid Dandridge would walk in on them. Cody had picked up on Lee's nervousness and was watching him closely.

Lee leaned toward Kay and said in a hushed undertone, "I called Jerome. He's coming—" Lee heard footsteps in the hallway and shut up.

"What are you talk—" Kay started to ask.

Lee waved his hands frantically to make her stop. "Not

now!"

CHAPTER TWENTY-FIVE

Dandridge walked into the kitchen and took his seat between Kay and Lee. Cody was directly across from him.

"Would you like something more to drink?" Dandridge's voice was emotionless.

Everyone declined his offer.

"Maybe we should be going?" Kay said and started to get up, but Lee kicked her under the table.

"I think you should stay for a little while longer. Don't you?" Dandridge addressed his question to Lee, who could only nod.

"What's going on?" Cody asked innocently.

"I don't know." Dandridge frowned. "What do you think is going on, Mr. Lamberton?"

"Honestly, I'm not sure." Lee mustered all his nerve and met Dandridge's gaze.

"No, I really think we should be going." There was a sharp edge to Kay's tone as she stared at Lee.

"I'll take some coffee," Lee said and deliberately, almost

comically, reached out and took a cookie from the package.

"Of course. I'll brew some up," Dandridge said.

Kay didn't know what was going on and she didn't like being ignored, but seeing Lee's determination, she decided to sit back.

Cody was looking from one person to the other like a spectator at a sport that they didn't understand. He knew that nothing good was happening, but he couldn't understand the nuances of the situation.

The only conversation for the next half hour was about the weather and small talk about the University of Florida's football team. The doorbell caused everyone to look toward the hallway expectantly.

"I'll get it." Dandridge rose from his chair.

"I'll go with you." Lee also stood up.

Dandridge looked like he was going to say something, but instead he shrugged and started for the front door. Kay was right behind them, with Cody trailing at her heels.

There was more knocking before Dandridge got to the door. Lee stood ready to welcome Jerome as soon as the door opened. What he wasn't ready for was Sheriff Pratt standing at the open door, damp and looking decidedly unhappy.

"Keith, seems we owe you an apology." The sheriff held his hand out to Dandridge, who shook it.

"It's okay, Tom. I think they're just a little overzealous. No real harm done. I called you so we could talk this through before it got out of hand. Come on in."

"You know Deputy Sutton," the sheriff said, and to his dismay Lee saw the smirking face of Wade Sutton looking over the sheriff's shoulder. "And like you told us we would, we found one of my other deputies outside. This is Jerome Carter."

"We've met." Dandridge nodded to an unhappy-looking

Jerome who walked in behind Sutton.

Kay had let her mouth fall open as she watched the men enter the house. *I'm going to kill Lee*, she grumbled to herself. She knew this would spell the end to any investigation into Roger Harrington's death.

"I see we have the usual suspects," Pratt said, looking at Kay and Lee. "Who's the kid?"

"That's Cody Morgan. He lives up the road with his grandfather," Dandridge said and added, "He's all right."

"Morgan? I know your mother. An addict and a thief." The sheriff shook his head. "Now, would someone please explain what's going on?"

Lee looked at Kay, who stared daggers back at him.

"Lee called me because he had found something that he thought might be evidence in McKenzie's disappearance," Jerome said in an effort to make the situation seem reasonable.

"You can go over and stand with them," the sheriff told Jerome, earning a crooked smile from Sutton.

With gritted teeth, Jerome walked over and stood next to Kay and Lee. Cody continued to watch the scene play out in front of him.

"So what's this evidence you've got?" Pratt asked Lee, whose face turned bright red under the sheriff's mocking tone.

"I'll show you." Lee's voice shook a little as he thought about how lame the auto magazine was going to look to them.

Everyone followed him into the hallway where he pulled the magazine out from the pile. He flipped to a couple of the marked cars and noticed that there were more of them marked than he'd seen the first time.

"I... This... I think he's marked more of the cars." Lee stared at Dandridge, whose expression didn't change.

"What are you going on about?" The sheriff reached out and took the magazine from Lee, flipping through it. "Is this a joke? What does this prove?"

"When I looked at the magazine the first time, there were only a few cars in St. Augustine marked." The words rushed out of Lee.

"Are you on drugs?" The sheriff leaned forward and stared at Lee's eyes.

Lee swallowed hard and steadied his nerves before explaining the significance of what he'd seen.

"That's got to be the dumbest thing I've ever heard, and I've heard some stupid stuff." Pratt turned to Jerome. "And you came out here to harass a county employee, and one of our best citizens, over this stupid excuse for evidence?"

"I thought it was worth looking into." Jerome knew how lame the words sounded, but his only other option was to throw Lee and Kay under the bus, and he wasn't going to do that.

"I'm glad you already work for them part-time, 'cause I think you're going to need a job that doesn't involve wearing a star." Pratt's voice was getting louder as his irritation grew.

The more Pratt yelled, the bigger Sutton's smile became.

"I didn't intend on anyone getting fired," Dandridge said.

"You've been through enough hard times with your wife running off and now your friend going missing. You don't need one of my deputies coming here on the say-so of a couple of half-ass detective wannabes and harassing you."

"And what about your wife?" Jerome said, surprising everyone. "I did a little digging after the first time we talked to you, just out of curiosity. No one has seen your wife since she disappeared, including her sister."

"What are you talking about?" Dandridge's face flushed with anger. "Everyone knows my wife ran off."

"That's about enough out of you!" Pratt pointed his

finger at Jerome. "We did everything we could to find Keith's wife. You just can't satisfy that sister of hers."

"Still, don't you think it's odd. Your wife and now Dwayne McKenzie. Why do people around you have a tendency to disappear?" Jerome asked, going all-in.

"How dare you!" Dandridge stepped toward Jerome, who didn't back down.

"That's it, you're fired!" the sheriff yelled.

"Ask your good friend Keith here if we can search his house," Jerome told him.

For a minute, Kay thought Dandridge was going to hit Jerome. Instead, he stepped back, took a deep breath and visibly relaxed.

"This is insane," he said. "I have nothing to hide. Go ahead, search the house." He waved his hands around, indicating they could go wherever they wanted.

"Let's do this." Jerome looked pumped.

"Settle down!" Pratt told him. "We'll go ahead and look around since Keith says it's okay, but there won't be any tearing stuff up, dumping drawers or leaving things in a mess. We're just going to look around."

An hour later, they were all standing in the hallway again.

"Nothing. Not even a *Playboy* magazine. You've really screwed yourself this time," Sutton said to Jerome, Lee and Kay.

"I hope you're satisfied, because that's the last thing you're ever going to do as a deputy in this county," Pratt told Jerome.

"I don't know what you expected to find." Dandridge shook his head and looked at Jerome and the rest like they were students who'd gotten "F's" on their final exams.

"Ha! They thought you had McKenzie locked up in a closet and your wife's skeleton under the bed. They're crazy as bedbugs." Pratt waved his hand in front of his face as though trying to dispel a bad odor.

"McKenzie could have been here and you wouldn't care because Dandridge is your buddy." Kay was still inclined to think that Lee had gone off half-cocked when he'd called Jerome, but she was furious at the sheriff's attitude.

"McKenzie isn't here!" Pratt shouted. "He's probably run off with some floozy like poor Keith's wife! Did you see any signs of McKenzie? No! Any signs that this poor man killed his wife? No!" Pratt was shouting so loud that the dishes were rattling in the china cabinet.

"If he killed them, they're probably buried." Lee didn't want to let go of this. He still remembered the chill he'd felt when he saw the auto ads. He also knew that Dandridge had gone back and marked more cars after he'd heard Lee talking on the phone.

With fire in his eyes, the sheriff turned to Dandridge. "Tell me that these goons are trespassing and I'll lock them all up right now."

"I'll be glad to handcuff them." Sutton smiled and Kay had to stop herself from stepping forward and slapping the smile off his face.

"I think they just need to go," Dandridge said solemnly.

"You heard the man." Pratt gestured toward the door.

"Why'd you move the rock?" Cody's voice wasn't loud, but it caused everyone to stop and look at him. Most of them had forgotten he was even there.

"What rock?" Pratt narrowed his eyes and stared at Cody.

"The large one with the hole near the top," Cody said.

"What are you talking about?" Pratt said, waving everyone toward the door again without waiting for an answer.

"They're big limestone boulders from the quarry that line the path from McKenzie's property," Kay told them, then looked at Cody. "When did he move it?"

"I guess about a week before the Professor died."

Before anyone could respond, there was a thump from somewhere beneath the house.

"What was that?" the sheriff asked, looking around as if he expected another annoyance to walk into the hallway.

"I'm sure it was my cat," Dandridge said a little too quickly.

Kay saw his eyes shift back and forth like he was looking for an escape route. Then there was another small thump.

"Sounds like your cat is under the house," Sutton said.

Like the tumblers in a lock, everything clicked into place in Lee's mind. "He's under the house!"

Before anyone could react, Lee ran toward the front door. Sutton and Pratt spat out expletives and turned to watch as Lee flung the door open.

Everyone ran after Lee as he hurried across the porch and almost slipped going down the wet steps. For a second, everyone else came to a stop when they saw the sheets of rain coming down, and then, like a switch had been thrown, they continued as a group after Lee.

"Wait!" Kay yelled as she tried to catch up to her brother, who was hunting for a way to get under the bricked-up crawlspace beneath the house.

"Don't you see?" His words were hard to understand through the rain and his heavy breathing.

"Stop, damn you!" Sheriff Pratt was madder than a wet hen and just as wet as he slipped and sloshed across the soaked lawn, trying to keep up with them.

"I could fire a warning shot," Sutton told the sheriff, who just growled at him.

Only Cody noticed Dandridge slip away and head for the large shed at the back of his house. He watched Dandridge for a moment before turning and following everyone else.

Finally, Lee found one of the wooden doors that allowed

access to the space under the house. A new padlock gleamed from the door. Muttering in frustration, Lee looked around for a tool to bust the hinges. Under a bush, he found a concrete block that had been used as a guide for a hose and pulled it up. Kay tried to talk to him, but he didn't have enough breath to answer her.

The sheriff and Sutton caught up to them. Pratt, sputtering with rain and anger, ordered Lee to stop. Lee ignored him and walked over to the locked door. When Pratt grabbed his arm, Lee turned with the concrete block, and everyone thought he was going to club Pratt with it. Instead, Lee turned back to the house and hurled the block with all his strength at the door's latch. With a crack, the door bent inward, and Lee threw himself at it.

Kay didn't fully understand what was going on, but when Sutton went to grab Lee, she kicked him in the leg and sent him sprawling into the mud.

"Be careful!" Kay yelled as she rushed forward to help Lee pull away the wood from the opening. Jerome yanked Kay out of the way while Lee scrambled through the narrow opening they'd created. Once Lee was through, Jerome kicked the rest of the door in.

"It's dark and I can't see anything." Lee's voice came through the opening, sounding hollow and distant.

Jerome started to get down and follow Lee, but before he could, Sutton grabbed him while Pratt started yelling in his face.

"You're not just fired. You're going to jail for this!"

Jerome violently shook off Sutton's hand and raised his fist, but Kay grabbed him before he could swing.

"I can hear something!" came Lee's voice from the hole, barely audible over the rain. Something in his tone caused all of them to turn and look at the opening.

"I've got him!" Lee shouted.

Now both Kay and Jerome dropped to their knees and stuck their heads under the house. Jerome pushed his way past Kay until only his feet were visible. When he started backing out, Kay could hear him and Lee telling each other to be careful.

Jerome cleared the opening and Kay could see him helping someone else out. Slowly, a gagged and bound Dwayne McKenzie was birthed from the access hole. Lee was the last to appear as he helped to support and guide McKenzie's legs.

"Help me, dammit!" Jerome growled at Pratt and Sutton, who were standing there with their mouths open, staring at the scene before them. "One of you go call for an ambulance."

Pratt punched Sutton and pointed him toward their vehicles parked in the front yard. Sutton turned and trotted off through the rain and mud, climbing into his car to use the radio. Pratt eased himself down beside McKenzie and started to untie his hands while Jerome pulled off McKenzie's gag and Lee untied the man's feet.

"Thank you." McKenzie's voice sound dry and hoarse. He closed his eyes as if in prayer.

Kay felt Cody tap her shoulder as a deep growling sound emerged over the constant downfall of the rain. Everyone turned and looked toward the sound.

"He's out of his mind!" McKenzie tried to yell, but all that came out was a hoarse grumble.

A large tractor with a bucket rumbled from the shed and headed across the front yard. Later, they couldn't decide if the tractor purposefully changed directions or if the sheriff's truck and Sutton's unmarked car were simply in the most direct path. Either way, the bucket on the tractor slammed into the left front panel of the pickup and shoved it into Sutton's Ford LTD. Even through the rain, Jerome, Lee and

Kay could see Sutton's horrified expression through the windshield as his car was pushed fifty feet before the tractor broke loose and headed down the path toward McKenzie's property.

Jerome was the first one to start running after the tractor. Kay helped McKenzie up and made sure he was okay before she left him with Lee and followed Jerome and the tractor. Cody seemed unsure as he trotted through the mud behind her.

Meanwhile, the sheriff ran over to his truck. Seemingly as an afterthought, he checked on Sutton, who was cursing and trying to kick one of his car's doors open.

The rain had slacked up a bit by the time Jerome and Kay caught up to the tractor. A crazed Dandridge was using the bucket to dig a hole between two of the limestone rocks. The rocks were twenty feet apart, which gave him plenty of room to maneuver.

"Stay back," Jerome told Kay and Cody.

Dandridge drove the tractor back and forth, splashing up mud and digging the hole deeper. After a few minutes, the sheriff and Sutton, soaked to the skin and muddy from the knees down, joined the group standing around and watching Dandridge dig. They stared in silence until finally the bucket rose out of the hole with a skull perched on top of a pile of mud.

It took a second for everyone to realize what they were seeing, and then there were gasps and a few muttered curses. Dandridge started to dump the bucket when Jerome jumped forward, pulling his .38 and screaming in an effort to be heard over the sound of the diesel engine.

"Stop! Turn off the engine! Turn off the engine and get down from the tractor now!"

When Sutton saw Jerome jump into action, he pulled his own revolver and started yelling at Dandridge. Whether it was the two deputies screaming at him or a glimpse of the skull in the bucket, something caused Dandridge to idle back the tractor and look at what he had dug up. When he saw the skull, he turned the engine off and half fell from the seat onto the ground.

With Jerome and Sutton yelling at him to stay on the ground, Dandridge stumbled to his feet and walked to the edge of the hole.

"There she is! The cheating whore! I killed her. I killed her! I killed her and I'm glad I did!" He faced all of them and pounded his chest with his fists. "Shoot me if you want. I'm done. I'm just done."

His voice suddenly faded, and his body seemed to go limp. Sutton stepped forward and elbowed Jerome out of the way, placing handcuffs on Dandridge.

Jerome shook his head and re-holstered his pistol. Kay looked around and saw the sheriff with his mouth hanging open, staring at the scene before him. Cody was standing back, wide-eyed as if he'd just watched the best movie he'd ever seen.

The rain stopped and the wind died down, allowing them to hear footsteps coming down the path toward them from the house. Everyone turned to see McKenzie walking stiffly toward them with Lee beside him.

"Lock him up and throw away the keys," McKenzie said with anger in his voice.

"Why did he kidnap you?" Pratt looked totally confused.

"I figured out that he'd killed Harrington because Harrington had decided that the gold was under one of these rocks. No matter how much Dandridge tried to discourage him, Harrington kept poking around them. Dandridge even moved the stone he had placed over the body of his wife. But he finally decided he just couldn't take a chance that Harrington would stumble upon the body."

"Why did he torture Harrington?" Kay asked.

"He needed to make sure that Harrington hadn't told anyone else that the gold was under the rocks. What he didn't know was that Harrington kept a journal with enough information to tell me where he thought the gold was. Sunday morning, when I went to look at the rocks, I noticed one of them had been moved. Harrington couldn't have moved a one-ton boulder by himself. It had to have been Dandridge who moved it. I also remembered that when Dandridge's wife went missing, he'd moved the same boulder up from the quarry and placed it there."

"Were you suspicious of Dandridge?" Lee asked.

"Not as much as I should have been. I'd always had an odd feeling about the disappearance of his wife, but I never thought he'd killed her. When I realized the boulder had been moved around, I went to ask him about it. Instead of denying it, he broke down crying and told me the whole story. I counseled him to turn himself in, but as soon as I mentioned the sheriff, he went berserk and attacked me. Next thing I knew, I was tied up. He's spent the last few days telling me what good friends we are and how I should see things his way." McKenzie shook his head sadly.

"It's hard to feel much camaraderie with someone who's keeping you tied up under their house," Jerome said.

"I'm glad we were able to rescue you," Pratt said, stepping over to McKenzie with his hand out and a huge smile on his face.

McKenzie's face took on an ominous expression as he turned to face the sheriff. "Funny thing about a gag. It kept me from being able to call for help, but it didn't prevent me from hearing everything that was being said above me. You are a sorry-ass excuse for a lawman. If it wasn't for these other people, I would still be trapped under that house. Don't think for one minute that I'm not going to do everything I can to shorten the amount of time you're in office."

The smile had fallen from the sheriff's face, and he slowly backed away from McKenzie.

"What do you want me to do with him?" Sutton, who was still holding onto Dandridge, asked the sheriff.

"What the bloody hell do you think I want you to do with him? Put him in the back of your…" The sheriff realized that both of their vehicles were out of commission. "Contact the office and get them to send out some more cars and the crime scene unit."

"No!" Jerome barked at the sheriff and Sutton. "Call the office and get Townsend out here to make the arrest. He deserves to make the collar."

They looked at him like he'd gone mad.

"You wish!" Sutton yelled like a child on a playground.

"Do what he says," McKenzie ordered.

"Now see here—" Pratt started to say, but McKenzie cut him off.

"If you don't, I'll tell everyone what happened this afternoon and how you clowns had your cars crushed and looked like the idiots you are."

Slowly, Pratt turned to Sutton. "Get Townsend out here to take Dandridge in."

Without a word, Sutton pushed Dandridge back toward his half-crushed car and the crumpled truck. The sheriff, with one more quick look at McKenzie, followed after Sutton and the prisoner.

CHAPTER TWENTY-SIX

A week later, Lee and Kay were enjoying a celebratory dinner with their friends. Lester and Jerome were there, Lee had brought Alison and Kay had invited Alan Eckhart. Ruby was hovering over all of them, encouraging everyone to eat more.

"Yin and Yang were a big part of the investigation," Ruby said as she took her seat for the fifth time.

"How do you figure that?" Lee asked. "All I said was that having had to deal with Yang getting under the funeral home made me think that the noise we heard under Dandridge's house might be McKenzie."

"It's not like people don't bury bodies under houses all the time," Jerome said.

"Let's hope not all the time." Alison frowned at Lee. "I don't know if you're doing the right thing by not pressing charges against Harrington's ex-wife and that professor."

"They *did* send me a very nice letter of apology," Lee said.

"I'm not sure a letter of apology covers a kidnapping," Alan said.

"You don't have to worry about them," Ruby said. "I see travel in their future."

"They're lucky that Dandridge is going to plead guilty to the murders and Dwayne McKenzie's kidnapping, so their part in making the fake manuscript doesn't have to come out in court," Jerome told everyone, ignoring Ruby.

"Don't forget the rock that Kay stepped on. Yang got that out of the flowerbed and placed it in front of the door," Ruby reminded everyone.

"I don't get it," Alan said.

"A limestone rock was the solution. The body buried under the rock was the motive for the crimes," Ruby explained while Lee shook his head.

"I wish he'd found a better way to give us clues. I can still feel the bruise on my heel," Kay said. She wouldn't admit it to anyone else, but there was something truly strange about Ruby and her two cats. Besides the clues that the cats might or might not have provided, Kay remembered Ruby bringing up Bigfoot before they knew about Cody's obsession with the hairy biped.

"You said that Yin was also involved in solving the crimes. How?" Lester asked. He was a true believer and loved to hear Ruby's stories.

"The picture," Ruby said as if it was obvious. When she saw all their puzzled looks, she explained, "He broke that picture frame in the office and dragged the photo around."

"So?" Kay asked. Though she loved bear-baiting Ruby, this time she was genuinely confused about where Ruby was going with this.

"Yin scratched off the image of the wife in the picture. See, he was telling you that the motive for the crimes went back to a man killing his wife." Ruby smiled at the assembled guests.

"Wow, yeah!" Lester said, digging into another helping of mashed potatoes.

"I wish you would have invited that nice young man to join us." Ruby looked disappointed that she had lost the opportunity of stuffing someone else full of her food.

"Don't worry. You'll have plenty of opportunities to feed Cody. Kay and I offered him a part-time job helping out around here and he accepted." Lee had discussed it with Lester before offering the job to Cody, explaining to him that the extra help would come in handy with the way the business was expanding.

"Is the sheriff going to fire you?" Alison asked Jerome.

"Not this week. Mr. McKenzie got out in front of the sheriff by telling everyone he could that I'd been instrumental in rescuing him and solving the case. After that, Pratt couldn't fire me without looking more incompetent than he normally does. Of course, there's still the fact that Henry is going to run against him in the election. Not that I'm as worried as I once was. I told McKenzie we had a challenger for sheriff, and he agreed to back Henry."

"Have you seen the new cat lately?" Alison asked.

"Two days ago, I saw Yin watching the little tortie minx strut across the driveway." Ruby smiled.

"We need to keep an eye on that situation and nip it in the bud before we're overrun with cats," Lee said.

"Kittens would be f—" Lester stopped when he noticed everyone was giving him a hard look.

After dinner, Lee came out of the kitchen to find Kay looking around for Alan. She was a little worried that he might be upset because she'd told him that she wasn't going to take the job at the hospital. *Maybe in a year*, she'd told herself. While a bit disappointed, Alan had seemed to take it in stride and even joked that she clearly got plenty of excitement at the funeral home. Now she wondered if he was off pouting.

"I saw them looking at the caskets," Lester said, walking past them to see if there was any dessert left.

Kay and Lee went into the casket room and found Alison and Alan shaking their heads over the price of an oak coffin with gold-plated fittings.

"Looking at buying a casket?" Kay asked.

"I'm a doctor and even I couldn't afford this one." Alan laughed.

"At this price, I figured it should have a built-in stereo," Alison said with a grin.

"They aren't cheap. There's craftsmanship that goes into building one." Lee always got his nose a little out of joint when someone questioned the cost of the coffins.

Alison came over and took his arm. "Customers complain about the cost of TVs too." She gave him a light kiss on the cheek that instantly brightened his mood.

"Alison and I also decided that it would be great fun to go on a double date," Alan told Kay and Lee, who both looked shocked by the idea.

"Sounds like fun," Lee said hesitantly.

"I guess we should celebrate the little windfall that Chester Madison is going to send us for saving his insurance company a fortune." Kay didn't sound any more convinced than Lee that it was a good idea for the four of them to go out on a date together.

As they settled on a time for the next Friday night, Lee felt the strange sensation that life was changing, and he wondered what the future would look like. *Only one way to find out,* he told himself.

Kay and Lee will return soon in book 5 of the Mortician Murder Mystery series!

ACKNOWLEDGMENTS

The idea for this series owes a lot to my wife's own upbringing. When I first met my future father-in-law, he was the only funeral director in a small, North Florida town in the 1980s. My wife has vivid memories of playing hide-and-seek in the casket room, being driven to school in a hearse and being fascinated by the mysteries of the embalming room. I hope these memories add a little realism to this series about a challenging and often misunderstood profession.

Cover Design by Melody Barber
www.aurorapublicity.com

ABOUT THE AUTHOR

A. E. Howe lives and writes on a farm in the wilds of North Florida with his wife, horses and more cats than he can count. He received a degree in English Education from the University of Georgia and is a produced screenwriter and playwright. His first published book was *Broken State*. The Larry Macklin Mysteries is his first series and he released a second series, the Baron Blasko Mysteries, in summer 2018. The first book in the Macklin series, *November's Past*, was awarded two silver medals in the 2017 President's Book Awards, presented by the Florida Authors & Publishers Association; the ninth book, *July's Trials*, was awarded two silver medals in 2018. Howe is a member of the Mystery Writers of America, and was co-host of the "Guns of Hollywood" podcast for four years on the Firearms Radio Network. When not writing, Howe enjoys riding, competitive shooting and working on the farm.